Here's what critics are saying about Catherine Brun's books:

Readers are sure to enjoy this playful tale...this book is bound to please anyone that is looking for an easy, satisfying read on the beach.
—*InD'tale Magazine*

"If you like your cozy mysteries complete with a cast of zany characters this is one for you. And guess what? Recipes are included which makes me really wish I could bake."
—*Night Owl Reviews*

"TASTES LIKE MURDER is an intriguing start to the *Cookies and Chance Mystery* series. I want to visit more with all of the quirky characters just to see what crazy and outrageous things they will do next!"
—*Fresh Fiction*

"Twistier than expected cozy read--great for beach or by the fire"
—*The Kindle Book Review*

BOOKS BY CATHERINE BRUNS

SILENCED BY SUGAR

a Cookies & Chance mystery

Catherine Bruns

Acknowledgements

A huge thank you to retired Troy police captain Terrance Buchanan for his willingness to answer my questions and to Constance Atwater for serving as my wonderful beta reader. Special props to Kim Davis and Margaret Kehn for sharing their original delicious recipes with me. Thank you to my patient husband Frank for his assistance with "plotting" this novel. And as always, deep appreciation to publisher Gemma Halliday and her wonderful editorial staff (especially Danielle Kuhns and Wendi Baker) for taking such good care of Sally and her gang.

CHAPTER ONE

———

Josie stood at the front window of the bakery, hands perched on her hips as she stared out at the dismal January day. "Did you win Publishers Clearing House and forget to tell me about it, Sal?"

I glanced up from behind the display case to hand Mrs. Josten her change and the little pink box filled with jelly cookies. "Thanks so much. Have a great day." After the woman had departed, I joined my best friend at the window. "Why, what's up?"

Josie pointed her slim hand in the direction of a black stretch limousine parked at the curb. An attendant in a black Eddie Bauer jacket and chauffer hat exited from the driver's seat and then held the rear door open for his passenger.

Josie squinted, trying to see inside the limousine. "Maybe this person will buy everything we've got on hand," she quipped.

"Don't I wish." At this point, any sale would be a blessing.

A woman alighted from the back seat and said something to the driver. She was tall and thin with straight, fine dark hair that fell past her shoulders. She wore dark sunglasses and an expensive-looking, brown trench coat with suede boots to match. The boots had at least a four-inch heel, but she moved effortlessly and gracefully in them, despite the sidewalk being coated with freshly fallen snowflakes.

Josie clutched my arm tightly. "Oh my God. Is that who I think it is?"

I shrugged. "Beats me, but we sure could use a big order." My cookie shop, Sally's Samples, was in its second year of operation. We'd done fairly well so far, thanks in part to the free homemade fortune cookies we offered to customers with each purchase. After the busy holiday season, business had slowed to a crawl, and we were in desperate need of sales right now.

Josie dug her nails into my flesh, and I yelped. "It's Donna Dooley!" she shrieked.

Donna Dooley was a popular talk show host on the Food Network. She'd made her debut on television a few years ago when she'd been one of several people to audition for the host position of a new pilot show, *Delicious Dishes in Twenty Minutes*. Donna had won the job and risen to fame quickly. Her success was topped only by the likes of Rachel Ray, another native New Yorker. Rumor had it that they didn't like each other.

Donna's current talk show, *Someone's in the Kitchen with Donna*, featured different chefs and celebrity personalities who presented their original recipes to the public. I didn't see the program often since it aired while I was at work, but Josie religiously DVR'd it every day and watched it after her kids went to bed.

In shock, I stared out the window at the woman. Donna noticed us and gave a merry little-finger wave as she strolled in the direction of our front door. "What the heck is she doing here?"

"Maybe she wants to have you on her show." A small squeak of excitement escaped from between Josie's lips, and she turned and ran into the back room. "Oh my God! That's my favorite show. I need her autograph."

I struggled not to roll my eyes. "Jos, stop getting all crazy. She puts her pants on just like us, one leg at a time."

"No, she doesn't," Josie yelled back. "She has enough money to pay someone else to do it."

The bells over the door jingled cheerfully as Donna stepped inside my shop. She gave me an ethereal smile filled with gleaming white teeth. "Hi, I'm looking for Sally Muccio."

"That's me." I took a moment to study the woman. Her face was angular—not exactly what I'd call pretty but as my Grandma Rosa would say, full of character. She had a high forehead, alabaster skin that was striking against her dark hair, and brown eyes fringed with long lashes.

She extended a French-manicured hand adorned with a large ruby ring on her forefinger. "It's a pleasure to meet you, Sally. I'm Donna Dooley."

Josie handed her a piece of notebook paper. "Miss Dooley, can I have your autograph?"

Donna gave her a warm, genuine smile. She must have been used to the request because she graciously took the paper and pen from Josie's outstretched hand. "Of course." She wrote out a quick message with a flourish and then handed it back to Josie.

Josie's blue eyes widened in delight as she read the words aloud and laughed. *"There's no bitchin' in my kitchen. Love and hugs, Donna D.* Oh, this is great. I'll hang it in the back room."

"Would you like to sit down, Miss Dooley?" I gestured toward the three little white tables which were set up in front of my bay window. "Could I get you a cup of coffee? Or maybe an espresso?"

Donna placed her Dolce & Gabbana handbag on a table. "No thank you, dear. Too much caffeine isn't good for the complexion." She removed her coat, and Josie ran over to assist her.

Although I loved Josie dearly, I was tempted to shake her and yell, *Snap out of it!* This behavior was so unlike her. We'd been best friends since the age of eight. She was a superb baker and had even made my wedding cake last year. My shop would never have gotten off the ground without her. Sure, it technically belonged to me, and Josie was a paid employee, but she was also the backbone of the operation.

After we graduated from high school, Josie had attended the Culinary Institute of Buffalo. My background skills had been limited mostly to the fast food industry, where I'd been a server of ice cream, food preparer at Dunkin' Donuts, and then barista and eventually assistant manager at a Starbucks in Florida. Although I could bake almost anything Josie could—with proper directions—my expertise leaned more toward the financial side of the business.

Donna smiled as Josie placed her coat on one of the

brass wall hooks by the front door. "Are you one of Miss Muccio's employees?"

"Oh, forgive my manners," I stammered. "This is Josie Sullivan, my head baker." *And obviously your biggest fan.*

Donna watched Josie with newfound interest. "Ah, yes. You must be the one who appeared on Cookie Crusades with Miss Muccio last January."

"That's right." Josie grinned. "We kicked some serious butt on that show."

"My last name is Donovan now," I interrupted. "I got married last year."

"Congratulations," Donna beamed. "I'm thinking of featuring newlyweds on one of the shows in the near future. What line of work is your husband in? Does he cook as well?"

I laughed. "No, but he loves to eat. He owns a one-person construction company." Mike and I had been married for six months, and this was truly the happiest time of my life so far. We'd first dated in high school and then broken up on the night of senior prom over a stupid misunderstanding. I'd gone on to date and eventually marry another classmate, Colin Brown, which had ended in disaster when I'd caught him in bed with my high school nemesis, Amanda Gregorio. By two weird twists of unrelated fate, they were both dead now.

"Oh well, you never know. Maybe we can work something out." Donna glanced around the bakery with a satisfied air, and then suddenly her face lit up. I followed her gaze. She was staring at the certificate from our win on the Cookie Crusades competition a year ago. We'd taken home the grand prize of $20,000 and a lot of prestige as well.

"This shop is adorable," she said. "When I graduated from culinary school, I thought about opening a bakery. I love the smell of chocolate and cinnamon. It's like a distinct perfume to my nose. Do you know what I mean?"

Yes, I did know what she meant, but since I inhaled so many different scents on a daily basis, they sometimes tended to blend together.

"I'm actually here about your win on Cookie Crusades." Donna fingered the beige tablecloth in front of her that my Grandma Rosa had so lovingly crocheted for me. "My talk show is taking on a new theme this year. I've started a journey of sorts, where I go around to visit past winners then invite them to be on my show to make a popular recipe and talk about their business. Would you be interested?"

Josie squealed out loud then covered her mouth with both hands. I was dumbfounded. This was a golden opportunity for us and the bakery. "Of course we're interested, but you didn't have to come all this way to ask in person." I'd never heard of a celebrity doing that before, and frankly, it baffled me.

Donna tapped her perfect oval nails on the table. "I admit the producers are usually the ones who call people to set up appearances, but since I've bought the rights to Cookie Crusades, this is a personal interest for me. There are also two more winners located in Western New York that I need to visit, so it wasn't too much trouble. Besides, I'll be in the area for several days. I'm accepting an award at the Culinary Institute of Buffalo next week."

"Oh!" Josie's eyes grew wide. "I went to school there and heard you were going to be giving a speech. They were already sold out when I tried to get tickets."

Donna cocked a pencil-thin, fine eyebrow at her. "What year did you graduate? I'm sure it was several years after me, though. You look like you're just out of high school yourself."

Despite having four children and her thirtieth birthday looming, Josie did look much younger than her actual age. "Thanks for the compliment," she said, "but I didn't graduate. I left before school was over."

What Josie didn't bother to explain was that she had chosen to leave school when she became unintentionally pregnant with her first child. At the young age of nineteen, she'd found herself married and a new mother to a baby boy. Her four boys now ranged in age from eleven to twenty months old. Although she loved her children dearly, Josie always felt that she'd lost out on her one opportunity in life to make a huge splash in the baking world.

Fortunately Donna had too much tact to pursue the subject. "I would love it if you both would appear on the show the day after tomorrow," she said.

I gaped at her. "That soon? Uh, I'm not sure. What

would we make?" Heck, what would I even say? This appearance would be different from Cookie Crusades. We would actually have to chat with Donna while we cooked. Her show was filmed in front of a live studio audience, and I was afraid my nerves might turn me into a babbling idiot.

Donna reached across the table to pat my hand. "There's nothing to worry about. My assistant will take care of all the details. Of course you can make anything you like, but I've heard that you won last year thanks to your original fortune cookie recipe. Personally I adore them and would love it if you'd make them on my show. Perhaps you could do enough for our entire audience."

Sweat started to break out on my forehead. "I don't know. As I'm sure you're aware, fortune cookies can only be prepared a few at a time because they harden so quickly. How many people are in the audience?"

Donna wiggled her hand back and forth. "About 200 or so, but again, no worries. You can make them ahead of time. We'll only do one sample tray on the actual show."

Relief soared through me. "Okay, that sounds much better."

Donna laughed. "Relax, dear! This is supposed to be fun, and it should be great exposure for your business." Her phone beeped, and she stared down at the screen. "Excellent. My assistant is on her way over. She's been at the television studio arranging everything for tomorrow's taping. We're featuring the owners of the Magnolia Bakery."

Josie stared at Donna with unbridled adoration. "*The* Magnolia Bakery? That has to be one of the most popular bakeries in all of New York."

Okay, Josie was completely star struck, and even I had to admit that it was difficult not to be excited. However, we would need to stay calm and focused for the taping. This might mean a great profit for the bakery, which I hoped to expand within the next year and even add a small lunch menu. That had actually been my plan from the start, but a fire in our former location and my wedding had derailed things a bit.

"Kelly will stop by in a little while with the details," Donna said. "She'll tell you what time to be there, what to bring with you, all those important particulars. We'll be using the television station right in Buffalo, which is about a forty-five-minute drive from here. The owners of Magnolia Bakery have family in the area, so it's convenient for them as well. Speaking of which, if you'd like to have relatives attend the taping, you're more than welcome. Just let Kelly know so she can arrange seating for them."

Josie's face went white as flour underneath her freckles, and I knew what she was thinking. My parents were not exactly people you would want in the studio audience. I loved them dearly, but my father was the type to make catcalls while my mother, who dressed like a teenager most days, would show up in a provocative outfit two sizes too small and twenty years too young for her. "I'll let Kelly know, thanks."

"I'm looking forward to having you both on the show," Donna said. "To be honest, the ratings for Cookie Crusades have dropped in the past few months, and this appearance is as much for me as it is for you." She handed me a business card. "This is my office number. When you phone, my administrative assistant will get in touch, and then I'll return your call. But I'm almost positive that Kelly can answer any questions you have."

Josie wrinkled her nose. "I thought your assistant's name was Eve? I've seen her on a couple of episodes. Do you have more than one?"

"I do have other assistants, but Eve was my personal one," Donna explained. "She handled all the details of the show and was quite a fabulous baker herself. She recently found out she was pregnant with twins and had some health issues, so unfortunately she had to give up the job. Kelly started with me a couple of months ago."

Whenever I heard anything associated with babies, my heart went into overdrive. "I hope she and the twins will be okay."

Donna nodded. "Me too. Do either of you have children?"

Josie raised a hand. "Four for me. Sal doesn't have any—yet."

Yet. The momentary hesitation caused a pang in my chest, although I knew Josie had not intended to do so. More than anything, I wanted a child. We'd been trying since our honeymoon, but there was currently no baby on the way. Every month I said a little prayer, but they'd all gone unanswered so far. Mike had assured me it would happen eventually and not to worry. He was right, but there were still times when I tended to get a bit anxious.

I decided to change the subject. "Thank you again for this opportunity."

Donna opened the front door of my bakery and waved gaily at us. "Bye girls. So lovely to meet you both."

The bells chimed with Donna's departure, and we both watched as the driver held the limousine door open for her. She sidestepped the snow at the curb on her way into the vehicle, and it drove away shortly afterward.

"Isn't she wonderful?" Josie sighed. "Maybe I could have worked for her if I'd finished culinary school. She only hires people with the most experience."

She was thinking about missed opportunities again. Josie had been doing this quite often as of late and claimed it was part of her "turning thirty" crisis.

"Hey," I said. "Who cares about having a talk show? You're a fantastic baker and have had lots of requests lately to make wedding cakes. You're the biggest bakery success I know."

"Thanks, Sal." She continued to stare out the window with a solemn expression on her face that saddened me. When we were in high school, Josie had often talked about touring the world, working in a French restaurant, or perhaps even writing a cookbook. Real life had intervened, and she'd done none of those things. Josie had always been more of a restless soul than me, and it had been difficult for her to settle down at such a young age.

I knew what it was like to have dreams that didn't come true. Although content with my life and grateful for all that I had—a wonderful husband, house, cute little dog, and my business—I still desperately wanted a child more than anything.

I went to place a hand on her arm, but she quickly turned and strode into the back room, our kitchen and prep area. "Let's start cleaning up so that after this Kelly splits, we can get out on time. I promised the boys I'd make my homemade pizza tonight, and you know how they hate to be kept waiting. I'm using the crust recipe that your grandmother gave me."

"Sure thing." Josie wasn't the type to cry over spilled milk, and I knew better than to pursue the conversation further. "Grandma offered to make braciole for us tonight since it's our six-month anniversary."

"Your grandmother is the best cook I know," Josie said. Food and Grandma Rosa were always safe topics because everyone loved them both. "Are you going to your parents for dinner?" she asked.

I shook my head. "No. Mike said this morning that he has a surprise for me."

"I'll bet he does," Josie said wickedly.

My cheeks warmed. "Ha ha. I think he's planning to cook for me."

"No offense to your hunk of man there," Josie said, "but I think *I* would have taken the braciole. But then again, I'm not a newlywed anymore. Let me go put the garbage outside."

As she let herself out the back door, the bells jingled again, and a woman about my age walked into the shop. She had short, light brown hair in a blunt cut, hazel eyes, a pert nose, and a wide mouth. Although we were the same five-foot-three-inch height, she had at least ten pounds on me.

The woman approached me and tossed her head in an arrogant sort of way. "Hi, are you Sally Muccio? I'm Kelly Thompson, Donna Dooley's personal assistant."

"Nice to meet you." I extended my hand. After staring at it for a moment, she reluctantly shook it. Something about this woman registered high on my dislike radar, but I always tried not to judge people. "I've been expecting you. Would you like to sit down?"

Kelly pulled a chair back, flopped down on it, and pulled out a leather-bound notebook from a black designer attaché case. "Okay, let's see. Donna has you booked on Thursday's show. She's calling it "A Fortune Lover's Treat." Got any extras of the cookies lying around? I'd love to see what all the fuss is about."

"Sure." I went behind the display case, grabbed a piece of wax paper, and lifted two of the cookies from the tray. Both had been dipped in chocolate and sprinkles.

Kelly examined the cookies with interest and immediately broke one apart. As she read the enclosed fortune, her thin lips pressed together into a frown. "Wow. Is this some kind of a sick joke?"

She held up the paper so I could read it. *Too many sweets can be deadly.*

"The messages tend to be a bit weird at times," I admitted. "We don't write them. They come from a novelty store." Her fortune was not exactly great advertising for my bakery, but hey, it could have been worse. In the past year and a half, I had considered discontinuing the cookies because of their creepy messages, which always seemed to come true in some shape or form. However, they were a big attraction for customers, and with Thursday's show imminent, it looked like we'd be making them for quite some time to come.

Kelly threw the paper on the table and scowled. "I'm a diabetic and don't appreciate messages like that."

Of all the worse luck. "I'm terribly sorry. It certainly wasn't intentional."

She looked down her nose at me. "I own a bakery too, you know. It's located over in Colgate and called Naturally Delish. We're entirely sugar free." The pride in her voice was apparent.

"Oh yes, of course. I've heard of the place." It was more successful than my own, and I always saw paid advertisements for it in the newspapers. She had been in business much longer than me, at least seven or eight years. "I'll bet it's wonderful."

Kelly glanced around the shop, and I felt a surge of pride as her eyes traveled over the blue and white checkered vinyl floor, cream-colored walls, and the silver-framed artwork that adorned it. After the fire at our former location, Mike had managed to transform this shop into almost an exact replica of the previous one. Some days I still couldn't believe it was all mine. I felt certain that Kelly was going to return the compliment and perhaps say something about how cute my place was. The words that did fall out of her mouth were quite a surprise.

"Yeah. *My* bakery has a lot of class. Unlike certain others."

My mouth dropped open in shock, but somehow I

managed to turn it into a smile. *Wow. How rude is this woman?* I was still trying to think of a response when I spotted Josie headed in our direction. She was cleaning her hands off with a disinfectant wipe.

"Wouldn't you know that stupid bag broke? I had to—" Josie's voice trailed off when her eyes focused on Kelly's face. Kelly returned the gaze, and I couldn't help but notice how her tanned complexion quickly paled.

Josie's hands immediately balled into fists at her sides, and her clear blue eyes practically bulged out of her head. "What are *you* doing here?"

Kelly gave her a superior smile. "Hello, Josie. Long time no see."

Josie pointed at the door. "Leave now before I throw you out."

CHAPTER TWO

———

Baffled, I stared at my friend. "What's the matter with you? This is Donna's assistant, Kelly."

"Kelly Connors," Josie said as a way of explanation. "She sabotaged my dessert back in culinary school. *I* should have won that contest."

Josie had enlightened me several times with the tale of a flambé dessert gone wrong. She swore that one of her classmates, jealous of Josie's near perfect marks and desserts, had done something to make her creation resemble a forest fire.

"Thompson is my last name now." Kelly ignored the death glare Josie shot her and gaily showed off the impressive rock on her left hand. It was so large that it made my own one-carat diamond look like it had come out of a gumball machine. "I can't believe you're still sore about that. You have no one to blame but yourself."

Josie gritted her teeth together in contempt. "Get out of here this minute before I tear your freaking head off."

Unfortunately, Josie used another word similar to *freaking*. Startled, I rose to my feet and placed a hand on her arm. "Why don't you go ahead and take off. I'll talk to Kelly about the show on Thursday and then close up."

"Like hell." Josie shook my hand off. "She might try to set you on fire too!"

Good grief. "You're making a fool out of yourself," I hissed.

Kelly leaned back in her seat, clearly enjoying the show that we were putting on for her solo benefit. "Still the same old Josie Brooks. Oh, wait a second. What's your married name now? Didn't you leave school because you suddenly got a little *fat?*"

Josie started toward Kelly, and it took every ounce of my strength to push her in the direction of the back room instead. "Help yourself to a cup of coffee," I called to Kelly over my shoulder and then added a quick lie. "We need to have a quick chat about one of our orders."

Josie picked up a dish from the counter, and for a moment I was afraid she might hurl it in the direction of Kelly. Suddenly she took a deep breath and then dropped it into the sink. Despite the fact she was taller than I was, I placed my hands on her shoulders.

"I hate that woman!" Josie screeched.

"Okay, this happened—what, ten years ago?" I asked. "You need to calm down and let it go."

Josie closed her eyes for a moment, as if struggling for composure. "I can't believe that she's Donna's assistant. How is that even possible? From what I've heard, she barely passed culinary school."

She picked the dish up again, and I braced myself, waiting for her to fling it at the wall. When Josie saw my face, the anger began to dissipate from hers. "I'm sorry, Sal. I shouldn't be taking this out on you. The problem is that I'm angry at myself for allowing her to pull that over on me. I was such a laughing stock at school for weeks after the competition. It still pisses me off that she played dirty and got away with it."

"Look," I said. "Maybe this television appearance isn't a good idea. You're going to have to see Kelly during the taping and probably will have to talk to her." I remembered how in past episodes of the show, Donna sometimes called her assistant on stage to deliver ingredients or pass out prizes to members of the studio audience. I winced at the mental image of Josie flinging fortune cookies at Kelly's head. "Maybe I should call Donna and pass."

Josie looked startled. "No. You can't miss out on an opportunity like this."

"I'm more worried about your well-being." To tell the truth, I was also concerned about her and Kelly getting into a fistfight in front of the studio audience. Josie had been known to throw a few punches back in her day during high school, but fortunately, I'd never been the recipient of one. She'd even given her husband, Rob, a black eye once when they were dating, although he'd never laid a hand on her in return. He'd laughed about the incident with me and Mike and said it had only made Josie appear more endearing to him. Go figure.

For some reason I didn't think Donna would appreciate it if her assistant showed up at the taping with a fat lip. "I don't want Kelly upsetting you."

Josie shook her head. "That's not fair to you. It's your shop, and this will be a great opportunity for more business. I can control myself around her."

I deftly raised one eyebrow and wished that this was true but had my doubts. Josie was known for her quick temper, and if Kelly started something, she would be sure to finish it. "Jos, it's really not a—"

"No. We're doing it." Without another word to me, she whirled around and went back into the front room as I followed, mystified.

Kelly was texting on her phone but looked up as we entered. She gave us both a pretentious grin. "How are we doing, ladies? Ready to back out of the show on Thursday?"

"Not a chance," Josie growled. "We'll be there. Just make sure that you stay out of my way."

Kelly held her hands up in front of her face and shook them. "Ooh. Threats now. I'm so scared."

Okay, I needed to get this woman out of my shop—*now*. I sandwiched myself in between Kelly's seat and where Josie stood, hoping to serve as some type of buffer in case they started to smack each other around. "Do you have something for me to sign or instructions for the show?"

Kelly handed me a manila envelope. "All of the details are inside. You'll need to be at the station by one o'clock for the taping. It's being held at Channel 13's studio in Buffalo, WBSN, which is about 45 minutes away from here." She gave Josie a triumphant smile. "Right across the street from our alma mater. Well, *my* alma mater anyway."

Josie sucked in so much air that if she'd been a helium balloon, she might have burst at that precise moment.

"I know the place. How long will it take?" I hated to

close the shop for the entire day. Right now, with business so slow, we needed every sale we could get our hands on. We did have a part-time driver who helped out at the counter sometimes, but I wasn't sure if he could handle things alone. At least we could stay open until noon.

"You should plan on being there for the entire afternoon, although the actual taping segment should take under an hour." Kelly gathered her purse and briefcase and rose to her feet. She extended her hand to me. "Donna's going to be featuring *my* bakery next month. This is a great opportunity for your shop, so be sure that you don't do anything stupid."

My cheeks burned. "Excuse me?"

"Sorry, Sally," she said soothingly. "I meant make sure your *employee* doesn't do anything stupid." She handed me her business card. "Call if you have any questions." Kelly shot Josie an evil smile and then without another word pushed the door open gleefully, the bells jingling in time with her departure. She crossed the street to where her Lexus was parked.

The first round was over. Kelly one, Josie zero.

"That witch," Josie said between clenched teeth. "She hasn't changed a bit in ten years. Still the same conceited little snob who thinks she's better than everyone else."

I turned the *Come In, We're Open* sign around to *Sorry, We're Closed* on the front door and pulled down the blind. "I've heard of her bakery. There are always ads in the Colwestern Times for it." They were usually a half page in size and raved about how the place used no refined white sugar. Kelly must be doing quite well for herself. The ads in our local paper were too expensive for my meager budget. The only advertising I could afford was in the local college newspaper.

Josie had already whipped her phone out of her pocket, brandishing it as if she was in one of those old TV westerns. "Me too. But I didn't know *that* twit owned it. Check this out. Kelly even shows up under Wikipedia as the proprietor of Naturally Delish, a past winner on Cookie Crusades. We must have missed that episode because I'd know her mug anywhere. Then all of a sudden she's got an in with Donna and gets this job? She must have other people running her bakery. It's the only thing that makes sense."

"It's kind of hard to run a bakery if you can't bake yourself. Then again, I'm certainly far from being an expert." Since a child, I'd dreamed of opening my own business. While I'd made a lot of progress in the last couple of years, I would never possess Josie's talent. "I'd be lost without your expertise."

Josie flushed with pride. "Thanks, but don't sell yourself short, Sal. You have a great head for business, and you can make anything that I can."

"With directions," I chimed in. "For the record, I remember you telling me how someone had sabotaged your attempt to win the school's baking contest. I know I'm going to regret asking this, but what exactly did she do to you and why?"

Josie narrowed her blue eyes. "It was more than just one competition. If I told you everything that chick did to me back then, it would turn your curly, black hair into a straight blonde. Kelly told lies about me to the professors and said I cheated off the other students. One time I made these ginger cookies in class that were absolutely perfect. The texture, taste, everything. Out of this world." She brought her fingers to her lips and kissed them, an Italian gesture she'd probably gotten from my father. "The professor ate one of mine and almost choked to death right on the spot. So I tried one. How interesting. It seemed that someone had replaced the sugar with salt."

"Ouch." I winced. "But how do you know that—"

"Let me finish," Josie interrupted. "I had one test cookie, ate it, and was happy with the results. Then I left the room for a minute—I had to take a phone call in private. A classmate swore to me later that she saw Kelly heading toward my station with the salt container. She didn't actually see Kelly commit the deed, but hey, that was good enough for me."

Her voice choked up. "And then of course, there was the matter of the baking competition. The prizes were a gold apron and five hundred dollars. I could have used that prestige to help me hunt for a job after I learned I was pregnant. Cherries jubilee was my dish. For that dessert you normally use brandy as the liquor of choice. Someone replaced the brandy I had in the bottle at my station with Bacardi 151."

My hands flew to my mouth. "Holy cow." That stuff was almost potent enough to burn holes through clothing. Mike's mother had been an alcoholic, and I vividly remembered the empty bottles of Bacardi at their house when we'd dated in high school. Tonya Donovan had ended up dying of cirrhosis while I had been married to Colin. "You never told me what kind was used before."

Bitterness permeated Josie's tone. "It was too upsetting to talk about back then, even with you, so I skimmed over the details. Anyhow, it's a good thing that I only used a small amount. The smell of Bacardi is very strong, but I had a cold that week, and my senses were off. I used the torch to light the dessert and was lucky that the school *and I* didn't go up in flames. Good thing that there was a fire extinguisher nearby."

"What makes you think it was Kelly?"

"Later that night, I received a call from a private number. The person spoke only one line when I answered. 'Life's a cherries jubilee, but you're stuck with the pits.' I knew it was her voice, but how could I prove it? Kelly ended up winning the competition." Josie's lower lip quivered slightly.

This rendered me speechless. How could anyone be so cruel?

"Oh, and there's more," Josie went on. "Right before the competition, she found out through a mutual friend that I was pregnant and spread it around the entire school like wildfire. My professor treated me differently after that. Remember how bad I had morning sickness? It all became too much for me to deal with."

It hurt for me to hear this story, but I knew it was important for her to get this boulder off her chest. In the early stages of her pregnancy, Josie had confided to me that just looking at food she had to prepare for class made her ill. Things had gotten so stressful between her parents' attitude, school, and constantly being sick that she was afraid it might affect the baby and had decided to drop out.

I placed my arm around her shoulders. "What was Kelly's problem? Why would she single you out like that and be so rotten?"

She wiped her eyes with her apron. "There was a guy in our class she had a huge crush on. His name was Will Chester, and he made it obvious that he was interested in me. I told him repeatedly that I was dating someone else, but he was very persistent. Every time Kelly caught us talking, she looked like she'd just sucked down a bottle of lemon juice."

I burst out into laughter. "Well, I can certainly understand why you don't like her."

"Don't like isn't strong enough," Josie declared. "I hate her flaming guts. Yes, pun intended."

My phone buzzed at that moment. I removed it from my jeans pocket and saw Mike's name pop up on the screen. He didn't usually call during the workday. While my business was dwindling, he could not keep up with his. Winter was known as a slow time in the construction industry, but he had enough indoor jobs lined up to last him until spring.

Josie saw his name and waved me off. "Take the call from hubby. I'll finish cleaning up so we can get out of here." She walked briskly into the back room.

Still worried, I spoke into the phone. "Hi, sweetheart. What's up?"

"Hey, baby." His voice was low and sexy. "Any chance you'll be home soon?"

"We're leaving in a few minutes. Where are you?"

"I finished a little early today," he said, "so I thought I'd go home and cook dinner for my beautiful wife. It is our six-month anniversary, after all."

The words made my heart melt. He hadn't said anything this morning, so I wasn't sure if he'd remembered. All of a sudden I found myself wishing I had some wonderful news to share with him tonight like, "You're going to be hearing the pitter-patter of little feet soon," or, "Guess who's going to be a daddy?"

"What's wrong?" Mike asked.

"Nothing," I said quickly. He must have heard me sigh. Mike was well aware of my disappointment month after month, and there was no reason to ruin this special occasion with regrets. "I was thinking how lucky I am."

"Well, I know that *I* am. How's business? Did it pick up any today?"

"No, but maybe in a couple of weeks." I told him about the taping scheduled for Donna's show on Thursday.

"Wow." He sounded impressed. "That's fantastic, babe. Should I come down to cheer you on?"

"It's not necessary. I know how busy you are, and to tell the truth, if my parents find out that anyone else in the family got an invitation and they didn't, the result wouldn't be pretty." Josie was going to be stressed out enough without having to deal with my nutsy cookie parents, as Grandma Rosa referred to them, sitting in the audience. We'd been through this before on Cookie Crusades. "I'm worried about Josie, though. That Kelly knows how to push all the right buttons with her."

"I'm sure it will be fine. By the way, did you come home for lunch this afternoon?"

I laughed. "No, I never have time for that. Why do you ask?"

There was a distinct clinking of pots and pans in the background, and I was curious as to what he was making. He could boil water to make spaghetti and open a jar of sauce, but that was about the extent of his culinary skills. Not that it mattered much to me, though.

"No reason," he said. "The tire tracks in the snow weren't yours, so I thought maybe Josie had driven you over. There were also footsteps on the porch, but they were way too large to be yours."

"Sounds like someone's turning detective," I teased. "It must have been the mailman."

His voice was puzzled. "But we didn't get any mail today. I checked."

"Oh." I finished sweeping the floor and laid the broom against the wall. "Well, I guess we must have had a mysterious visitor then."

"A well-wisher for our half-year anniversary," he said in a low voice that made me tingle from head to toe. "As long as they don't stop by tonight. I have plans for you."

"I do love it when you make plans. See you soon, honey."

"Bye, princess. Drive safe."

I clicked off and saw that Josie had her coat on. "All set?"

"We're good." I set the alarm before grabbing my coat

and purse then followed her out the back door into the alley. After I had shut and locked the door behind me, she put a hand on my shoulder. "What's wrong?"

She bit into her lower lip. "Sal, I'm aware that this appearance on Donna's show could mean a lot of business for the shop, which we really need right now. I hope you realize I'd never do anything to jeopardize it."

"Honey, of course I know that. Now stop worrying, and go home to make pizza for those four loveable boys of yours. Oh, wait. I forgot Rob. Make that five."

Josie's face spread into a wide grin. "See you tomorrow, partner. Have fun tonight, and happy one-half of an anniversary." She winked.

I secured my seat belt around me and watched as she drove off in her minivan. Perhaps I was worrying for nothing. There was no doubt in my mind that Josie would do whatever was necessary to ensure the bakery's success.

Just in case, though, I might ask Grandma Rosa if I could borrow her rosary beads on Thursday.

CHAPTER THREE

Less than 48 hours later, Josie and I found ourselves backstage for the taping of *Someone's in the Kitchen with Donna* waiting for our cue to go on. Among the papers Kelly had delivered to us was a request from Donna that we come dressed in black slacks, pink shirts, and our white bib aprons with *Sally's Samples* written in large pink letters. We donned our pink baseball hats with the bakery's name as well. Sure, we were a walking advertisement for the shop, but hey, that was fine with me. I would have been more comfortable in jeans, but Donna strictly prohibited them on the set.

We'd already been prepped by another one of Donna's helpers and had spoken with the head cameraman and assorted crew members. I'd mentioned the taping to Grandma Rosa and my sister, Gianna, but asked them to please keep it a secret from my parents. Despite Josie's assurance that she would be fine will Kelly, I worried that my father's presence in the audience, along with shouts of "Give me one of those fortune cookies. I'm feeling lucky today" might send her straight over the edge.

I had never been to this television studio before. The layout was similar to the one used for Donna's regular tapings in New York City. The entire set was an open-floor design with furniture that looked the same as hers—everything from the white, leather sectional couch, glass coffee table trimmed with plated gold, and an electric fireplace surrounded by a white and black brick design.

A high archway led to the kitchen which also occupied the largest area. All appliances were gleaming stainless steel, and I could picture crew members endlessly wiping fingerprints off the surfaces. The appliances were situated at one end, while oak cabinets ran the rest of the length of the room. There was enough space available on the light blue Formica countertops to make a seven-course meal. A burner top stove dominated one counter, with all of our fortune cookie ingredients set out on the counter next to it. I spotted five-pound bags of both flour and sugar, along with a canister of cinnamon, a tray of eggs, and two large bottles of pure vanilla. These were all for effect of course, to make it look as if we'd be slaving away for hours. A few eggs had already been cracked and waited in a glass Pyrex cup. Sometimes Josie chose to glaze the dough with them.

Josie walked back and forth behind me muttering something unintelligible. She was clearly nervous, and despite my best efforts, I hadn't managed to calm her down yet. We had seen Kelly briefly upon our arrival. Donna had two other assistants who reported to Kelly, and they had explained to us what would transpire during the actual taping.

I always tried to give everyone the benefit of the doubt, but Kelly had even enraged me yesterday. She phoned to inform us that Donna had forgotten to mention one small item—that instead of two hundred fortune cookies, we would need to make four hundred ahead of time and bring them to the taping. Each member of the audience took two home in a lovely silver designed bag that Donna provided, along with a ten-dollar coupon toward their next order at my shop and a cookie scoop gifted by another vendor. Although Kelly tried to sound apologetic on the phone, I was certain I'd detected a note of glee in her voice.

Since Donna was reimbursing me for the coupons, I couldn't complain, but it had been quite a chore to make four hundred fortune cookies at last minute's notice. We hadn't left the shop until after nine o'clock last night. Despite Mike's best attempts to relax me with a wonderful back massage, I'd still had trouble sleeping. Once I had finally dozed off, images of Josie choking Kelly by the throat had permeated my dreams.

Donna started her show in the same manner every day. She was seated on the couch reading select phrases of letters and emails from fans that delighted her. She *ooh'd* and *aah'd* over several and had even telephoned one star-struck woman to inform her that she was the daily winner of a hundred-dollar

Visa gift card to enjoy dinner at a favorite restaurant. Everyone seemed to like Donna, but there was something phony and pretentious about her—at least to me. Then again, weren't all television hosts like that?

"Stop fidgeting," I whispered to Josie. "You're making me nervous."

She leaned against the wall and sighed. "When this is over, I'm going to need a stiff drink. Make that an entire bottle. Jack Daniels should do it."

"Don't let Kelly get to you," I said. "We might not even see her for the rest of the show."

"Two minutes, ladies," one of the assistants called.

I grabbed Josie's hand. "Think positive. This is going to be great." *How could it not be?* We were already ahead by two thousand dollars, and who knew how many more orders might trickle in thanks to this appearance. Maybe we'd have to start shipping cookies through the mail. I might need to make up some catalogues—

"Okay, ladies." Susan, Donna's assistant, pointed at the speaker located high up on the wall. "Donna's talking about you now."

Donna's voice suddenly filled the room. "As many of you know, I bought the rights to Cookie Crusades a few months ago and have been traveling throughout the country to meet several of the past winners in person. I'm pleased to have one with me here today. She and her head baker will be making a tray of their famous original fortune cookies, and I personally can't wait to see what the future holds for me. Please give a warm welcome to the proprietor of Sally's Samples in Colwestern, New York—Sally Donovan and her baker, Julie Sullivan!"

I was taken aback by Donna's mistake and stood there frozen, unsure what to do. Susan gave us both a little shove forward. "Go!"

Josie and I walked onto the stage amidst polite clapping from the audience. We both shook Donna's hand, which was soft and cool to the touch. She had moved from the couch and was now standing by the kitchen counters. Everything had been timed down to the minute.

"How are you, ladies?" Donna asked in a cheerful tone.
I recited my speech, which had been among the papers
Kelly had given us. "Josie and I are very excited to be here."
Donna looked startled, as if she realized the guffaw with
Josie's name. I wondered if someone else—a certain assistant,
perhaps—had written down the wrong name on purpose. To
Josie's credit she looked calm and ready for action as she
positioned herself behind the counter and arranged the mixing
bowls in front of her.

"Now, Sally, can you tell us a little about your shop and
what makes it unique?" Donna inquired.

I went to stand next to Josie, while Donna remained on
the other side of the counter. This was very different from the
last time Josie and I had appeared on television. During the
appearance on Cookie Crusades, there had been three other
teams of contestants to share the limelight with. Today we were
the sole focus of the show, and it was much more intense.

"Of course." My voice began to shake as it always did
when I grew nervous. After a moment to steady myself, I
continued. "We've been in business about a year and a half, and
some of our specialties include jelly cookies, fudgy delights,
oatmeal crème, biscotti, and of course chocolate chip and double
chocolate chip cookies. Our trademark, or rather what makes us
unique, is that we offer a free fortune cookie with every
purchase. These cookies are homemade by Josie and me."

"Marvelous," Donna beamed. She turned to address the
audience. "As a special treat Sally and Josie will be making
enough cookies so that everyone in the audience can take some
home, along with other goodies too!"

The audience whooped and clapped at the
announcement. Yes, it was always about the freebies.

"Now tell me," Donna asked, "are the fortune cookies
difficult to make?"

"They're not difficult at all," I said. "But they do harden
quickly, so you can only bake one or two trays at a time."

Josie started to mix the ingredients into a bowl while I
named each one off. "We have original fortunes too."

"I love it!" Donna squealed. She leaned over the counter
for a better look and then stared directly into the camera lense.

"Be sure that you visit Sally and Josie over in Colwestern, New York at 13 Carson Way. The shop is open nine to six every day but Sunday." She rattled off the phone number. "We're going to take a break because Sally and Josie have a lot of baking to do! But don't go away because..." Her voice trailed off, and she looked over at the studio audience expectantly.

"Someone's in the kitchen with Donna!" everyone yelled.

"Cut," the cameraman shouted. "That was perfect, Donna."

Donna turned off the mic that was clipped to her designer, beige blazer and spoke into the Bluetooth positioned by her ear. "Kelly, have Susan and Lisa bring the tray of fortune cookies out to the stage." She flashed a brilliant smile at both of us. "That was great, ladies. When the taping starts again, I'll sample a cookie, read its fortune, and you can both wave good-bye. Any questions?"

We both shook our heads as Lisa appeared on the stage holding a silver platter laden with fortune cookies. Susan and Kelly followed with two rolling carts that held gift bags for the entire audience. The fortune cookies had already been placed in each one, along with the other treats Donna planned to give away.

Then I saw the distinct look of hatred pass between Josie and Kelly and sensed that World War III was about to commence.

Donna seemed oblivious to the death glares around her and went to stand next to Josie. "You have such a way with dough," she marveled. "It must be those delicate hands of yours. Why, you're a natural at this."

Josie practically glowed from the praise. "Thank you. I've enjoyed baking since I was a child and always knew I wanted it to be my career. When you love something that much, it doesn't even feel like work most days."

The disdain on Kelly's face was evident. I wasn't sure if it was pure loathing for Josie or the fact that her employer was fawning praise on public enemy number one. Whatever the case, it was enough to turn Kelly's hazel eyes green with envy.

"Kelly told me before the show that you two were at CIB

together. What on earth are the chances?"

What indeed.

Josie smiled so wide for Donna that her cheeks must have hurt. "That's right. We were both in the pastry program." A sly grin formed at the corners of Kelly's mouth. "Josie didn't graduate. She, um, had a little problem."

Josie and I both stared at her in disbelief. I could not believe Kelly would sink so low as to embarrass my friend in such a horrible manner. Josie had tried hard not to cause any waves, but this woman was a major monsoon.

"Kelly, I don't think that's relevant to the conversation," I said calmly.

Josie's face was scarlet as she stared at Kelly, almost as if daring her to go on.

Donna looked from Kelly to Josie, her eyes anxious. "Okay, Kelly, why don't you get Lisa and Susan ready to pass out—"

"Josie got pregnant." Kelly's voice resonated across the stage. "She didn't finish culinary school because she was busy baking other things—in her *own* oven."

The entire audience watched us, their mouths hanging open. Donna was the first one of us to recover and reached over to yank the mic off of Kelly's jacket. "What's the matter with you?" she hissed. "I don't want to wind up on the cover of the National Enquirer tomorrow!"

"One minute," the cameraman yelled.

Josie walked toward Kelly, an open bag of sugar in hand. "You haven't changed a bit. The same old vindictive troll. You couldn't make a decent dessert if your life depended on it."

Kelly reached out her hand and shoved the sugar bag straight into Josie's chest. About half of the contents spilled out and landed all over her.

"Uh-oh." Donna motioned across the stage to the cameraman, who was preoccupied with something else. "Bill," she shouted, "we're going to need a couple of extra minutes."

Josie's eyes narrowed at Kelly. "You know what your problem is?"

"Besides you?" Kelly sneered back.

"Diabetic or not, you need serious sweetening up." Josie

dumped the rest of the bag over Kelly's head. "Maybe this will help."

"You're on!" the cameraman yelled.

"No!" Donna screamed. "I need to get them off the stage first."

"Josie, don't stoop to her level!" I moved in front of my friend. "She's not worth it."

Kelly rewarded my statement by pelting me in the face with a bag of flour. My mouth was wide open, and a good portion landed inside. I heard Josie gasp out loud as I stood there half blinded by the white cloud and trying desperately not to gag. By the time I could see somewhat clearly again, it was too late. Josie and Kelly were already on the floor, rolling around like two little kids fighting over the last cupcake at a birthday party. There was even screaming and hair pulling.

I watched, dumbfounded, as Josie reached up onto the counter, and her fingers connected with the Pyrex cup of eggs which she then proceeded to dump all over Kelly's head. Kelly returned the favor by dousing Josie in the face with a bottle of vanilla. The audience shrieked and howled with laughter. Some were even snapping pictures with their phones.

"Hey, this isn't *Someone's in the Kitchen with Donna*!" someone shouted from the audience. "It's *The Jerry Springer Show*!"

Donna's expression was pure horror. "Security!" she screeched then grabbed me by the arm and shoved me toward Josie. "Get your friend off the stage. She's ruining my show!"

"Your so-called assistant started it!" I yelled back and then lost my balance in the slippery mess on the floor, landing on top of Kelly. She let out an *oof*, cracked an egg on my forehead, and then continued to work it into my hair along with the flour mixture.

"Time to make cookies," she taunted.

Three beefy-looking security guards appeared on stage, and each took hold of our arms.

"I was trying to break it up," I shouted in defense to my guard, who was well over six feet tall and about three hundred pounds. He refused to listen as he picked me up off the floor like a rag doll then threw me over his shoulder in his best Tarzan imitation.

"I hate you!" Kelly screamed at Josie.

"You'll be sorry you messed with me!" Josie yelled back as her guard half dragged, half carried her off the stage. "I should have torched you years ago when you ruined my flambé!"

We were left to cool down backstage with my monster guard, who had arms like an orangutan. "Don't even try to go back out there," he growled at me.

Why would I? All I wanted was to leave this disaster behind and never return. It was a safe assumption to say that our television career was over—forever.

I shook myself off like a wet dog, scattering flour everywhere. Lisa scurried back and forth with a broom and handed us warm, wet towels to clean our faces. I was a sticky mess on the outside and flaming hot on the inside. Kelly stalked off toward one of the dressing rooms without a word to anyone.

"You two can go to Dressing Room B down the hall and finish getting cleaned up," Lisa said in a meek tone. "I'm sure Donna will want to speak with you both afterward."

Oh, I was betting she would too.

"Not if that witch is with her!" Josie screamed. "Just wait until I get my hands on her!"

"Shut up," the guard growled. "They're taping out front."

Donna's voice filled the room. "We're back. Unfortunately Sally and Josie had to head back to their shop, but Susan will be passing out goodie bags to all the members of our studio audience. First, though, I need to open my fortune cookie."

Oh, dear God. Please let her get a normal one.

There was silence as Donna snapped the cookie, and then her light, airy laugh was heard. "It says *You will receive a surprise tonight.* Oh my. Do you think that means I'll win the lottery?"

A chill traveled down my spine. Personally, I was betting that neither the lottery nor Publishers Clearing House would happen. The message didn't say *what kind* of surprise Donna might receive, and that concerned me. It might mean anything from a temperamental baker with red hair burning down her set to being nominated for an Emmy. There was no way to tell.

Everyone laughed as the theme music blared through the speakers, followed by tumultuous applause that indicated Donna's show was over. Thank God for small favors.

Lisa showed us to the dressing room, and we started to clean ourselves up as best we could. After Josie washed vanilla off her face, I tried to remove the flour out of my clothes and hair. I didn't want to make a further mess, so I went into the adjoining half bathroom, removed my clothes, and wrapped myself in a towel.

Donna opened the door to the bathroom without even knocking. Panicked, I clutched the towel tightly around me. "Do you mind?"

Her cheeks flamed red, and her pupils had dilated to twice their usual size. "Your check will be mailed to you later this week. I can only hope that the press doesn't get wind of this horrible fiasco and try to ruin me with it."

"I'm sorry about what happened," I stammered. "It wasn't our intention to—"

The scent of vanilla wafted through the air. "Don't apologize for me, Sal." Josie stood behind Donna in the doorway, her red hair loose and disheveled around her solemn face. The front of her blouse was stained almost everywhere with the cookie ingredients. A determined look that I knew all too well had settled in Josie's enormous blue eyes. "That bitch started it. And I should have finished it."

The door to the dressing room slammed, and we all walked out of the bathroom to find Kelly standing there. She was in worse shape than Josie or me. Kelly's white linen pantsuit was stained down the front, and her hair was matted and greasy looking from the eggs Josie had dumped on her head. She held a small vial in one hand and a syringe in the other.

"Eggs are supposed to be good for your hair," Josie snickered. "They'll give those dyed roots a nice shine."

Kelly turned her nose up in the air and addressed Donna. "Why is this no-talent slut still here?"

Josie's face suffused with anger, and she started toward Kelly. Alarmed, I jumped in front of her while Donna wrenched Kelly's arm in such a tight grip that she nearly jerked her off her feet.

Ouch!" Kelly yelped. The syringe fell out of her hand and landed on the floor, directly in front of me. "What do you think you're doing?"

"Get out of here," Donna hissed. "You'll be lucky if I let you keep your job after this catastrophe. Call me in the morning."

Before Kelly could reply, Susan poked her head inside the room. "Miss Dooley, can I have a word?"

"Not now," Donna snapped. "Can't you see I'm busy?"

Susan cowered in the doorway. "Kelly, your husband's waiting out front, and your sister is with him."

"Don't forget this." Josie flung the syringe, hitting Kelly squarely on the side of the head with it. Kelly picked it up, muttered something that sounded like a swear word, and slammed the door, almost hitting Susan in the process.

Donna placed a hand over her heart in dramatic fashion. "There are rumors flying around that someone in the audience has already put this nightmare up on YouTube. I can only hope that you have not managed to tarnish *my* reputation with your vulgar food fight."

I'd finally had enough. "Excuse me, Donna, but at least I tried to break the fight up. I didn't see *you* doing anything about it."

She glared at me. "Look. I know Kelly may have started this, but I have to think of my show's reputation first. You're welcome to stay and clean up for as long as necessary, but then please leave quietly, and don't make any more trouble."

Josie stepped forward. "Donna, I hope this won't affect the endorsement you were going to give Sal's shop. I'm really sorry for my behavior."

Her voice sounded anxious, but Donna gave her a doubtful look. "I will still pay for the gift certificates and give the shop my seal of endorsement. But to be perfectly honest, I never want to lay eyes on either one of you again." She noticed Susan still standing there and frowned. "Was there something else?"

Susan's head jerked up suddenly from the floor that she'd been staring down at. "Um, Anita is here again. She'd like to have a word with you."

"Tell her I'm busy."

"She's already in your dressing room," Susan said in a meek voice.

Donna stared at the woman in disbelief. "You know better than that. What the hell is the matter with you?"

Susan placed her hands out in front of her, palms up. "I didn't let her in, honest! She must have found her way backstage somehow."

"Great." Donna cursed under her breath. "What's the sense of having security when you have to take care of everything yourself?" Without another word, she flew past Susan like a tornado. The sound of her high heels clicked angrily on the linoleum in the hallway and then started to fade into the distance.

Susan looked from me to Josie and attempted a smile but couldn't quite pull it off. She uttered a squeaky good-bye then scurried away like a mouse who had just found its way out of a maze.

Josie shut the door behind her. "I'm really sorry, Sal. When it comes to Kelly, I seem to lose all sense of reason."

"Forget it," I said wearily. "This wasn't your fault. Let's grab our stuff and get out of here. I've had enough of television studios for a while."

"You and me both." She slung her purse over her shoulder. "I need to go call Rob, so I'll wait for you in the van. Take your time."

I threw my clothes and boots back on, fussed a bit with my hair, which was hopeless at this point, and then grabbed my purse, anxious to leave. Backstage was quiet, and the studio audience had emptied out. I spotted a couple of crew members still on the set. One was talking on his cell phone in Donna's kitchen, and the other was leaning over the counter, making notes on a pad. Everyone else had abandoned the place like it was the *Titanic*. It had been destined to sink the moment Josie and Kelly laid eyes upon each other.

Josie had left the van unlocked but wasn't inside. As soon as I settled myself into the passenger seat, she emerged from the back door of the studio with a plastic bag. "I almost forgot my apron," she said.

I rolled my eyes. Josie was so practical some days. "We do have spare ones back at the shop, you know. Besides, it's probably more trouble than it's worth to clean."

She shrugged. "Let Donna get her own. At least she's still willing to give you the money for the gift certificates. I was worried about that."

I tried to turn the serious moment into a joke. "As my grandmother says, there's no great loss without some small pain."

Josie shook her head. "Rosa does come out with some classic ones." She drove out of the lot, her expression forlorn. "That Kelly brings out the worst in me. She always did. I was so stressed out last night that I yelled at the kids over some really stupid stuff. I hate when people get to me like that and thought I could handle this."

"Hey, no worries. I can imagine how difficult this must have been for you."

We both rode in silence for a few minutes then I reached into my purse for my phone to text Mike. "What the—"

Josie looked over at me. "What's wrong?"

I groaned. "My phone. I must have left it in the dressing room when we were cleaning up." Of all the worst luck.

"No big deal." Josie steered her van toward the upcoming exit. We traveled down the road for about half a mile until we saw signs for the Thruway and hopped back on in the opposite direction. It was only an extra ten minutes, but my head ached, and I longed to see my husband. The fact that he was waiting for me brought a ray of sunshine to my otherwise dismal and dreary day.

When we arrived back at the studio, there were only three vehicles parked in the lot—a beat-up Chevy station wagon, a television van, and Kelly's car. I sucked in a breath. "Great. She's still here."

Josie gripped the steering wheel tightly between her hands. "If Kelly comes outside, I am not responsible if she gets run over."

Good grief. I opened the door of the minivan. "Hopefully I can still get inside. You stay here and turn off the engine so you won't be tempted to do something crazy."

I shut the door before she could respond. To my relief

the back door of the studio was still unlocked. The hallway was eerily quiet and encompassed in semidarkness with a few lights still burning on the nearby set. A male voice could be heard on the stage. It was probably the same crew member, Grady, who had been on the phone when we'd left. I headed straight for Dressing Room B, anxious to get my phone and leave. My watch announced that it was seven o'clock already, and I was starving. I hadn't eaten since breakfast and thought about asking Josie to stop for a quick burger on the way home.

I opened the door to the dressing room and walked in the direction of the vanity, certain that was where I'd set my phone earlier. My gaze traveled down to the rug, and I froze.

A body was lying in front of the table.

My heart stuttered inside my chest. It was definitely a woman, but her face and neck had been covered completely by a white substance that appeared to be sugar. Her arms were spread out wide on each side of her body, as if she'd been making snow angels and been interrupted. A small vial of insulin and a syringe were on the floor next to her.

With a dry mouth and weak knees, I lowered myself beside the body. I felt the woman's wrist for a pulse but found none. My hands trembled as I felt along the surface of the dressing room table until my shaking fingers connected with my phone. Ignoring the several text messages displayed on the screen, I dialed 9-1-1.

"9-1-1, what is your emergency?" a brisk female voice asked.

"Please send help to WBSN's studio. There's a woman lying on the floor, and I'm pretty sure she's dead."

There was silence for a beat. "Do you know the woman's name?" the operator asked.

Even though I couldn't see her face, I recognized the stained white pantsuit, brown stiletto heels, and the shiny rock that adorned her fourth finger—the same one she'd flashed in my bakery a couple of days ago. There was no doubt in my mind who the victim was.

A face flashed through my mind, but it didn't belong to the victim. The vivid picture of Josie waiting in her minivan for me was enough to make my blood run cold. If that video ever leaked out, Josie would be everyone's prime suspect.

"Ma'am?" the operator asked. "Are you still with me?"

In somewhat of a daze, I answered. "Yes. Her name is Kelly Thompson."

CHAPTER FOUR

———

I should have known.

For the past year and a half, the story of my life had been murder, plain and simple. Ever since I came back to my hometown after the divorce and had started Sally's Samples, a perverse fate had trespassed into my life. Before that, I had lived a normal, somewhat boring existence.

The fortune cookie message Kelly received the other day had burned itself into my brain. *Too many sweets can be deadly.* Cripes. Was that foreshadowing at its best or what? Was there any way I could have determined that the message meant she'd die two days later with a bag of sugar poured over her head? *No.* I wasn't responsible for Kelly's death, but it all made for a weird coincidence.

I was seated next to Josie on the small, white leather loveseat in the dressing room Donna had used earlier. We were in the middle of being interrogated by one of Buffalo's finest who had responded to my call. Grady, the crew member I'd seen talking on his phone earlier was being questioned by another officer in the next room. The medical examiner was with Kelly's body.

Our policeman resembled my father—he was close to Dad's age and had the same physical attributes, which consisted of a protruding stomach and balding head. Apparently not everyone had hot-looking cops like Colwestern did.

Officer Trenton eyed me suspiciously. "Did you touch anything at the crime scene, Mrs. Donovan?"

"No, sir. Only Mrs. Thompson's arm to look for a pulse." I had learned from prior crime scenes never to disturb anything since it could potentially interfere with the police's investigation.

I hadn't even attempted to remove the sugar from Kelly's face, and to leave her in that condition had been disturbing. What a sick way to treat a dead body. Then again, the thought that someone had killed another human being was beyond sick. No matter how many murders I'd stumbled upon, I would never get used to it. Did the killer know about Kelly's diabetic condition? Or had they performed the act after witnessing the food fight between Josie and Kelly? I prayed that my face looked stoic enough for the officer, as a sick feeling of dread spread throughout my entire body.

Josie's hands trembled slightly as she clasped them in her lap. She stared straight ahead, saying little. This was unusual behavior for my friend who was all about snark and sarcasm. I had no doubt about Josie's innocence. We'd been best friends for over 20 years and knew each other better than we knew ourselves at times. The idea that Josie had anything to do with this crime was ludicrous.

Josie had telephoned Rob, and I'd also spoken to Mike. He'd wanted to come and get me, but I didn't like the idea of Josie driving home alone, especially in the current frame of mind that she was in. Rob had to watch their four kids and he worked nights, so Josie had told him not to come either. She said she was fine, but I had my doubts.

Officer Trenton cleared his throat. "When was the last time you saw Mrs. Thompson alive?"

"Right before we left the building." I winced at the memory of Josie and Kelly screaming at each other and Josie hitting her in the head with the syringe. "She came into the dressing room where we were—uh—getting changed."

He made some more notes on his pad, and I shifted in my seat. We'd already been subjected to a half hour of his relentless questioning. "Can you tell us how she died?" I asked.

Officer Trenton narrowed his charcoal-colored eyes at me. "I'm not at liberty to divulge those details, ma'am."

Okay, I knew the man was just doing his job, but this was beyond frustrating. I wanted answers. It was a crazy notion, but what if they somehow thought Josie was responsible? How many people had already seen the food fight?

There was a tap on the door, and a good-looking male

cop with dirty blond hair and brilliant green eyes stuck his head in. "Excuse me. Officer Trenton?"

I gave a sigh of relief and rose to my feet. "Brian. Thank you for coming."

After phoning 9-1-1, I'd made another call—to a member of Colwestern's police force. I'd first met Brian Jenkins when I had returned to town a year and a half ago, and he'd been the cop to investigate a homicide on the front porch of my bakery. We'd become fast friends, and he'd made it clear that he wanted to be something more as well. It wasn't long afterward that I'd reconciled with Mike, and Brian had taken my decision hard at first. For the past six months, he'd been happily dating an old high school acquaintance of mine, Ally Tetrault, who was a nurse at Colwestern Hospital. He still stopped in the bakery occasionally for chocolate chip cookies, or as he called them, his personal fuel.

Brian was almost an exact opposite of Mike regarding looks and mannerisms. He had a Greek god-like profile that could make any woman swoon. My husband was dark haired with midnight blue eyes, which had never failed to mesmerize me since the first day we'd met, and more of a rugged, tanned look to his face. Mike had been aware of Brian's interest in me, and for a while this had made for an uncomfortable situation between the two. However, my husband had come a long way from the jealous insecurities that led to our breakup back in high school.

Officer Trenton frowned. "Who are you?"

Brian extended his hand. "Brian Jenkins from the Colwestern Police Force."

The Officer cocked his head to one side to study him. "Steve Trenton. Pardon my saying this, Officer, but it seems that you're out of your jurisdiction here."

Brian's voice was self-assured and smooth as silk. "It would seem so, but my father, Cody Jenkins, was on the job with your Chief, Ed McKenna, back in Boston years ago. I explained to the chief that I know both Mrs. Donovan and Mrs. Sullivan personally, and he's agreed to let me take part in this investigation."

"I see." Officer Trenton suddenly looked as if he'd lost

his best friend. He closed his notepad and placed it under his arm. "Well, I guess I'll go see how Officer Petreky and the medical examiner are making out. These ladies are all yours, Officer."

Officer Trenton tipped his hat at us but said nothing further as he closed the door behind him.

To my surprise Brian folded his arms across his chest and scowled at me. "Sally, what exactly is it with you and murder scenes? How many does this make now? I seem to have lost count."

I rolled my eyes. "Brian, it's not like I go around looking for dead bodies." Somehow, they just seemed to find me. I'd started to think—or perhaps hope—that the period of doom and gloom was over in my life. Last summer someone had burned down my bakery, and the body of one of Gianna's clients had been inside. A few weeks later, someone had tried to kill me days before my wedding. After that, things had mercifully settled down, and I'd actually started to believe that Mike and I could have a normal, happy life together. It seemed that I might have been wrong about the normal part.

"Maybe not." Brian echoed my thoughts. "But they always manage to find *you*. You're lucky I know the chief of police in this town, or that other officer would have kept you here all night. I wouldn't have even been allowed to question you if Chief McKenna hadn't given his permission. What exactly is the deal with this woman? Did you know Kelly Thompson personally?"

"We were here to tape an appearance for *Someone's in the Kitchen with Donna*," I explained. "Kelly was Donna Dooley's assistant."

"I'm aware of who she was," Brian said evenly. "I've already watched the footage on YouTube of the three of you and your food escapade—or shall I call it a brawl. One million hits so far and counting."

Josie sucked in a long, raspy breath while I brought a hand to my mouth in horror. What I was afraid might happen had in fact just come true.

Brian went on. "What I'd like to know is how she connects to both of you. Did either of you have a previous relationship with her or somehow manage to piss her off during the taping?"

"This is crazy." I clasped my hands together and stared back at him in earnest. "You know that we would never do something like that. Kelly was a schoolmate of Josie's years ago. They, uh, didn't like each other."

"I hated her," Josie admitted, "but I never would have killed her."

Ugh. Did she always have to be so brutally honest? Or maybe Josie thought there was nothing to fear since the cop in charge was Brian. Then again, she might not have been thinking at all. "You're not exactly helping your case here," I hissed.

Brian rubbed a hand wearily over his eyes. "Kelly was already dead when you found her, Sally?"

I nodded. "After the fight we went backstage to get cleaned up and left, but I forgot my phone. When I returned to the dressing room, she was lying on the floor with an insulin vial next to her."

Another tap sounded on the door, and Officer Trenton's face reappeared. "Excuse me, Officer, but Donna Dooley's out in the hallway. I've already taken a statement from her. Would you like to speak to her as well?"

Brian flipped a page in his notepad. "Yes, I would, thanks. Please send her in."

Officer Trenton stepped back, allowing Donna to enter. Her somber brown eyes moved to me and Josie then over Brian's intimidating figure leaning against the white vanity table opposite us. I almost did a double take when I saw her. Donna's face was pale and devoid of makeup, and she was dressed casually in jeans, sneakers, and an oversized, purple designer T-shirt. She always seemed so put together with an ethereal air about her. Seeing Donna with no makeup was like picturing Buffalo without snow in the dead of winter—unnatural.

"Did Kelly have an accident?" she asked, her voice hollow.

Brian extended his hand. "Miss Dooley, I'm Officer Jenkins from Colwestern's Police Department. I can't comment on how Kelly died yet, but I would like to ask you some questions."

She sank down onto the couch next to me and placed her Fendi purse in her lap. "Yes, of course. Ask away."

Brian gestured at me and Josie. "You two need to leave the room."

"It's all right," Donna said weakly. "I don't mind if they stay."

By the look on Brian's face, I knew *he* minded and didn't want nosy little me possibly tampering in the investigation. To his credit he refrained from further comment. "When was the last time you saw Mrs. Thompson?" he asked Donna.

Donna's forehead creased into a frown. "It was right before I left. Everyone else was gone, except for a couple of crew members. Sally and Josie may have still been here too. I don't know. As a matter of fact, Kelly came into my room while I was getting dressed. She didn't even bother to knock but marched in as bold as brass. She was very angry about—" Donna hesitated for a moment and cut her eyes to Josie. "There were some problems during taping."

"I'm aware of the problems," Brian said dryly. "It's all over YouTube, in fact."

Donna's face turned as white as powdered sugar. "Yes, so I've heard." She twisted the brown leather strap of her bag. "How am I supposed to explain this to my fans? What happened to her?"

"We're not able to reveal the mode of death yet," Brian said. "How close were you and Kelly?"

She wiggled her hand back and forth. "Kelly had only been working for me for a short time. We got along well enough, but she seemed to have an agenda."

"What do you mean?" Brian asked. "Was she after your job?"

Donna laughed. "Officer, *everyone* is after my job. That type of thing I can handle. I got the impression that Kelly might be using this job as a stepping-stone to her own show. Her husband is some type of hack writer, and I suspected they were in the middle of developing an idea to pitch to the Food Network."

"Has he been notified about her death?" I asked Brian.

Brian shrugged. "From what I've heard, it appears that

they haven't been able to track him down yet."

Donna looked puzzled. "That's odd. He was at the taping this afternoon."

Brian raised an eyebrow. "Really? Did he come to the shows often?"

"Often enough," Donna admitted. "Like I said, I think they might have been looking for ideas. Her sister Shelly was here too. They were sitting right next to each other in the studio audience."

"What's Shelly's last name?" Brian asked.

Donna bit into her lower lip. "I don't remember. I only met the woman once before. Each staff member is allowed to have a couple of guests in the audience. Some only come for the goodie bags or in hopes to be seen on television. Hey, it is what it is. Shelly works at Kelly's bakery, Naturally Delish. From what Kelly said, her sister doesn't have a great deal of culinary skills. On the other hand, Kelly's résumé was so impressive— especially with owning one of the top bakeries in the state—that I hired her on the spot."

"Too bad Kelly didn't have culinary skills either," Josie retorted.

Brian narrowed his eyes at her but didn't comment. "Go on, Miss Dooley."

Donna flushed at Josie's remark. "I'll admit that I was fascinated by the idea of her owning a sugar-free bakery. That kind of sealed the deal for me. I like to hire candidates who have a public presence."

Josie clenched her fists. "Kelly couldn't bake, let alone cook. Charlie Brown could have fixed a better pumpkin pie than she could. She sabotaged my dessert during a baking competition back in culinary school, and there were rumors that she even slept with one of the instructors. I'm guessing it was to ensure that she passed. Perhaps you should think about checking references the next time you hire someone, Donna."

A muscle ticked in Brian's jaw, and he pointed toward the door. "Josie, it might be better if you wait outside."

Her mouth dropped open in surprise. "What for?"

Brian's face was crimson. "*Now.* Sally can go with you or stay here if she prefers."

"I'd like to stay." I whispered in Josie's ear. "He's afraid you'll say something incriminating. Go out to the hallway, and I'll be there in a minute."

"I have nothing to hide," Josie said in a loud, upset voice. "Brian, are you afraid *I* might have killed her? Because I didn't."

Good grief. Even though Brian knew Josie wasn't killer material, this speech of hers wasn't exactly making her sound good.

"Outside, Josie. *Now!*"

It appeared that Brian had finally had enough. I was startled by his tone, and apparently so was Josie who sat there in silent shock.

"Do as he says," I whispered. "Please?"

Josie cast a wounded look upon me, as if I'd suddenly announced to the world that her fudgy delight cookies tasted like mud. Her mouth set in a firm, hard line as she stood, swung her purse over her shoulder in a defiant air, and then flounced out of the room. Oh yeah, it was going to be a fun ride home.

Donna broke the ice. "Officer, I wasn't aware that Josie and Kelly knew each other or that there was bad blood between them. If I'd been apprised of the situation earlier, I would have arranged for Kelly not to be on the set today."

I bristled inwardly. "What does that mean? You mentioned on the set that Kelly told you they went to school together."

Donna was visibly annoyed by my remark. "Yes, but she didn't mention that they disliked each other. How was I supposed to know that? Am I Nancy Drew now?"

Brian sighed and glanced at his watch. It was after nine o'clock, and I hoped that we were almost done—Mike would be worried that he hadn't heard back from me. "All right, ladies. That's enough for tonight." He stared at Donna. "I may have more questions for you in the next few days. Are you flying back to New York City tomorrow? That's where you do most of your taping, right?"

She nodded. "Yes, but I'll be in the area until next week." She drew a business card out of her purse, jotted something down on the back, and then rose to hand Brian the card. "This is my personal cell. I'm staying at the Hilton until next Wednesday. In the meantime I'm doing a couple of more tapings and accepting an award at the Culinary Institute of Buffalo next Wednesday. I'll be leaving for the airport right after the ceremony."

Brian placed the card in his shirt pocket. "I don't know if you'll be able to use the studio tomorrow, given the circumstances. But I'm sure someone will be in touch with you about that."

Her face was pained. "Yes, I understand. We can postpone it for a day, if necessary, or try to make arrangements at another local studio. But as they say, the show must go on."

"I'm sorry for the inconvenience," Brian said, his voice tinged with a note of sarcasm.

Donna didn't seem to notice. "You and me both."

After she had left I remained sitting on the couch, lost in my own thoughts. Brian waved a hand in front of my face. "Your husband's probably worried about you. Or maybe you're planning on staying here all night?"

"Josie must be having a conniption by now. Thanks for coming all the way out here." I hesitated. "Can you please tell me how Kelly died?"

Brian pursed his lips. "I don't want this to leave the room. Understood?"

I nodded.

He folded his arms over his chest. "I stopped to see the medical examiner before coming in here. It seems that someone replaced the insulin in Kelly's vial with antifreeze, and she injected herself with it. The examiner thinks she grew ill too quickly to call for help. He also said it probably wouldn't have done her any good."

My stomach muscles constricted. "Oh God. What a horrible way to die."

Brian nodded. "Just when I thought I'd seen it all."

"Yeah, me too."

He examined my face closely for a moment. "You've got something else on your mind, I can tell."

The man knew me well. "This crime feels way too personal."

"How do you mean?" Brian asked.

"The fact that she was a diabetic," I explained. "Only someone who knew her fairly well would know about that, right? Plus they were able to get a hold of her vial to switch it out or replace it."

"We already know this," Brian said. "Why—"

"I'm not finished," I interrupted. "Then there's the matter of the sugar dumped over Kelly's head. It's like the killer was taunting her for being a diabetic."

Brian seemed impressed by my statement and made a note on his pad. "That's a good assumption, but I have a different theory. I'm wondering if the person who killed her was enraged. Sure, they wanted her dead, but why dump the sugar on her head afterward? It's like they were trying to make a point. Or maybe they wanted to finish what they started earlier."

I understood his meaning. "Brian, please tell me that you're joking."

"Sally," he said, "I saw the footage. Kelly started the fight when she hit Josie with the bag of sugar."

My voice rose an octave. "Josie would never hurt her."

"Was she with you the entire afternoon?" he asked.

Remembering how Josie had gone back for her apron, I decided to clam up. "I'm not even going to dignify that with an answer." Annoyed, I grabbed my purse off the couch and headed for the door.

He put a hand on my arm to stop me. "Look. I'm sorry. Go home, and get some rest. No one is being arrested tonight."

"You know that Josie wouldn't hurt anyone," I protested.

Brian leaned back against the wall, hands in his pockets. "I've seen people do things when they're angry that they would never do under normal circumstances, Sally. All I'm telling you is that it *can* happen. For now Josie's a suspect, same as you."

"Me?" Incredulous, I pointed at myself. "Come on, Brian. You don't think—"

He held up a hand. "It doesn't matter what I think. I'm telling you how it works. We've been down this road before. Everyone who was here today is a potential suspect. That includes you, Josie, Donna, crew members, the studio audience, and whoever else might have been around Kelly. My advice?

Pray that no evidence comes to light to prove Josie was involved because then it will be a totally different scenario."

CHAPTER FIVE

―――

"How'd it go today?" Mike asked.

We were on our way to my parents' house for dinner. It was Friday evening and had started to snow a couple of hours ago, with the weatherman predicting several inches by morning. My mind transported me back to our honeymoon in Hawaii last summer. I would give anything to be there now—away from the snow, homicides, and empty bakeries.

"Awful." I sighed as he reached for my hand and kissed it. "The word must have already leaked out about our so-called involvement in Kelly's death. I don't think we even had a dozen customers today."

"Well, you've been through worse," Mike remarked. "As soon as they find out who killed Kelly, it will all blow over. Try not to worry, princess."

"I tend to worry about everything lately." It was after six o'clock, and the sky was already pitch black, but streetlights illuminated my husband's handsome profile as he drove. If there was one thing I didn't have to worry about, it was my marriage. We were closer than ever since our wedding last July. After breaking up in high school, we'd been apart for more than ten years before finally finding our way back to one another. That had been a lonely time for me, and I'd always known, at least subconsciously, that something was missing from my life. Except for children, I had everything I could possibly want.

Mike realized my mind had shifted direction. "Don't be upset. It's going to happen, okay? No stress. We have plenty of time."

True, we did have plenty of time and had only been trying for a baby since our honeymoon. "My mother doesn't make it easy for me some days."

I used to look forward to dinner at my parents' house. We would go by once or twice a week if Mike wasn't working late. Grandma Rosa was a fantastic cook, and tonight she was making my favorite—pasta with braciole, which was tender, thin slices of beef pan fried with a filling of herbs and cheese then dipped into her rich tomato sauce. The icing on the cake, so to speak, was that she had also made tiramisu. Next to her famous ricotta cheesecake, it was my favorite dessert.

As we pulled into the driveway, an exasperated sigh fell from my mouth. Every time my mother saw me, the first question that popped out of her mouth was if I was pregnant yet. I knew she meant well and was anxious to be a grandmother, but it was difficult to answer her with the same discouraging "no" every time.

My grandmother met us at the front door. From her appearance no one would have dreamed that she'd spent the entire afternoon cooking in the kitchen. There wasn't one trace of sauce on her spotless apron or a single white hair out of place. Her short hairdo framed her wide face in a pleasant manner. Although she was seventy-six years old, her skin and face were devoid of wrinkles, except around her dark, calm eyes that were filled with endless wisdom. Some days I wondered if she was a bit psychic as well.

She smiled as I hugged her, and Mike gave her a kiss on the cheek before he shut the door behind us. As we hung our coats in the foyer's closet, she touched my arm. "I am out here to warn you."

Uh-oh. "What now?"

"Your mama went shopping today. Baby shopping. She thought it might motivate you somehow." Grandma Rosa put a finger to her ear in a circular motion.

I stifled a groan as Mike put an arm around my shoulders. "She has to let up, Rosa. It's not like we aren't trying."

My cheeks burned. "Mike! This is my grandmother, after all."

Amusement settled in Grandma Rosa's eyes. "What? Do you think you are the one who discovered sex? It has been around for a long time before you, my dear."

Mike barked out a laugh, and I raised an eyebrow at both of them. "Well, some things are—you know, private." My grandmother's comments managed to render me speechless some days.

"As they should be," Grandma Rosa agreed. "I did not ask for details. But your mama thought somehow this might help if you saw what she had bought. Do not ask me why. The inside of her head is a very strange place. Even when she was a little girl, I suspected she was off her chair."

Mike and I stared at each other in confusion. "Do you mean off her rocker, Grandma?"

She nodded. "That is good too. Come now. I do not want the food to get cold."

My mother, father, Gianna, and her boyfriend, Johnny, were already seated around the cherrywood dining table. Johnny raised a glass of wine in greeting to us. He was the grandson of Nicoletta Gavelli, who had lived next door to my parents since I was a baby. Johnny had come home to live with his grandmother when she had been diagnosed with bone cancer last year and worked as a history teacher at a local school.

"Hey, guys. Saw you on the news this morning, Sal." His saucy black eyes laughed at me. "You do such great things with flour."

I made a face at him. "Thanks for that, Johnny."

He reached for the Parmesan cheese. "Come on. Give us all the dirt."

Gianna nudged her boyfriend in the side with her elbow. "Can't you wait for them to sit down before you start grilling them?"

"That's your job anyway, my love," he teased. "You are the lawyer in the family, after all."

Mike took the bowl of tomato sauce filled with braciole that my grandmother handed him. "Sal always has the misfortune of being in the wrong place at the wrong time."

"Yep, she does that a lot," my father grunted from the head of the table. He chewed on a piece of braciole then dropped a spot of tomato sauce on his T-shirt stretched tight over his belly. When it came to dinnertime, Domenic Muccio didn't wait for his family. He ate when he felt like it, and then everyone else was welcome to join in when they saw fit. From the looks of things, he was already on his second plate of pasta. In his late sixties he was growing stouter daily, and the bald spot in the middle of his scalp seemed to be increasing along with his weight.

My mother dunked her napkin in water and went to work at the spot on his shirt. "Poor Josie. People have been leaving such nasty comments online saying how she killed that girl. Why are people so cruel?"

"It's all about the media," my father said, his mouth full. "They like playing with your head."

I tried to concentrate on the food in front of me. It looked delicious, but the conversation was already doing a number on my appetite. Josie had said very little at the shop today, which was unusual for her. We'd had a number of hang-ups too. Once, when I answered the phone, I'd been greeted by an elderly man who yelled, "You should be ashamed, you murdering, brazen hussy!"

The YouTube video and pictures that had appeared in our local paper today certainly had not helped business either. The cause of death had leaked out somehow, and I wondered if Kelly's sister or husband might have been responsible. A member of the press had even managed to dig up Josie and Kelly's class picture from pastry school. Ironically they had been standing right next to each other, both smiling brightly for the camera. There was also another shot of Josie and Rob's wedding day when she had been about eight months pregnant. My heart had broken in two when I'd seen her staring at it this morning.

My father was right about the media. By running these photos, they were making things worse for Josie and perhaps even implying they thought she was responsible for Kelly's death. In my opinion this was sabotage, and I wanted it stopped.

"Isn't there anything we can do about those pictures they printed in the paper?" I asked Gianna. "They also included an entire paragraph about how Josie left culinary school when she got pregnant. That's private information. Who leaked this to the paper?"

Gianna shook her rich chestnut hair and brought her wineglass to her lips. My baby sister was my pride and joy.

Three years younger than me, she was so beautiful that everyone always thought she was a model instead of a public defender. People mentioned that we looked like twins, but frankly I didn't see it. My hair was ebony with more curl to it than hers, and in the summertime humidity made it a perpetual frizz. Gianna's framed her angelic-looking face and was always perfect, no matter what the temperature.

"I wish there was something we *could* do," she said, her soft brown eyes fixated on my face. "Unfortunately, it's public information. Reporters are great at sniffing that kind of stuff out. They'll do anything for a story, especially a front page one."

Grandma Rosa sat down on the other side of me. "It is not right. Josie has had a tough life and does not need this gratitude."

"Attitude, Grandma." Gianna drained her glass.

Grandma Rosa nodded in approval. "That works too."

My mother rose from her chair with a package in hand. She had a perfect size-four figure that was accentuated by the strapless, black minidress decorated with rhinestones that she wore. She trotted over to me on her tiny four-inch stiletto heels and brushed her long, dark hair back from her face. "I picked up some sleepers today for you today, honey. Pink, blue, and yellow."

Mike took a healthy sip from the beer in front of him and gave me a piteous glance. I bit into my lower lip and reluctantly reached for the package. "Thanks, Mom. I'll put these with the rest of the inventory."

Johnny glanced from me to Gianna in confusion. "You didn't tell me Sal's eating for two. When did—ouch!"

Gianna's elbow had moved so fast into his ribs that I'd barely seen it. "I'm not pregnant, Johnny. My mother's planning early—like she always does."

Everyone laughed.

My father tapped his fork against his wineglass. "Enough about babies and murders. I have some great news to share. I'm going to be in a commercial!"

Gianna's wineglass shook in her hand. "You're kidding."

"Nope," my father said cheerfully. "It's for a funeral parlor over in Colgate. They advertised on my blog and said that their business has doubled since." He stuck his nose into the air proudly. "Of course my blog *is* the hottest thing to hit this town since snow shovels."

Johnny coughed loudly into his napkin.

"What the heck will you be doing?" Gianna wanted to know.

My father puffed out his chest. "I'll be like a car salesman, except in this case it will be coffins I'm hawking instead."

Gianna's wineglass hit the table with a loud thud and a few drops spilled out. "Oh my God. We'll all have to leave town."

"What do you think, Sal?" my father asked. "After all, you're a big television star now. Want to give your old man some pointers?"

I scrunched my eyes shut. "No offense, Dad, but I've had enough of television for a while. Are they paying you well?"

He nodded eagerly and pointed at Gianna. "I need my lawyer to go over the contract. But it's a good figure, and I even got some extras thrown in."

Gianna frowned. "What kind of extras? Like a burial plot?"

My father's eyes shone. "I hadn't thought of it, but yeah, that would be great. The only problem is that your mother and I already have spots in Paradise Cemetery. Maybe I could sell one of those."

Johnny's body shook from head to toe with laughter, and he made a strangled sound low in his throat.

Gianna shook her head in apparent disbelief. "I'll look at it after dinner. I'd like to think that this won't have you making a fool out of yourself, but I'm pretty sure I already know the answer to that."

"No need to worry." My father assured my sister as he helped himself to another glass of wine. "It will all be very dignified."

Gianna raised an eyebrow at me but said nothing. I knew she was afraid that my father would turn out to be the talk of the town with this commercial. It seemed like we were always the talk of the town anyway, so I didn't know why she bothered to get so upset.

"Stupido," Grandma Rosa muttered under her breath as she brought the tiramisu to the table. "Some things never change around here."

I hadn't been able to eat much dinner but wasted no time digging into the dessert. It was one of those days when I needed chocolate—badly. As usual, Grandma Rosa had outdone herself. The rich, creamy taste of coffee and mascarpone rolled over my tongue, and I lingered over every bite, wanting it to last forever. I closed my eyes in contentment.

When I opened them, Mike was watching me with a bemused expression on his face. He leaned over and whispered in my ear. "I know of something that will make you feel even better than tiramisu."

I suppressed a giggle. "Sounds good to me." My phone buzzed from my purse under the table, but I chose to ignore it. My father hated cell phones at the table. Meal times were for eating, not staring at your screen, he always said.

My mother, who had been unusually silent for the latter part of the meal, now spoke up. "I don't think it's fair, Domenic."

Dad scraped the plate with his fork and then reached for another piece of cake. "What's that, hot stuff?"

Mom's lovely face had twisted into a frown. "That you get to do a commercial before me. I'm the one who had the modeling contract, after all. They didn't even use my pictures."

Gianna stifled a groan. "Mom, it's no one's fault that the magazine canned the ad. You still got paid for it. Sometimes they run out of room. They told you they might feature it in a future issue."

My mother gave a loud harrumph and folded her arms across her chest. "Let them stand there for six hours in their underwear and five-inch stilettos posing, and they might get a better sense of what it was like for me. And I swear that the cameraman was ogling me the entire time."

Ew. Mike lowered his head, but I could see the smile forming at the corners of his mouth. Gianna shot Johnny a sideways glance in warning, and he meekly reached for his wineglass without comment. Grandma Rosa muttered something under her breath as she went to answer the house phone out in the kitchen.

My mother had received a modeling contract for winning first place in a beauty contest last summer. They had told her at the time that there was a possibility some of the ads would wind up on television. Her big dream, besides being a model, was now to be an actress. She still was employed as a real estate agent but never made any sales. One of these days she and my father might come full circle in their career paths. A retired railroad worker, he was actually making a living from his morbid blog, where he proudly referred to himself as Father Death.

My father patted my mother on the knee and wolfed down the rest of his cake. "I know you're the better looking one of us, hot stuff. When I get my own commercials, you'll be the star. I personally guarantee it."

"This is nuts," Gianna mumbled and reached for the wine bottle.

Grandma Rosa stood in the doorway of the kitchen and crooked a finger at me. "You have a phone call, *cara mia*."

Puzzled, I pushed my chair back. "Who would be calling me here?" Even as I said the words, my gut warned that something was wrong. I grabbed the phone and spoke into the receiver. "Hello?"

"Sal, it's Rob." His tone sounded off, and I could hear the kids shouting in the background. "I couldn't get you on your cell and hoped you'd be at your parents. I was wondering if you could do me a favor."

Cripes. Maybe Josie was sick and he wanted us to watch the kids tonight. Mike would freak. We'd watched them a few months ago, and it had not gone well. "Ah, sure. What is it?"

Rob's voice was hoarse. "I need some money and fast. I hate to ask, but you and Mike are the only ones I know that might have it."

I stared at the phone mutely. Rob had never asked to borrow anything from us before. He and Josie were too proud and independent. A chill swept over me. "What's going on? Where's Josie?"

He hesitated for a moment. "In jail."

CHAPTER SIX

———

"She's in *jail*?" I repeated incredulously. "How? What happened?"

Rob breathed heavily into the phone. "The cops just left the house with her. They—" His voice shook, and I knew he was trying to control his emotions. "They waited until I took the kids upstairs. When they asked where mommy was, I told them she'd left to go to a party. They cried because they didn't get to go too."

Mike was at my side. "Oh my God." I whimpered and reached out to him, afraid I might burst into tears.

"Yeah." Rob sounded angry. "When she answered the door and the cops told her why they were there, she didn't even put up a fight. It was like she'd been waiting for them."

"What's wrong?" Mike whispered in my ear.

I covered the receiver. "They took Josie to jail! Get Gianna for me." I removed my hand and spoke into the phone again. "Rob, how could they arrest her? There's no evidence that she did anything."

"Gianna," Mike yelled into the dining room. "We need you."

Rob lowered his voice. "That's where you're wrong. Apparently they found Josie's fingerprints on Kelly's syringe. I guess the footage of the fight on television was more fuel to add to the fire."

I had forgotten all about the syringe. "That's crazy. I was there when she touched it. Kelly dropped the syringe, and Josie threw it back at her. That's all that happened. I'll talk to the cops."

"They won't believe you, Sal," he said. "You're her best

friend, and they'll probably figure you'd say anything to protect her."

"Where is she? I mean, which jail?" I asked.

"The one out in Buffalo," Rob replied. "I'm headed that way now. My mother just got here to watch the kids."

Gianna put her hand out for the phone. "Let me talk to him, Sal."

My body and brain were both numb as I stood there, helpless and confused. I listened as Gianna calmly asked Rob a couple of questions, and then I couldn't even remember what she'd said.

Gianna hung up the phone then pulled hers out of her pocket and scrolled through the contacts for a number. I couldn't stand it anymore. "What's going on? Why did Rob hang up?"

Gianna placed a finger to her lips. "*Shh*. I'm trying to get ahold of a bail bondsman. Rob's coming to get me, and we'll go out to the jail together. I doubt that I can get Josie bonded out this late at night though." Her face was grim. "She's probably going to have to spend the night there, Sal."

The thought sickened me. "She can't stay there! Josie doesn't belong in jail."

Gianna spoke into the phone. "Chuck, this is Gianna Muccio. Please call me back as soon as possible at 716-229-9999. It doesn't matter how late." She clicked off and then gripped me tightly by the shoulders. Her lovely face held that determined look I knew so well. "You need to calm down. I'll get Josie out of there. She has no prior record, right? If I'm acting as her lawyer, they'll let me talk to her. Then I'll go back in the morning with the bail money."

Johnny had joined us. "Let me drive you, babe."

She gave him a quick peck on the lips. "Not necessary. You've got all those essays to correct before class. It's better if just Rob and I go. You'd be stuck waiting around for me, and I don't know how long it might take."

"Shall I wait for you at your apartment?" Johnny's tone sounded a bit anxious.

Gianna looked away from him. "No. Stay at your grandmother's tonight so I don't disturb you. I'll call you when I get in."

Johnny nodded solemnly but said nothing further. I briefly wondered if something might be wrong between the two of them, but would have to find out later. My mind was preoccupied with concern for Josie right now.

"I want to go too." I sounded like a whiny five-year-old.

Gianna frowned. "Didn't you hear what I told Johnny? There's nothing you can do, and they won't let you see her. If you want to do something, get your checkbook ready. Rob hasn't got close to what they'll need for bail."

"It's not the full amount though, right?" Mike asked. "Doesn't she just need a percentage?"

"Yes," Gianna agreed, "but from what Rob told me, they haven't got much to spare."

A shiver ran down my spine as I remembered how I'd had to raise bail money for Mike when he'd been arrested for Colin's murder. My grandmother had been kind enough to lend me the money. I glanced at my husband and could tell from his expression that he was thinking the same thing too. Josie, like Mike, was a proud person. They'd both had less than idealistic childhoods and been denied many things that I'd taken for granted while growing up. The knowledge that we had to lend her money for bail would no doubt humiliate her. Under the circumstances Josie might not want me to see her like this.

Mike ruffled my hair. "Your sister's right, princess. You can see Josie when she gets out."

"Is it okay—about the money?" We had about twenty grand in the bank, thanks in part to some leftover insurance money when my previous shop had burned down.

He nodded soberly. "Of course it's okay. You don't even need to ask me that, Sal."

Our eyes met, and once again I was reminded of how lucky I was to have this man in my life. "Thank you."

A horn sounded from outside. Johnny handed Gianna her coat, and she ran back to the doorway. "Night, Mom, Dad. Thanks for dinner, Grandma. It was amazing as always."

"Be careful, *cara mia*," my grandmother called.

"Knock em' dead, sweetheart," my father yelled from the dining room. His voice was garbled, probably from polishing off another piece of tiramisu.

Gianna rolled her eyes at his comment. As she reached for the knob, the door opened, and she let out a small shriek.

Nicoletta Gavelli stood on the porch, clad in her usual depressing outfit that consisted of a dark, drab housecoat, despite the cold weather. Johnny's mother had died when he was five, and Nicoletta had raised him by herself. She'd never been a fan of mine, especially after she had caught Johnny trying to play doctor with me in her darkened garage when I was six-years-old. Of course it was my fault since Johnny had always been absolved of blame.

She shook her finger at Gianna. "What you do with my grandson? Why I chopped liver? No one invite *me* to dinner. No one think about poor Nicoletta."

"Fool." My grandmother stood behind Gianna. "You were invited, but you decided to go out with Ronald tonight."

Ronald Feathers was in his eighties and Mrs. Gavelli's main squeeze. He was also hard of hearing, which is probably why her mouth, which ran constantly, didn't bother him.

Gianna gave Mrs. Gavelli a little finger wave and ran down the steps. "I don't have time to talk right now, Nicoletta. Good night." She hurried toward Rob's waiting car.

Nicoletta watched as the car backed out of the driveway and then gave Johnny a hard swat to his shoulder. "You let some other man take your girl? What the matter with you?"

Johnny managed to contain his smile. "Come on in before you freeze to death, Gram. Gianna's going to the jail to try to bail Josie out."

Mrs. Gavelli's dark eyes shone like a cat's. "Aha. I knew it! I always say that girl would come to no good. For shame. What she do? She make poisoned fortune cookies, no?"

Grandma Rosa's voice was a low, angry growl. "You do not know what you are saying, old woman. It is all a mistake."

Johnny put an arm around his grandmother's shoulders. "Have some of Rosa's tiramisu, Gram. I'll come back to the house with your afterward."

Mrs. Gavelli snorted. "Bah. She put too much coffee in it." She glanced at her grandson suspiciously. "And what the matter with you and little miss fancy pants lawyer? She too busy to see you last night. She want to break up with you? These

Muccios—they think they too good for everyone."

"Hush, *pazza*." Grandma Rosa scowled at her.

"I no crazy," Mrs. Gavelli announced.

The smile disappeared from Johnny's face. "Gianna and I are fine, Gram." He cut his eyes to me and then looked away abruptly. "Come on. I could use a piece of cake."

I watched them disappear into the dining room then turned to Mike and my grandmother. "I feel so helpless."

Mike rubbed my shoulders gently. "Gianna will handle everything. She knows what she's doing, Sal. Don't worry."

Grandma Rosa's expression was grim. "I do not like this at all. It stinks like that monster cheese your grandfather used to love to eat."

"I think you mean Muenster cheese, Grandma."

She made a face. "Whatever."

"What exactly are you trying to say, Rosa?' Mike asked. "Are you worried about something?"

Grandma Rosa shrugged. "I am not sure. But I will tell you this. Someone is very happy that Josie is in jail tonight."

* * *

The bakery was slow the next day, but as most of our stock had been depleted, I needed to make more dough, plus we had an order of cookies for a bridal shower to fill. My first choice of helper was always my grandmother, despite her age. Unfortunately, she had already promised to take Mrs. Gavelli to visit a mutual friend and wasn't available. Mike was starting a new job but said that he could postpone it until later this afternoon and give me a hand for a while.

While I appreciated the offer and loved spending time with my husband, I cringed at the thought of Mike helping with the actual baking. When he tied on one of our bib-style aprons and even donned a pink and black ball cap without complaint, I started to giggle. He made the apron look quite sexy, but then again, the man made anything he wore sexy. He was smart, sensitive, and loved me unconditionally. Plus he could fix anything around the house. When it came to culinary skills though, Homer Simpson probably had him beat.

He grabbed a bag of ready-made dough balls to be used for sugar cookies out of the freezer and dumped them onto a cookie tray. He then reached for the piping bag as I watched, mystified. "What are you doing?" I asked.

Mike waved the bag at me. "I was going to frost the cookies. I've always wanted to use this thing."

I blinked. "You do know that you have to *bake* the cookies first, right?"

Mike's smile faded. "Oh, right. I forgot about that."

Ugh. The bells jingled over the front door, and I gave him a slight push in that direction. "You go wait on the customers. I'll prep the cookies."

"Sure." He looked disappointed. "Can I frost them later?"

I shook my head in disbelief. "You never made cookies with your mother when you were a kid?"

His expression darkened as he looked down at the tray. "Nope. Mom was too busy hitting the bottle back then."

My heart twisted at his words. Mike hardly ever talked about his childhood, and I understood why. From the small snippets of information I'd gathered and seen first-hand when we'd dated in high school, I knew that his stepfather was abusive and his mother had neglected everything but her alcohol. His biological father had left home when he was five, and he'd never had any further contact with him. I knew better than to press for details but always hoped that over time he might divulge more.

For the next hour we worked well together, and I managed to finish the bridal shower order. Fortunately Josie had made the dough ahead of time, so all I had to do was frost them and arrange the packaging, with Mike's help. While I enjoyed it, I didn't possess the talent Josie did.

It was past noon, and I still hadn't heard from Gianna yet. I tried to remain calm and tell myself that everything was fine, but my concern continued to mount as the clock ticked away precious minutes.

Our delivery boy showed for the order, and after that, things slowed down a bit. A few young women lingered in front of the case, openly flirting with Mike as he rang up their order. After they left I went out front to place some fortune cookies in the case, and he wrapped his strong arms around me.

"No public displays of affection in the shop," I teased. "You never know when Mrs. Gavelli might walk in."

He grinned and kissed me softly on the lips. "That woman needs to lighten up a bit. Maybe that's her problem—she isn't getting any PDA. I feel sorry for Gianna, having that woman for a grandmother-in-law. I lucked out big time compared to her. Well, compared to anyone, actually."

I cocked an eyebrow at him. "What are you talking about? They've only been dating for six months."

Mike's grin faded. "Uh, forget I said anything."

"Wait a minute." I pulled on his T-shirt as he started to walk into the back room. "What do you know that you're not telling me?"

He sighed. "Johnny asked me not to say anything. Remember how last week he stopped by the house because he's thinking of buying my bike? He told me out in the garage that he was planning on asking her something very important soon."

"Oh my God." Maybe Johnny had asked her already, and that was why Gianna had been acting strange last night. "It's definitely time for a sister heart-to-heart talk."

Mike groaned. "Great. Me and my big mouth. What if he hasn't said anything to her yet? You'll ruin it."

"I have to give her some warning that it's coming." Cripes, didn't men understand anything? "You don't know my sister like I do. I'm not sure Gianna's ready for marriage yet, and this would totally freak her out."

"Women," he muttered under his breath. "I'll never understand them."

I wrapped my arms around his waist. "Oh, come on. You know you love it."

He ran a finger down my cheek. "I love *you*. I know that much." His gaze turned somber. "Sal, I'm worried about you getting involved in this mess with Josie."

"What are you talking about? She's my best friend. When you were accused of murdering Colin, she stood by my side. Is this about the money? You know they'll pay it back."

Mike raised a hand in the air. "I'm not worried about the money. Rob's been a good friend, and I hate seeing them go through this. I didn't mean to imply that you shouldn't help her financially. But this feels more like someone is out to get her. You know, with the entire YouTube catastrophe and now her being arrested. I don't want it to affect you too."

"It already has," I said sadly. "I texted Gianna but haven't heard anything back yet. Hopefully Josie's out of jail by now. She's my best friend, and I plan on doing anything I can to help her."

Mike sighed. "Okay, but please be careful. I worry about you. You're collecting dead bodies in your life the way that some people collect baseball cards. It looks like this has started to affect your business too. I'm guessing that the only reason you had any customers today is because they heard about Josie's arrest. Nothing is a secret in this town, remember."

"We were slow before the murder too." My tone sounded a bit defensive.

Mike's phone buzzed. He unclipped it from his jeans and stared down at the screen. "I've got a client with a leaky roof. I wish people would learn how to brush snow off them occasionally so they wouldn't have these problems."

"But then *you* wouldn't have any business," I reminded him.

He grinned. "You do have a point. Would you mind if I bailed, princess? I don't like leaving you here all alone, though."

I waved my hand dismissively. "All the baking is done for the day, so I'll be fine. But I don't like to think about you up on an icy roof." The proverbial worrier in me would not be silenced today.

He gave me a swift kiss. "It's what I do, my love. How about I bring home some takeout and my beautiful wife and I grab some wine and cuddle in front of the fireplace all night?"

"That sounds like heaven. Maybe we can even watch a chick flick," I teased.

Mike groaned out loud then laughed. "Man, I am such a pushover for you."

After he was gone, I went into the back room and popped a batch of butter cookies into the oven along with some more chocolate chips. I wasn't sure we would need them at this rate, but I could always drop some off at my parents' house later along with fortune cookies. I grabbed some out of the display case and started to place them in a Ziploc bag. A message that had come loose from one was now staring me right in the face. There was no way to avoid it.

I chuckled to myself and waved the message gallantly in the air. "Oh, enchanted fortune cookie, what words of wisdom do you have for me today?"

We'd had a long talk about these somewhat cryptic messages on our honeymoon. Since then, I thought I'd done an okay job of not letting them bother me as much. Mike had told me in no uncertain terms that I was taking them a bit too seriously, and I'd agreed to try to lighten up. The fortunes hadn't seemed so ominous as of late. Perhaps there was something to the whole mind over matter thing. Hopeful, I opened my eyes and read the strip of paper.

Sometimes the past can haunt our future.

Great, another oddball one. Why couldn't I get a normal message like *You have a nice smile* or *Life is short, so eat the cookie.* Was there such a thing as a *normal* message in my shop? With a shiver I threw the message in the trash and went about my business.

My phone buzzed with a message from Gianna. *Josie's out. Paperwork took forever! We'll be leaving in a few. She wants to stop over and see you.*

I sighed in relief and texted back. *Thanks for everything. Does she seem okay?*

Her reply came back within a minute. *She says yes, but I have my doubts. She's acting kind of strange. We'll see you soon.*

No problem, and thanks again. I breathed a sigh of relief about Josie but wished I'd had more of an opportunity to talk to Gianna before her dinner date. What if Johnny was planning to propose tonight?

The bells over the front door were put into motion, announcing I had a customer. I blew out a sigh and put the phone away. Customers were in rare supply these days, so I wiped my hands on my apron and went out into the storefront.

A man, who I guessed might be in his early fifties, was standing in front of the display case, hands stuffed inside a navy blue L.L. Bean jacket. He looked up when I entered the room and smiled. He was very good-looking, with silver-colored hair and piercing blue eyes. Something about him seemed familiar, although I was quite certain I'd never seen him before.

"Hi, can I help you?"

He nodded. "Are you Sally Donovan, the owner?"

"That's right. What can I do for you?"

The man glanced into the display case. "Well, the cookies look great, but I'm actually here to see you. I confess I've wanted to meet you for quite a while."

Oh, jeez. Please don't let this be a reporter or have anything to do with Josie's arrest. "Sorry. I didn't catch your name."

He extended a hand. "Sam Donovan. I'm your father-in-law."

CHAPTER SEVEN

My knees started to buckle underneath me. I reached out a hand and grabbed the edge of the display case in an effort to steady myself.

Sam was quick to step forward and placed a hand under my elbow to support me. "Are you okay, Sally? Your face is the color of chalk."

I nodded and opened my mouth but couldn't get any words to tumble out.

Sam led me toward the tables by the front window and helped me into a chair. "Would you like some water?"

"No," I managed to choke out. He sat down across from me and said something, but my heart pounded so loudly in my ears that I couldn't make it out. All I could think about was my husband. How would he react when I gave him the news that the man who'd walked out on him 25 years ago was back?

Not well. That was for sure.

Sam's blue eyes smiled into mine. "My son has very good taste. Congratulations on your marriage. I saw the announcement in the paper a few months back but figured I'd wait until after the holidays to pay a call."

Breathe, Sal. Breathe. I hoped that I wouldn't sound like a babbling idiot. "Have you been in town for long?"

"Since the fall," he replied. "I've been renting an apartment over on Woodside Boulevard. Before that, I lived in Massachusetts for the last twenty years. I'm getting on in age and decided that it was about time to make amends with my boy."

Make amends. That's what he called it after walking out on his only child 25 years ago. It wasn't my place to judge him. Plus I didn't know this man or his personal circumstances. Still, thanks to his desertion, Mike's only vivid memories of fatherhood were of the stepfather who used to smack him around all the time. Call me crazy, but I didn't think he was about to welcome this man back with open arms.

"Can I get you a cup of coffee?" At least it would keep me busy for a minute, and maybe by then I could think of something to say that didn't sound accusatory.

"Please," Sam said. "Decaf if you have it."

I rose to my feet, a bit steadier this time, and went to the Keurig behind the display case. As I placed the K-Cup inside the machine, I stole a glance in his direction. He was studying the shop with interest. Sam had a lot of physical similarities to Mike. Although they both had the same eye color, his were not the midnight shade of blue that Mike's were. Sam had the same strong defined jaw and rugged face, but his complexion was lighter. He was about the same height as his son, and though his body looked to be a bit on the soft side, it appeared that he once might have had the same muscular build as my husband.

"Cream and sugar?" *Why did you walk out on your son when he was so young? Didn't you know his stepfather abused him?*

"No thanks. I take it black."

I brought the paper cup over to the table and sat across from him. There was an awkward silence as we both tried to decide what to say next. I needed something to occupy my hands and fumbled with the lace tablecloth. "So, I take it you haven't seen Mike yet."

Sam took a sip from the cup and eyed me thoughtfully. "No. I figured I'd start with you and find out if you thought he might be receptive to seeing me."

"I can't answer for him."

He nodded. "Of course. Sally, I'm sure you have questions, and I'm positive Mike won't be thrilled to see me. He's moved on, started a new life. I'm not in the best of health these days and was hoping to set things right with my son—before anything happens, that is."

Uh-oh. A knot formed in the pit of my stomach. So that was it. Sam was dying and wanted to repair his relationship with his son before the fatal day came. I was sad for the man, but my first allegiance was to my husband. Sam had traumatized him enough, and now he was about to do it all over again. "I'm very sorry to hear that."

"Where's Mike today?" he asked. "I stopped over at your house a couple of days ago, but no one was home. The wedding announcement in the paper said he ran his own construction company while you owned a bakery. You two must be doing quite well for yourselves. I always knew he was a go-getter."

I smiled. "It's a one-man company, but Mike does okay. He can do anything with his hands." I flinched as I said the words, hoping he wouldn't take the statement out of context.

Sam didn't seem to notice. He stared down at the paper cup and blew out a long sigh. "He must have learned that trade from Ray. I can barely nail a board in place, but Ray could do everything, or so I was told."

For some reason I thought he'd never had contact with Mike's mother. "You knew that Tonya had remarried?"

He nodded. "Of course. We corresponded a few times a year. I paid alimony—well, when I could afford it, that is. I have to admit it was a blessing to hear that she'd remarried." He watched me with interest. "Does Ray still live at the house with you?"

I drew my eyebrows together in confusion and shook my head. "Mike said that his stepfather took off when Tonya got sick. Then Mike moved back in to take care of her." I had been living in Florida with Colin when that happened. "Did you go to her funeral?"

The color rose in Sam's face. "No, I'm ashamed to say that I didn't. I sent flowers though."

How freaking noble of you. I usually prided myself on being a tolerant person, but right now anger bubbled dangerously close to the surface for me. I counted to ten in my head before I spoke again. "If you'd kept in touch with Tonya, why didn't you ever go to see Mike?"

He stared down at the table, refusing to meet my gaze. "I thought I should stay away. Mike was better off without me."

Sure, he was better off without you. He had to contend with a drunken mother and an abusive stepfather, thanks to your absence. To me, it sounded like a lame excuse. Furious, I scraped the chair against the floor and walked angrily behind the display case to fix myself a cup of coffee in the Keurig, even though I'd already had four today. I didn't want to look at Sam any longer. To my surprise he got up from his chair and followed me.

"Sally, please try to understand," he began.

I whirled around and spoke in a tone that sounded surprisingly cold to my own ears. "Do you have any idea what your son went through back then? Did you know that Ray used to hit him all the time? Once he even came to school with a broken rib." Tears lodged in my throat as I remembered the incident, which is why I hadn't let myself think about it for years. We'd only started dating a few weeks before. Mike had been in horrible pain that day and could barely walk. When I'd figured out what had happened, he refused to confirm it. I'd phoned my grandmother who had met us at school and driven him to the emergency room, where he then lied to the doctor and said he'd fallen off a roof.

The expression on Sam's face was of pure shock. "I had no idea." He was silent for a moment and rubbed a hand over his face thoughtfully. "So Ray has never been back?"

I wasn't sure why he was so curious about Ray. "No." Mike once mentioned to me that his stepfather hadn't even attended the funeral. I'd wanted to go but had been living in Florida with Colin at the time. Tonya and Ray had divorced shortly before she died, and I wasn't sure if Sam knew that either. If he wanted any more information, he could ask his son.

"Sally, I'd like to see him," Sam said. "I just want to talk to him for a little while. Could I stop by the house tonight after dinner, say around seven?"

I hesitated. The shop closed up at six, and Mike had indicated that he might beat me home tonight, which was rare for him. There was no way to know for sure if he'd even want to see Sam, but the decision was entirely his to make, not mine. "I need to talk to Mike first. Is there a number where I can reach you?"

Sam nodded. "Do you have a piece of paper?"

I grabbed a Post-it note and pen from the counter so that he could write down his information. He gave the paper back to me and then reached for my hand. "It was wonderful to meet you."

I forced myself to smile in return. "It was nice to meet you too, Sam."

"Call me Dad." His eyes had an eerie quality to them that I couldn't quite make out. Sadness about the past, perhaps? And no way was I calling him Dad. I had one father, and he was more than enough. Yes, he was a bit strange at times, but at least he'd always been there for me.

I gave a small wave as Sam exited the building then immediately withdrew my phone from my jeans pocket and typed out a text to Mike. *I need to talk to you when you have a chance.*

I had just finished the message when the bells chimed again. For the second time in less than half an hour, I received a surprise. I stared at the woman who stood in front of me and figured I must be hallucinating.

Kelly Thompson was standing there, her hazel eyes surveying me with mild amusement. "Hello, Sally."

My jaw dropped, and I blinked several times. "How? You—I found you—they said you were—"

To my surprise she gave a hollow laugh. "I'm not Kelly. I'm her twin sister, Shelly." Her mouth twisted into a frown. "Who killed my sister? Was it you? No, wait. It was that partner of yours. I hope she's still in jail where she belongs."

For some strange reason *The Wizard of Oz* and Margaret Hamilton's green face popped into my head. "Josie didn't kill Kelly."

Shelly gave me a surprised look. "Please. I saw the whole thing. I was sitting in the studio audience. Kelly even told me how jealous Josie was of her when they went to culinary school together."

I clenched my fists at my sides. "Josie didn't do this. I'd stake my life on it."

She looked around the shop with a defiant air. "Hmm. What about your business? Would you stake that as well? I hope Josie doesn't own a share of your shop. If she does, Barry might try to take that in the lawsuit."

The nerve of this woman. "Who the heck is Barry?"

"My brother-in-law," she replied. "Kelly's husband. He's

planning a wrongful death suit against Josie."

I couldn't believe my ears. "You need to leave. I'm sorry for your loss, but my friend had nothing to do with Kelly's murder. I was with her the entire time."

"No, you weren't," she sneered. "I saw her wandering around the set before you guys left, and she was alone. Josie had plenty of time to switch Kelly's vial or empty the insulin out. There was a fridge in the employee's break room where Kelly kept it."

"How do you know? Have you been to this television station before?"

Shelly scanned me up and down. "Once. They're all set up the same way, though. I heard Josie's fingerprints were found on Kelly's syringe, too. More than enough proof for me."

I took a step closer to Shelly and tried to control my anger. Until recently, I might have been intimidated by someone like her. I'd always hated confrontation and tried to avoid it, but this was my best friend we were talking about. After twenty-nine-years on this earth, I had finally started to exert myself. Okay, perhaps not to Josie's level, but that was a special quality she'd been born with.

"You're wasting time here," I said. "You should be out looking for the real killer. I'll do whatever it takes to prove my friend's innocence, so please don't mess with me."

Shelly seemed a bit shell-shocked at my response and then lowered her face to the floor. "I only want justice for my sister. Everyone loved Kelly."

Somehow I doubted that last remark. "Was there perhaps maybe one person who didn't like her very much? Someone who might have been jealous of her success—like the job with Donna or her bakery?"

Shelly reached into her pocket for a tissue and wiped at her eyes, but I couldn't find any tears. "The only other person I can think of is Anita."

I struggled to remember where I had heard that name recently. "Does she work at Kelly's bakery? Is she the manager?"

Shelly stuck her nose proudly up in the air. "*I'm* the manager at Kelly's bakery. I've been overseeing everything there since Kelly started working as Donna's assistant. It works out great because when people see me, they think I'm Kelly. Get it? We've played that switcheroo game since we were kids."

"You didn't answer my question," I said. "Who's Anita?"

For someone whose sister had been murdered a couple of days before, Shelly didn't appear to be grieving much. Like an eager child, she spread her hands wide apart on the display case. "I thought your fortune cookie spiel on the show was a bit tiresome. It lacked originality."

How I wished I had a special fortune cookie message just for her.

"Anita was supposed to get the job on Donna's show," Shelly explained. "Donna was all set to hire her, but when she saw Kelly's impressive résumé, she changed her mind, and poor little Anita was left out in the cold."

Now I remembered the connection. Anita had been backstage the day we taped the show and had asked to see Donna. Suddenly I wondered who else might have been wronged by Kelly, besides Josie and Anita. "Who gets the bakery now that Kelly is gone?"

Shelly cocked her head sideways to look at me. "What are you implying? I loved my sister. We were twins for God's sake. Don't you know anything about the bond between twins? There's nothing stronger."

Growing up, I'd gone to school with a set of identical twins—Janet and June Fishbone. Every time I ran into them, they were either pulling each other's hair out by the roots or screaming at the top of their lungs at each other. Their mother had specifically requested that they always be placed in separate classrooms. I had no doubt that some twins did have a close, loving bond but knew first hand that others fell into Janet and June's category.

Shelly hoisted her enormous Gucci handbag over her shoulder. "The wake is tomorrow, if you'd care to pay your respects. It's at Gavin Funeral Home in Colgate from three to seven. Please don't bring the killer, though."

"Stop calling her that." I wasn't familiar with the town but figured my father would know the place. How could I ask without him wanting to tag along, though? He loved wakes. My father had an annual subscription to both *Coffins Are Us* and

Funeral Homes Unlimited. It was difficult to imagine that people would pay money for magazines like that, but he happily obliged. Maybe GPS was the way to go this time.

"Yes, I would be glad to come pay my respects. Do you think there could have been anyone else besides Anita that wanted your sister dead? How was Kelly's relationship with Donna?"

"She loved Donna," Shelly crooned. "Personally, I think that chick is a bit stuck on herself, but I suppose fame will do that to a person. Now that's a job that someone would kill for— literally. I'm telling you, Anita was livid when she got passed over for Kelly. If your friend hadn't done the deed, Anita would be my next guess."

I sucked in a sharp breath. "Please stop referring to my friend like that. Again, I'm sorry for your loss but think it would be better if you left now."

Shelly's eyes swooped over me like a hawk. "I have to admit there's a bit more to you than meets the eye. You looked like such a meek little thing at the studio the other day."

I lifted my chin in defiance. "Perhaps some of Josie has rubbed off on me over the years. She's as tough as nails." They didn't come any more resilient than my best friend whose life had been rough compared to my somewhat pampered upbringing. With Gianna's help and mine, she'd get through this mess. I was certain of it.

Shelly gave me one last cool, superior look and started for the door. Before she could open it, the bells jingled, and Gianna and Josie entered, stomping snow from their boots.

Josie looked tired and her face a bit gaunt. She was dressed in faded blue jeans and a brown parka. Her eyes met Shelly's, and she immediately turned pale underneath her freckles. She emitted a low, guttural sound from her throat.

Shelly turned to me. "Tough as nails, huh?" Her mouth turned upward at the corners. "How's our jailbird doing today?"

"She's alive!" Josie squeaked and pitched forward onto the linoleum floor.

CHAPTER EIGHT

———

"It's nothing to be embarrassed about." I patted Josie's hand and motioned to the cup of tea on the table. "Come on. Have another sip."

"Right," Gianna chimed in. "Sal fainted at her confirmation. Dad was all upset. He thought she was pregnant."

Good grief. I narrowed my eyes at my sister. "It was 95 degrees in that church. I wasn't the only girl who fainted that day either."

"No," Gianna agreed. "But you were the only one who *wasn't* pregnant."

Josie released my hand and wrapped both of hers around the mug. "I've never fainted before in my life. The shock must have been too much. I never knew Kelly had an identical twin."

"Have you been home to see the kids yet?" I asked.

She shook her head. "My mother-in-law kept them last night, and Rob's with them now. They think that you and I went away somewhere for the weekend. Rob's mom is keeping them until tomorrow. When we left the jail, I phoned him and said that I was stopping by the bakery first to thank you for the money." Her lower lip trembled, and her eyes started to cloud over. "Please thank Mike for me as well."

"Hey. There's no need for thanks. You would have done the same for me."

Her hands shook slightly as she brought the mug to her mouth for another sip. I hated to see her like this. Josie was always such a firecracker—a strong, wise-mouthed force to be reckoned with. Now it was as if someone had suddenly extinguished her fuse. "Gianna's going to get you out of this mess." I stared at my sister hopefully. "You'll represent her, right?"

Gianna drained her coffee cup. "Of course I will. You didn't even need to ask. The grand jury will be meeting in a couple of weeks. In the meantime I'll see what I can find out from the police about the investigation."

"Brian was given permission to work on this case, even though it's out of his jurisdiction," I explained.

"It's always good to have an ally," Gianna agreed. "I may be able to do some snooping around myself. For example, check into how Kelly's bakery was doing financially. If she had outstanding bills, etc."

"What about her will?" I asked. "Can you get access to it?"

She frowned. "If I knew the lawyer, there might be a slim chance. But it's highly unethical. I really don't want to go that route."

My sister took her law career very seriously and always went by the book, so I said nothing further. Still, I didn't care a great deal about what might be deemed unethical right now. My only concern was to help my friend. "I was invited to stop by the wake tomorrow, so I'm going to do a little snooping around myself. Want to join me?"

Gianna nodded. "Sure. What time's the service?"

"Shelly said it was from three to seven. I'd prefer to go as early as we can."

"Well, don't tell Dad," Gianna warned. "I don't want him tagging along. And now people are starting to recognize him from that dumb blog. It's so embarrassing."

The shocking part was that my father's new career was actually taking off, thanks in part to funeral homes that chose to advertise on his blog. Who knew such a thing was possible?

Josie cleared her throat. "I'm coming too."

"No, you're not," I said.

"Sal's right," Gianna chimed in. "God knows what those people would do to you."

Josie bit into her lower lip. "This is my life we're talking about. I want to be in on the investigation."

If Josie walked into that funeral parlor, there was a good chance someone would recognize her from the video and attack her. Heck, it might not be a good idea for me to go either, but Shelly had invited me. Plus I wanted to find out what was going on. "I am thinking about your life. I don't want someone to try to jeopardize it. We don't know anything about Kelly's family or what they might try to do to you. What if we compromise? You wait in the car while Gianna and I go inside. You could observe the people in the parking lot—who seems genuinely distraught, who comes out for a cigarette break. We have to think about this in a rational manner."

Josie's nostrils flared. "So that's it? I'm irrational because I'm a jailbird now?"

"As your lawyer I'm telling you to do as Sal says," Gianna put in. "If someone sees you there and starts a fight, you could wind up back in jail. Do you want your kids to witness that?"

Josie lowered her eyes to the table and didn't answer. My chest constricted with pain as I watched her. She'd been through so much that I only wanted to make this all go away for her.

"All right," she said quietly. "I'll stay in the car."

"Good." Gianna checked her watch and rose. "I need to get going. There's another client for me to see, and then Johnny and I are going out."

"I'll walk you outside." I turned to Josie. "Do you want me to drive you home or have Gianna take you?"

Josie started toward the back room. "There's still over an hour until closing, so I'll wait for you, Sal. I'd like to make some dough. It would be nice to keep my hands busy for a while."

"Okay." I went outside with Gianna. It was freezing, and I hadn't bothered to grab my coat, so I stood there shivering while she unlocked her car. "What are her chances, Gi?"

Gianna wiggled her hand back and forth. "You know I'll do everything I can. But Josie had a clear motive, and they found her fingerprints. Plus you can't be an alibi because you weren't with her every minute. Does this sound familiar?"

I exhaled a sharp breath and watched it form a perfect round circle in the cold air. The same thing had happened to Mike after Colin had been murdered. They'd gotten into a public brawl at a local bar when Colin tried to attack me. Unbeknownst to me, Mike had gone to his hotel room in the middle of the night to confront him. Nothing happened, but the police had found Mike's fingerprints, and he was the number one suspect when Colin was discovered shot to death the next morning.

"I don't want to think about that," I said. "Kelly started the fight with Josie. She did some awful things to her in culinary school, and I'm sure that she must have been rotten to other people as well. Shelly said that another woman was all set to get the job with Donna until Kelly appeared out of thin air. If we go to her wake tomorrow, we might discover some more potential enemies."

"Say no more. I'll pick you up about 2:30 and grab Josie too." Gianna gave me a warm hug. "I want to talk to you alone at some point though."

My mind traveled back to dinner last night. "Are you and Johnny okay?"

She stared at me in wonder. "What makes you say that?"

"Because you acted annoyed with him last night."

Gianna's cheeks were tinted pink. "Was it that obvious?"

"To me it was," I admitted. Undoubtedly it was to Grandma Rosa as well. She never missed anything. "What's going on?"

She watched as I continued to shiver in the cold. "You're freezing, and I really have to go. We'll talk later."

"Come on," I implored. "You always tell me everything."

"Josie needs you now. Like I said, we'll talk later." Without another word she got into the car, started the engine, and zoomed off.

Cripes. A couple of days ago my life had been in a humdrum state, and now chaos was my middle name. I checked my phone but had no new messages from Mike. When I went into the back room to clean up, Josie had finished making her batch of cookie dough and was preparing to store it in the walk-in freezer.

"Be careful with the door," she said. "It seems to have trouble unlatching. If you need to go inside, use something to keep the door wedged open."

"Oh, jeez. It was fine earlier today. I'll ask Mike to look at it." I went back into the front room, locked the door, switched the sign over to *Closed*, and then grabbed my coat. "Is Rob at the house?"

She shrugged into her parka. "By now he should be. The kids are staying at his mother's tonight. I almost don't want to go home."

Confused, I stared at her. "Why?"

Josie turned anxious blue eyes upon me. "Because he's going to be angry. He always says that I'm too quick with my temper and don't have enough restraint. He thinks I should be more laid back like him. Do you think I'm too impulsive?"

I gave her what I hoped was a disbelieving look. "Do you really want me to answer that?"

She put her phone in her purse. "Not necessary. I wish I had more patience like you, but it's hard for me. All my life I've had to fight for everything. It's the only way I know how to react."

"Kelly started it." I locked the door behind us.

"Yes, but I should have ignored her." Josie settled herself into the front passenger seat of the Kia Sportage I'd bought last summer when my Toyota had been totaled. "It's been ten years for God's sake. Sure, it was a missed opportunity, but last night showed me how much I have to be thankful for." Her voice broke. "Now I may lose it all."

A tear rolled down her cheek, and I had to blink my own back as well. It wouldn't do any good for me to start crying. I had to be strong for my friend and let her know that she could always count on me. "That's not going to happen. I won't let it." I wrapped my arms around Josie, and she rested her head on my shoulder as she continued to weep in silence.

After a minute Josie straightened up and wiped at her eyes. "You can drive me home now." She then turned her head and stared out the window.

I knew better than to argue with her, and the remainder of the drive was quiet. When I pulled up in front of the little yellow bungalow where Josie, Rob, and their children lived, the usual cozy look to the house seemed to have disappeared. There was one light on in the living room, while the rest of the house was mired in darkness. Rob's Hyundai was parked in the driveway, and Josie glanced at it nervously.

I squeezed her hand in reassurance. "Do you want me to come in with you?"

She shook her head. "I'm sure Mike's waiting for you. Besides, I need to do this by myself."

Her voice was not encouraging and sounded as if she was gearing up for one mother of a fight. "Hey, Jos, let me—"

"Thanks for everything, Sal." Josie opened the car door in a sudden rush then slammed it shut behind her. I watched as she trudged toward the front door, her head bent against the chilling wind, and I was overwhelmed with pity for her.

No. They'll be okay. Josie and Rob had been married for eleven years, had four beautiful boys, and they loved each other. They'd work it out, and I was determined to learn who was trying to ruin Josie's life. The wake for Kelly tomorrow was a good place to start.

Before I pulled out of the driveway, I checked my phone, and as I'd suspected Mike had texted. Usually I arrived home before him, and he always worried when he hadn't heard from me. This was not a sign of distrust on his part. Given my past dealings with murder and mayhem and assorted psychopaths, his concern was justified. His message was short and to the point as always. *What did you want to talk about, princess? Where are you?*

Since I was only about ten minutes away, I decided to wait until I got home to give him the news in person about his father. *Just dropped Josie off. Be home soon.*

I tucked the phone back into my purse and placed the car in drive. What in the world was I going to say to Mike? His reaction concerned me. Would he be happy or angry with the news that his father was back? I knew this man better than anyone else on earth did and was betting on the latter.

The lights were all ablaze in my comfortable little home, and Spike barked as I hurried up the steps of the front porch. I loved our small ranch house that had belonged to Mike's mother until she succumbed to cirrhosis. To Mike's credit, he had taken good care of Tonya in her final days—something that must have been difficult for him, although he'd never complained about it to me.

The smell of egg rolls and fried rice were in the air, and

my stomach began to growl. Mike could make a mean steak on the grill, but that was about the extent of his culinary talents. I was a fair cook but didn't even come close to my grandmother's expertise. With our hectic schedules it was easier to order out a couple of times a week.

Spike met me at the front door. He was a black and white Shih-Tzu who I'd helped Mike pick out at the shelter shortly before we'd broken up in high school. Even though he was almost 13 now, he still acted like a puppy most of the time. He rolled over and gave me permission to scratch his belly. "Who's a good boy?" I crooned.

"I know I am," Mike teased as he came out of the kitchen with a beer in one hand and a wine cooler in the other for me. He handed me the drink and leaned down to kiss me then nuzzled my neck. "Hmm. I've wanted to do that all day. How was your day after I left?"

"Long and weird," I said wearily as he helped me out of my coat. "I'm worried about Josie."

He took the coat from me and hung it by the front door. "Yeah, I know. I've been thinking about her all day. This does kind of hit close to home."

I shivered as he put his strong arms around me. "It was almost a year ago when this happened to you—us. It's like some freaky kind of déjà vu."

He ran his hands up the inside of my shirt. "It's not something I enjoy reminiscing about. Look. I don't want to sound insensitive to Josie's plight, but I'm starving, and I'm not just talking about food."

My entire body tingled. "Oh, really? What exactly did you have in mind?"

He gazed down at me with those beautiful midnight blue eyes of his. "I think you know what I have in mind. Do you want to eat dinner now—" He paused. "Or wait until later?"

"Hmm." I took a sip of my wine cooler. "Chinese food tastes great when you reheat it."

"My sentiments exactly." Mike placed his lips over mine.

A knock sounded on the front door. We broke apart, and I groaned. "Who could that be?"

He shooed me in the direction of the bedroom. "Go slip into something sexy while I get rid of whoever it is. Probably the paper boy. He left a note earlier saying he'd be back tonight for his money."

I found a pretty white nightie that Mike had given me for Christmas and covered it with a satin, pink robe. Spending an intimate, relaxing evening alone with my husband was my favorite part of the day. I hated to ruin the moment by telling Mike about his father but couldn't wait any longer. Hopefully he'd still be feeling romantic afterward.

Muffled voices could be heard coming from the living room, and then there was complete silence. The front door shut, so I assumed that Jimmy, the paperboy, was on his way home. I hadn't seen car lights from the window, so he must have walked the short distance from his parents' house down the block. I fussed with my hair in the mirror, tied the robe around my waist, and called out to my husband. "Ready or not, sexy, here I come."

Mike stood in front of the fireplace, his hand on the mantel as he stared down at the roaring fire. His back was to the man who stood by the front door, also in silence, hands thrust deep into his coat pockets. Both men looked up when I entered the room.

My hands flew to my mouth when I saw who it was. "Sam, what are you doing here?"

Sam shifted nervously from one foot to another as he took in my appearance. "Hello, Sally. I see that I'm interrupting something here."

Mike fixed his gaze on me. His eyes, which minutes ago had been inviting and warm, now smoldered away like an inferno as they glared accusingly at me. "Next time you invite my father over, maybe you'll let me know about it first, Sal."

CHAPTER NINE

Panic seared through my body. I stared at Sam, expecting him to come to my defense, but he remained silent. *Thanks a lot.*

"It's not what you think," I stammered. "I told Sam I'd call and let him know if it was all right for him to come over. He was *not* invited by me."

"She's right, Mike," Sam said. "This isn't Sally's fault. If you want to be angry at anyone, be mad at me."

Mike suppressed a laugh as he turned to look at his father. The resemblance between the two was striking and also eerie at the same time. "Why would I want to waste any kind of emotion on you? I have no feelings at all toward you. For the life of me, I can't even figure out why you bothered to come here."

Oh, boy. This was worse than I'd feared. "Mike—"

"Stay out of this, Sal." His voice was a low, angry growl—one that I hadn't heard directed at me in years. It reminded me of our high school prom when he'd punched out a guy who'd asked me to dance.

Sam stepped forward. "Son, I know that it's been a long time. Too long, in fact. I just hoped that maybe we could talk for a little while and get to know each other better."

Mike drew his eyebrows together in disbelief. "Well, you thought wrong. I never knew you at all. Now please get out of our house."

Sam glanced around the room and a prideful smile played out on his lips. "You've done a great job with the place, son. It was falling to pieces when you were a kid. I remember one time when a huge chunk of the ceiling fell out during dinner. We had people over too." He chuckled. "Yeah, it was pretty embarrassing."

Mike clenched his jaw. "I asked you to leave."

Sam glanced from his son to me, as if expecting me to say something in his defense. I moved closer to Mike, where my loyalty laid, and placed a hand on his arm. It became rigid at my touch. An icy chill engulfed me, and for a second I wondered if Sam had left the front door ajar. No such luck.

Sam at least had the decency to look embarrassed. "Sorry about this. I should have checked first, but I was anxious to see you."

His statement provoked no further response from Mike, who looked at the man as if he didn't really see him. In desperation Sam turned to me. "Sally, you have my phone number. I hope to hear from you soon."

As he grabbed hold of the doorknob, he stole a backward glance at Mike, perhaps hoping his son would have a sudden change of heart. My stomach convulsed as I watched the emotions play out across Mike's face. He didn't stay and watch Sam leave. Instead, he turned on his heel and strode angrily toward our bedroom without a word to either one of us.

Feeling helpless, I held the door open for Sam. He leaned down and gave me a kiss on the cheek. "I hope I haven't caused any trouble between you and Mike."

"It's fine," I lied. "But you should have waited for me to call you first. He's obviously upset, so if you'll excuse me, I need to go see how he is."

Sam scratched his head in a thoughtful manner. "You're right. I've really screwed things up, and now he's probably angry at you too."

"No worries. Everything will work itself out." I glanced out into the night and scanned the driveway. "Where's your car?"

Sam looked apologetic. "I parked down the street. Guess that was kind of a cowardly thing to do, huh? I thought that if Mike was caught off guard, he'd be more willing to talk to me."

Oh, you certainly caught him off guard all right. I said good night to the man and then shut and locked the door behind him. With caution I approached the bedroom, unsure of what state I might find Mike in. He was standing in front of the window, hands on hips, staring out into the darkened night. The lamppost on our front lawn reflected off of the snow that had started to fall. The overall scene was picturesque with a cozy feel to it. Inside our bedroom was an entirely different atmosphere, though.

Mike sensed me behind him but didn't move. I placed a hand on his arm and felt him tense against me. "I didn't invite him here, Mike. I'm telling you the truth."

He turned to look at me with an expression I'd never seen before. Those beautiful eyes of his were masked with pain that he always managed to hide from me. I wrapped my arms around his waist, anxious to take it all way, and watched as his shoulders sagged.

"I'm not angry with you, baby. But I didn't want to see him. He was the last person I expected to find on my doorstep tonight."

I pressed my face against his chest. "Maybe it would help to open up about your childhood. To talk about him."

Mike's body grew rigid. "I have nothing to say about that man." He removed my arms gently and walked past me into the living room then grabbed his coat off the hook.

"Where are you going?" I hurried after him and clutched his arm in a sudden panic.

He took his truck keys out of the pocket and ran a soft finger over my lips. "I need some air. I need to think this through. It's—I just don't know what to do anymore."

"Please don't leave like this." Tears welled in the back of my eyes. "Don't shut me out. Let's talk about this together."

Mike shook his head. "I can't talk about this, Sal. I've spent too many years trying to forget. I'm sorry. Don't wait up." He kissed me on the forehead and shut the door quietly behind him. I watched as his truck backed out of the driveway and roared down the street.

The snow made a sharp splat sound as it pelted the front window. Rumor was that we could expect a fresh foot of the white stuff by tomorrow morning. The weather only added to my current state of depression.

This was all too reminiscent of what had happened a year ago when Colin had been murdered. The pain was still vivid in my memory—how Mike had made bail after being arrested and then become furious with me for borrowing money from Grandma Rosa to pay for it. He hadn't wanted me involved with the mess, so he'd thought the best solution was to take off for Canada the minute my back was turned. I'd been sick with worry the entire time he was gone, but when he returned, our relationship was much stronger.

A lot can happen in a year, and that held true for my life. Still, it was funny how when things changed, they often remained the same. I was self-assured enough in our relationship to know Mike loved me and that he would be coming back this time. But I hated to think of him driving around alone in this current state of mind. I knew why he didn't talk about his childhood—it made him feel insecure and weak when he reflected back. As my husband he was strong and protective, warm, loving, and everything I desired in a man. Mike always took care of me. What hurt was that he wouldn't let me do the same thing for him.

Spike jumped up onto the couch beside me, and I hugged him to my chest as my tears flowed freely onto his fur. The phone rang and startled me out of my thoughts. "Hello."

"*Cara mia*," my grandmother said. "How is Josie? I asked you to call and let me know."

I wiped my eyes with the back of my hand. "I'm sorry, Grandma. She's okay. I took her home a little while ago."

There was silence on the other end. "Did you and Mike have a fight?"

How she always knew what was wrong was a mystery to me. My grandmother was the cleverest person in my life, and I could only hope to inherit her wisdom someday. She had an uncanny knack of knowing when dramatic events were about to unfold, but she handled it in a nicer way than the fortune cookies did.

I blew out a long breath and stroked Spike's soft fur. "His father came back. He stopped by the house tonight and— well, let's just say it didn't go well. Mike won't talk to me about it, and he took off in his truck." I babbled and sobbed through most of the exchange. Grandma listened without saying a word.

"It will work itself out, *cara mia*," she assured me when I finally came up for air. "He will be back soon. Sometimes it is more difficult to talk about these things with the people we love than with a complete stranger."

I blew my nose into a tissue. "Mike won't talk to anyone, and it's not good for him to keep this all bottled up. I only want to help."

"Then be there for him when he comes home," she said gently. "He needs you more than ever now."

Grandma Rosa always said the right things. "I love you so much. Thank you for listening."

"And I love you. Sleep well, my sweet girl."

After a few minutes I made myself a cup of hot chocolate and went to bed. I heard Mike come in at about midnight and turn the television on in the living room but decided I'd wait and let him come to me first. When I finally went out to the kitchen for a drink of water about three o'clock, I found him fully clothed, asleep on the couch, and snoring softly. Spike was sitting on the arm of the couch next to his head, as if watching over him. The fire was only a flickering ember now but gave me hope as it refused to die out. I longed to lie down on the couch next to Mike and hold him in my arms but decided to give him some space. Exhaustion had settled into my bones, so I went back to bed and immediately sank into a deep, dreamless sleep.

At eight o'clock I awoke to the sound of a shovel scraping the steps outside. When I looked out the bedroom window, I spotted Mike, clad in jacket, boots, and gloves, clearing the sidewalk. He probably hadn't started the snow blower for fear of waking me. Still sleepy, I went to the kitchen and poured myself a cup of coffee from the pot he'd already made then proceeded into the bathroom to take a shower. I spent a long time under the hot spray, wishing that I could wash away my problems as easily. Afterward, I wrapped myself in an oversized pink towel and went to work on my hair in front of the bathroom mirror.

The door opened quietly, and Mike stood there, watching me with those expressive eyes of his. He looked tired, and his face was drawn. The normal five o'clock shadow I always associated with him resembled something more akin to a mountain man.

"Did you sleep okay?" I couldn't think of what else to

say to him.

He leaned against the doorjamb. "I never sleep well when you're not there with me."

"You could have come to bed." I swept my hair up into a ponytail, with an extra effort to keep my eyes fixed on the mirror.

"Sal." His voice was gruff. "I'm sorry, baby. I didn't mean to hurt you. Please forgive me."

His words were my final undoing, and I dropped the indifferent act. "There's nothing to forgive," I said tearfully as he wrapped his arms around me. He tilted my head up and kissed my lips, my hair, and the hollow of my throat. Within seconds my towel was on the floor, and it was as if last night had never happened.

We both slept a little afterward and woke shortly before one. I had to get ready for the wake soon but didn't want to leave him, and for a long time we lay there together in comfortable silence. That was the beauty of being with someone you loved. Words weren't always necessary to communicate.

I kept my head pressed against his rock-hard chest and listened to the steady sound of his heartbeat, wishing time would stand still for a while. "Do you want to talk?" I asked softly. "You shouldn't keep it all inside, sweetheart."

He kissed the top of my head. "I don't like feeling helpless, Sal, and that's always how I feel wherever that man is concerned. It's like I'm five years old again and waving good-bye to him while he promises to be back soon."

My throat clogged with tears as I pictured the image in my head. I reached up to kiss his cheek but said nothing. What could I possibly say to a comment like that?

"What lame excuse did he give you at the bakery yesterday?" Mike asked. "It figures he'd go to you first and try to smooth everything over. No surprise there."

"Your father didn't say much," I admitted. "He kind of implied that he wanted to make amends with you. I think he might be sick."

Mike was silent as he stared up at the ceiling. "So that's it. He wants to clear his guilty conscience before something happens to him." He turned my face up gently so that he could study it closely. "Do you want me to see him again?"

"Forget about me. I want whatever makes *you* happy," I said. "This is your decision, and anything you decide is fine because I love you."

He ran a finger down the side of my face and smiled. "I love you too. As long as I have you, everything will be fine." He hoisted himself into a sitting position. "I'm starved. Did you throw out the Chinese food? How about we go see a movie this afternoon?"

With a pang I now regretted the wake, although I still felt it was necessary for me to attend. "Uh, Gianna's picking me up at 2:30. We're going to Kelly's wake."

"That's okay." He kissed me again and pulled on jeans and a T-shirt. "I should run to Home Depot and pick up a few things for tomorrow's job anyway. What time do you think you'll be back?"

I shrugged as I dressed in a pair of black slacks and an oversized sweater. "Hopefully by six. It depends how much trouble we can get into."

He glanced at me sharply. "Josie's not going, is she?"

"She's waiting in the car for us."

Mike shook his head. "This is like asking for trouble, Sal. Big time. You're getting yourself involved in a murder investigation again. I don't want my wife to be the next victim."

"Give us a little credit. I have managed to solve a few crimes before. Plus Gianna will be with me."

He stared at me in disbelief. "You're like those two women in the movie—what were their names again?"

"Cagney and Lacey?" I asked hopefully.

Mike snapped his fingers. "Now I remember. Thelma and Louise."

I rolled my eyes at him as he went out into the living room and called to Spike. He took the dog for a walk while I fixed my hair again since it had become slightly mussed from our time together. Then I added some lip gloss and a coat of mascara, wishing my lashes were long and thick like Mike's. How men always got the best eyelashes was beyond me.

I had just finished a turkey sandwich when the horn on Gianna's car sounded outside. I pulled on my boots and coat and went to Mike for a kiss. He was making a list of supplies at the dining room table but promptly put it down when I came over. "See you soon."

He wrapped his arms around my waist. "Please be careful. Don't do anything—"

"Stupid?" I teased.

"Sal," Mike warned. "Don't joke about this. You seem to have a special knack for finding psychos. The sort of way a bowl of kibble attracts a stray cat."

"Come on. We're Thelma and Louise. We can handle anything." I pressed my lips against his. "Love you."

He tried to look stern, but his mouth dropped into a sexy, lopsided smile. "I love you too, princess. Never doubt that."

CHAPTER TEN

———

Before I could change my mind about going to the wake, I hurried outside to Gianna's car. The urge to stay with my husband continued to pull at me, especially after what had happened last night. He seemed okay for the moment, and Josie needed my assistance now. She was in the front seat with Gianna, so I settled myself in the back. "What's new?" I tried to sound casual.

Gianna took a left turn off of my street. "Nicoletta invited me over for breakfast. I think she's finally realized that it's serious between Johnny and me."

"She made you breakfast? When did Nicoletta become so charitable?" Josie asked.

"Okay, it wasn't really to eat," Gianna confessed. "She decided to show me how to *make* breakfast. Because, and I quote, 'a woman must cook for the man.'"

Josie snorted. "That old lady is a walking ad for sexism. Let a man cook his own breakfast."

Gianna eyed me suspiciously in the rearview mirror. "Something's going on with you, I can tell."

Cripes. Why did everything have to show on my face? As quickly as possible I relayed the events that had transpired last night. By the time I finished, Josie had turned around in her seat with her piercing blue eyes fixed upon me while Gianna's mouth hung wide open like a guppy's. The light turned green, but she continued to sit there, motionless, until the people in the car behind us laid on their horn with impatience.

"Holy cow," Gianna breathed. "Talk about a blast from the past. And Mike still won't talk about him?"

"He's saying very little. It's hard for him."

"How does that make you feel?" Josie asked.

Sad was the first thought that crossed my mind. If there was only some way to ease the pain for him. "I'm worried about him, but at least things are okay between us now."

"You're lucky," Josie remarked. "I can't remember the last time Rob ever apologized to me for anything."

Gianna brought the car to a stop in the funeral home's parking lot, and we both looked over at Josie. "How did it go last night?" I asked.

She swallowed hard. "It didn't. We had a huge blow out. Rob said that I'm a loose cannon, it's hurting the kids, and he's afraid this entire incident with Kelly is going to affect them at school." She heaved a sigh of frustration. "Then I told him to get out."

Gianna and I glanced at each other, thunderstruck. "You did what?" I asked.

Josie whirled around to face me. "Rob made me so angry. I love those kids more than anything in this world, and I know he does too. But it's like he has no regard for my feelings anymore. He thinks I went looking for trouble with Kelly. I asked him that point-blank, and he didn't deny it. To me that says he doesn't trust me enough, and if you don't have trust in a marriage, what's left? Nothing."

"Jos," I interrupted.

Her mouth was set in a thin, determined line. "Let me finish. Then I said that maybe he never really loved me in the first place and perhaps he should get out. If Rob wants a divorce, you'd better believe he's going to have one hell of a custody fight on his hands."

Gianna stared at Josie, wide-eyed, but was smart enough to keep her comments to herself. Not me. Desperately, I tried to wrap my head around this mess. "You can't be serious. You two have been married for eleven years! I know how much you guys love each other. If you only—"

Josie raised a hand in the air to silence me. "Sal, you're my best friend, and I love you to death, but don't try to talk me out of this. And I don't want you to worry about this affecting my work either."

"That's the last thing I care about. Listen. If you need—"

She cut me off. "Rob's staying with a friend, but he'll still come over to the house and watch the kids while I'm at work. Things will go on like before. We just won't be sleeping together at night—that's all."

"This is ridiculous!" I blurted out.

She folded her arms across her chest. "It's a matter of principle."

Gianna shot me a dubious look. "Let's go inside, Sal. We'll stop at the bakery afterward for a cup of coffee and talk about this further."

Josie's blue eyes hardened like steel. "There's nothing to talk about. Oh, and be sure to give Shelly and the gang my love, okay?"

Without another word Gianna and I let ourselves out of the car and walked carefully through the paved lot. The sidewalks had been salted after last night's storm, and for once the sky was clear, but the brisk wind whipped through my coat. I shivered, not sure if it was from the weather or Josie's indignant remarks. "I can't believe it. She spends one night in jail for something she didn't do, and now they might be talking about divorce?"

Gianna's breath was visible in the cold air. "This doesn't exactly surprise me. Rob was really angry the other night, Sal. On the way to the jail, he kept saying how he always knew that Josie's temper would end up getting her into trouble. You know that I adore her, and Rob's a good guy. But sometimes a situation like this can break apart the most solid of marriages. There's nothing you can do. They have to try to work things out for themselves."

As we walked up the porch steps of the funeral home, I mulled Gianna's reasoning over in my head. She was a lawyer and therefore had been trained to think like one. Still, I couldn't believe something so unsubstantial might mean the end of their marriage. My first one had ended for a totally different reason— infidelity. Divorce was painful, messy, and especially heartbreaking when children were involved. Josie and Rob couldn't give up yet—for their kids' sakes.

An elderly man with white hair and a matching, well-trimmed goatee opened the door for us. He was dressed in a perfectly pressed black suit and black dress shoes that shone in the sunlight. His name tag identified him as Andrew. He nodded pleasantly and showed us where to sign the register.

Gianna picked up one of the mass cards. Kelly's picture was printed with her name and the words *Remembered with love.* Beneath her picture was an endorsement for Naturally Delish with its address.

"Unbelievable." Gianna clicked her tongue against the roof of her mouth in disgust. "The woman was murdered, and now they're trying to promote her bakery through her death? This is in such poor taste."

Several mourners walked around chatting amongst themselves, some even laughing out loud. The scene resembled more of a party atmosphere than a mournful one. Boy, my father would be sorry if he knew he'd missed this. I found the overall effect disturbing, and it made me want to leave—fast.

There was no one waiting to pay their respects, and to my surprise, the only family member receiving mourners by the casket was Shelly, whose eyes followed Gianna and me as we made our way to the kneeler. Her face remained stony as we both positioned ourselves and then bent our heads in prayer.

"She's creeping me out," Gianna muttered. "And I don't mean Kelly."

Kelly looked peaceful and serene in a pink, silk dress with short sleeves and a rounded neck. Her white lace apron, with the words *Naturally Delish* printed above a chocolate sprinkled cupcake, was displayed in a corner of the coffin. I gave Gianna a gentle nudge. Kelly was wearing a silver choker around her neck that held assorted tiny charms of muffins, cookies, and brownies. A pair of silver earrings with tiny cupcakes on the ends dangled from her ears.

"Wow," Gianna whispered, her head still bent. "They've set this up like she was the next Martha Stewart."

After making the sign of the cross, we moved toward Shelly, who still regarded us with unbridled suspicion.

Gianna held out her hand. "I'm very sorry for your loss."

Shelly's eyes started to cloud over. "Thank you for coming." She stared pointedly at me. "And thank you for leaving your psycho murdering friend at home."

Egad. Okay, I knew this was a wake and that she was mourning the death of her sister, but she needed to stop attacking Josie. "Please don't talk about her that way." I gestured toward Gianna. "Especially in front of her lawyer."

Shelly stared at my sister with horror. "You've got to be kidding. You're an attorney? What other tricks do you guys have up your sleeves?"

I was still groping my way through this disaster and had no tricks to speak of, but maybe it would be better to let Shelly think otherwise. If I could catch her with her guard down, all the better. "Guess that's for us to know and you to—not find out."

Shelly started to say something, but there were two mourners waiting to speak with her, so we moved out of the way. Her "please excuse me" rang full of anger then she turned a sunny smile on the elderly couple, who each took hold of her hands. "Hello, Bill and Janice. It was so nice of you to come."

"I want to talk to her again when she's done," I whispered to Gianna. "I'll bet Kelly had other enemies, but for some reason, her sister is determined to pin the crime on Josie."

As we stood in the corner of the room and stared at the pictures of Kelly arranged on an easel, a man approached us. He was probably mid-thirties with light brown hair in a crew cut and a full well-trimmed beard that slimmed his face. He was not much taller than me and by his stick-person size might weight less too. He ignored me and observed Gianna with interest, his eyes sweeping over her figure in her dark brown wool coat and high-heeled leather boots of the same color. He returned his gaze to Gianna's face, licked his lips, and grinned. "Well, hello there, gorgeous."

Gianna, who'd been examining the pictures on the easel, glanced up in surprise. She narrowed her eyes and nodded coldly at him then returned her attention back to the easel.

He leaned in closer. "Were you a friend of the deceased?" he asked.

She shook her head. "I didn't know her. How about you?"

"Yep, I knew her." He shook his head. "Damn shame about what happened."

My curiosity piqued as I watched him. He stood between

us but never even glanced my way. I hoped Gianna would turn on what I called her "legal questioning voice" so we could find out more about this guy.

"Who do you think did this to her?" Gianna asked.

He snorted. "Please. It's so obvious who the killer is. They arrested the redheaded chick on TV who assaulted her. Did you catch that food fight?"

"You mean when it was on YouTube?" Gianna asked.

The man ran a suggestive finger down Gianna's arm. She smacked it away and stepped back from him in disgust. Steam must have been coming out of my ears. What kind of a man tried to pick up a woman at a wake? *Low-down, dirty letch.*

"I was in the audience and saw the whole thing," he bragged, in an obvious attempt to impress Gianna. "So how about you and me get together sometime?"

"It's not going to happen," Gianna announced. "*Ever.*"

Even though I knew that Gianna was perfectly capable of taking care of herself, I didn't want this man anywhere near my baby sister. Infuriated, I tapped him on the shoulder. "She's not interested, buddy, so please get lost."

He whirled around to face me, and his eyebrows shot up immediately as recognition set in. "Holy cow. It's you! You're the one who was at the show with that red-haired chick. The one who killed Kelly."

Much to my dismay, we were starting to attract unwanted attention. "And who are you?"

Before the man could respond, Shelly ran over and grabbed him by the arm. She practically dragged him away from Gianna. "What the hell is the matter with you?" she hissed. "You're making a mockery out of Kelly's life here."

"Sorry, babe." The man turned around and let his eyes rest on Gianna one last time. "But a man gets lonely pretty quickly. And we all have needs."

Ew. I was afraid I might throw up.

Shelly's face was a brilliant shade of red. "Get back over by the coffin," she whispered to the man. "I'll take care of you later." She watched him walk away and then approached the shell-shocked Gianna. "Sorry about that. He's not himself today."

"Well, whoever he is, I don't want to be anywhere near

him," Gianna declared.

We continued to watch the man as he started to shake hands with people. An uneasy feeling crept over me, enough to make my skin crawl. "Shelly, by any chance is that your husband?"

She shook her head vehemently. "No way. I would never marry a loser like that."

What a relief. "I'm sorry. I didn't mean to insult you."

Shelly pressed her lips together in disgust. "No, that—ahem—fine specimen of a man is named Barry, and he belonged to Kelly." She raised a deft eyebrow at Gianna. "How does it feel to know that the deceased's husband just hit on you?"

CHAPTER ELEVEN

———

Gianna and I both stared at Shelly in disbelief. "Please tell me you're joking," I said.

Shelly watched Barry with obvious contempt as he hugged a couple of attractive female mourners. "I wish. Scum of the earth is too high of a compliment for Barry Thompson. What my sister ever saw in that piece of crap is beyond me." She fixed her gaze on me thoughtfully. "As far as I'm concerned, add him to the list of suspects after Josie and Anita."

I couldn't stand this anymore. "Josie didn't kill your sister, but maybe someone else is responsible."

Shelly narrowed her eyes. "What exactly are you implying?"

"Look. I won't let you continue to talk about my friend in that manner. Yes, she and Kelly didn't like each other, but I *know* Josie. She'd *never* take someone else's life. For a minute let's assume someone else replaced Kelly's insulin with antifreeze. Who knew about her diabetes?"

Shelly shrugged in an indifferent manner. "Everyone, I guess. There's even a sign displayed in her shop which informs customers that the owner is diabetic, which was her reason for opening a sugar free bakery. She's been one since she was four, so it wasn't exactly a secret."

"That means anyone at the studio who knew about her condition and had access to the backstage area could have done it," I continued.

My face must have betrayed me because Shelly stared at me angrily. "Who the hell are you to accuse me? I loved my sister. Maybe you should leave now."

I held up a hand in protest. Shelly was perhaps the only

person close to Kelly who was willing to distribute any useful information, and I didn't want to alienate her. "I'm not accusing you. But for a minute could you please look at someone else besides Josie? Stop and think. Was there anyone who didn't like your sister or who might prosper from her death?"

Shelly's nostrils flared. "Barry recently took out a large life insurance policy on her. I just found out about it last night. I don't think my sister even knew."

It seemed that there was a lot Kelly didn't know about her so-called adoring husband. Gianna's eyes gleamed with that *I know he's guilty* look. "Are the police aware of this?" I asked.

Shelly did a palms-up. "I haven't talked with the police since the night of Kelly's death. Yeah, I guess he could have done it. But she knew about his affairs and didn't seem to care. Kelly had lovers of her own."

Wow, what a great basis for a marriage. "What about Kelly's, um—boyfriends?"

Shelly glanced around the room uneasily and then crooked her finger at a nearby door marked *Private*. "This way."

Having no choice, Gianna and I followed her into a small adjoining room reserved for family members who might need a break during the service. As I shut the door behind us, I spotted Barry looking very chummy with a pretty blonde in a short red coat and designer jeans. When he noticed my stare, he pinned me with a cold, dark gaze that spoke volumes as to what he might be capable of. I'd have to talk to Brian about him.

We watched as Shelly straightened a tablecloth that held chips, bottled water, assorted cut-up vegetables with dip, and chocolate chip cookies. The ones Josie and I made would blow these away.

Shelly popped one into her mouth. "Kelly wasn't serious with any particular guy. I think she even dated Grady a few times."

Puzzled, I drew my eyebrows together. "The one who's part of Donna's television crew?"

Shelly shrugged. "Sure. He's good-looking, so hey, why not? She broke it off a few weeks back though. Said he was too possessive. Look. I want to find this killer as much as you do. I still think it's Josie, but Barry—" She stopped. "I might as well tell you who he was fooling around with. The cops already know, so it makes no difference if you do too."

There was only one person I could think of. "Donna Dooley?"

Shelly let out a bark of laughter. "Please. That pretentious snob couldn't stand him. Kelly must have told her about their marital problems because whenever he came backstage, Donna headed in the opposite direction."

"Did he go to all the tapings?" I was intrigued. How would Barry have managed to travel to all of them if he worked? For that matter, how had Shelly gone as well?

"Donna occasionally tapes episodes on the weekends. More convenient for her, I guess. Sometimes I would fly out to New York City to watch a show, and Barry would tag along as well. He stays home while Kelly supports his sorry butt. Oh, wait. He tells everyone he's working on a novel. Mr. Big-time-author-to-be. Translation: he tweets and Instagrams all day. He got let go from his job about a year ago and hasn't made a real effort to find one since. Barry adores the life of leisure."

I couldn't imagine Mike not working, even if we didn't need the money. On Sundays, he was always puttering around the house doing some type of repair. He was never idle. To each his own, I guess. "Who is this woman that Barry was fooling around with?"

Shelly narrowed her eyes. "Did you see the blonde he was talking to?"

"The one in the red coat?" I asked.

She pursed her lips. "Yes. That's Kelly's best friend, Olivia Nigel."

Ouch. Your husband fooling around with your best friend. It didn't get much worse than that. "Holy cow. That must have destroyed Kelly when she found out."

Shelly shook her head. "She didn't know about Olivia. Oh, she knew he had affairs, but she didn't know who they were. I, uh—well, I kind of walked in on them together last week at the house. I'd borrowed an outfit of Kelly's and wanted to return it."

Gianna gave her a disbelieving look. "And you didn't tell your sister?"

A tear rolled down Shelly's cheek. "I was going to but

wanted to wait for the right moment. Barry tried to talk to me about it, but I told him to go to hell. Bastard. I wish I'd spoken up sooner."

If I'd ever caught my sister's boyfriend with someone else, I'd deliver the news to her in record time. Right after I broke a cookie tray on top of his head, that is. Could Shelly be lying? "How long were Kelly and Olivia friends for?"

Shelly paused to think. "Since Kelly got out of culinary school. They met while they worked together at an assisted living home in Datson. This was before Kelly bought the bakery."

Gianna spoke up. "Datson. That's about twenty minutes away. Are you talking about Mount Eden Assisted Living?"

"That's right." Shelly's eyes widened in surprise. "What, do you have a client there or something?"

Gianna tossed her head in a proud, defiant manner. "Maybe. Sorry, but that's confidential information."

"Figures," Shelly snorted. "I don't even know how that place is still in business. There have been rumors of thefts and even the residents fighting amongst themselves."

"Sounds like a great place," I agreed. "What did your sister and Olivia do there?"

"Olivia was a nurse's aide," Shelly explained. "Kelly worked in the kitchen as an assistant chef. She was thrilled to get the job right out of culinary school." Her arrogance shone through as she smiled. "With her skills though, it was no surprise. Your friend could learn a few things from her."

I didn't trust myself to speak for a moment and was grateful that Josie wasn't in the room. If she'd heard the remark, her fingers might have been wrapped around Shelly's throat by now. Josie had true talent, unlike Kelly, who probably just barked out orders to her staff on a daily basis. "Let's get back to your sister and Olivia. They remained good friends all these years?"

Shelly nodded. "They even lived together for a while. Kelly met Barry at some dive bar one night and instantly went nuts over him. I guess Olivia was there too. When Kelly and Barry bought a house last year, she gave Olivia a job in the bakery. Now that I'm the new owner, I fired her yesterday."

Wow. This was like real-life soap opera material. "Did Olivia ask why you fired her?"

Shelly gave me a disbelieving look. "Olivia knows. To her credit she didn't ask any questions. She picked up her stuff and left without another word."

Barry looked like the guilty party, but from the investigations I'd been involved with in the past, the obvious choice wasn't always the correct one. Still, he'd had opportunity, and he'd had motive. A large green motive. Olivia registered a close second for me. I hadn't met Anita yet, but she was a suspect in my book as well. After all, Kelly had taken away her job at the last minute.

I moved closer to the door and checked my watch. It was almost five o'clock, and I was anxious to get home to Mike. "Any chance I could stop by the bakery sometime this week if I have more questions?"

Shelly stared at me hard. "Why are you so interested? Donna promoted your bakery, and you got the money. So why do you care so much about my sister's killer?"

I shot her what I hoped was an incredulous look. "This has nothing to do with my bakery. Isn't it obvious? My best friend was arrested for a crime she didn't commit. If you ask me, someone saw the food fight and then decided to frame her because they figured Josie was an easy target."

My voice quivered with emotion as I continued. "Josie doesn't need this. She's got four kids and is concerned about how it might affect them. She isn't in the best position to clear her own name, so I'm going to do everything in my power to help her."

Without another word I reentered the viewing room. It was filled to capacity, and laughter rang out through the walls as I spoke into Gianna's ear. "We need to leave. Josie must be going stir crazy in your car."

As we moved through the room, I glanced over at Barry again, who was still stationed by the coffin as he wept visibly into a handkerchief. It was an acting performance that would have disgusted Steven Spielberg. Standing next to Barry was Olivia, talking in earnest to a petite, white-haired elderly woman. Olivia caught my look, frowned, and then turned back to the woman.

Gianna placed her hands on her hips. "They're not exactly being discreet. I mean, you'd think that they'd be on opposite ends of the room. Maybe they don't know Shelly spoke to the cops about them yet."

This was baffling. I wanted to talk to Olivia, but with Barry right there, I probably wouldn't get far. Maybe she'd recognized me from the video as well. In any case, I'd discovered some useful information and planned to share it with Brian. "We'd better go. Maybe we can track Olivia down later on. What time are you done with work tomorrow?"

Gianna barely managed to avoid colliding with a short, elderly woman who cut us off in a hurry on her way out the front door. "Why, what's up?"

An idea was brewing in my head. "I was thinking about shutting down an hour early and taking a ride out to the assisted living home. Want to come along?"

"Tuesday night would work better for me. Looks like Sal's on the job again," my sister teased. "I thought things had calmed down forever."

"Yeah, me too." It had been a wonderful six months with no bedlam, murder, or other serious distractions. Now real life was coming at me from every direction.

A firm hand fell upon my shoulder, and I stiffened, afraid it might belong to Barry. Brian stood next to me in a black leather bomber jacket and jeans, looking about as un-police-like as possible. He surveyed me with a slight smile on his lips. "Fancy meeting you here, Mrs. Donovan."

"Hello, Brian," Gianna greeted him.

He nodded to my sister and then turned his attention back to me. "I didn't know you were on such friendly terms with the deceased."

I blew out a sigh. Brian was no fool. He'd seen me in action before, so there was no reason to play games. "Someone is setting Josie up for this crime. I thought if we came here to pay our respects, we might get a line on who else might have a motive for wanting Kelly dead."

Brian arched an eyebrow. "Can I ask you a question, Sally?"

No. "Sure."

He propped a hand against the wall and leaned in closer. "Why can't you ever stay out of police business? Do you really dislike me that much?"

To my surprise, his tone sounded injured. I moved to the side to allow an elderly man to pass. He headed for the front door in a hurry. "Brian, I'm not looking for trouble, honest. My best friend was arrested the other night. You know that Josie is not a cold-blooded killer. I'm only trying to help her."

"The business is suffering too," Gianna added. "Sal barely had any customers yesterday."

I doubted Brian would care how much business the bakery was doing, so I said nothing further.

He ran a hand thoughtfully over his chin. "Did you find out anything?"

"Are you aware that Barry Thompson recently took out a life insurance policy on his wife?" I asked.

Brian nodded. "Yes. For a million dollars. We're watching him, but we don't have any proof to arrest him at this point. *His* fingerprints weren't found on Kelly's syringe, Sally. And he didn't have a public brawl with his wife shortly before she died either."

Touché. "No, but he was having an affair with Kelly's best friend."

This got his attention. "You do work fast, don't you?"

Before I could respond, the door of the funeral home flew open, and a woman in an expensive, gray, Burberry down coat rushed in. She almost trampled the elderly gentleman at the door in the process.

"Madam, please. There's a service going on," he reproached her.

It was Donna Dooley in the flesh. Her hair looked like someone had run a rake through it, and her dark eyes held a wild, terrified look.

"Call 9-1-1!" she shrieked as she caught sight of me. "There's a riot going on in the parking lot."

People rushed in from the viewing room as Brian approached Donna. "Miss Dooley, what kind of riot are you talking about?"

Donna stopped to catch her breath. "There's a group of people who've surrounded a car in the lot. They started to shake it, and there's a woman inside screaming back at them. She might be hurt. It's a silver Ford Fiesta with a vanity plate. *LAWLOVER*."

Gianna's eyes almost bugged out of her head. "Oh my God. That's my car! And Josie's inside it!"

CHAPTER TWELVE

———

In a panic Gianna and I rushed out the front door of the funeral home. Brian reached the porch first and held out a hand to stop us. His other was positioned on his belt, where I presumed he was carrying his gun, concealed. He spoke quietly but firmly. "Let me go first. You two stay here." Without another word he calmly walked down the steps toward the bedlam that was in full swing.

Gianna let out a small yelp and covered her mouth with a gloved hand. In the middle of the lot was her car, bouncing up and down. My stomach did flip-flops as I watched the scene play out in front of us. Surrounding the vehicle were six people. I blinked twice and at first didn't comprehend what I was seeing. My first reaction had been that a bunch of teenagers or some beefy adults close to my age were causing the commotion. Instead, the car was being shaken by a group of white-haired men and women who looked closer to my grandmother's age. Josie was in geriatric hell.

"What is this?" Gianna's eyes widened in surprise. "Colgate's version of *The Golden Girls*?"

We rushed down the steps in Brian's direction but stayed a few paces behind him. I couldn't believe the language spewing out from between their lips. If my grandmother had been here, she would have washed everyone's mouths out with soap.

"Murderer," a woman shorter than me with well-defined wrinkles and blue veins sticking out from her ungloved hands yelled at Josie through the car window.

"This is insane," Gianna muttered. "Are they all on steroids?"

Another seventyish woman who wore bright red lipstick

on her liver-spotted face brightened as Brian approached her. "Hey, we got us a fine young thing here to help," she shouted to her friends. "Hello there, handsome."

Brian's mouth twitched slightly. "What exactly are you people doing?"

His admirer pointed at Josie, who had stopped yelling and looked like she might be sick. "She killed that girl on the Donna Dooley show. We spotted her standing next to the car. I'd recognize that murdering puss of hers anywhere. Why is she out of jail?"

"Step away from the car, please." Brian waved his hands at the crowd.

The tiny woman with blue veins laid a hand on Brian's arm. "Please, sugar. We're trying to get justice for poor Kelly. A lot of nerve that chickie's got showing up here."

"She's not a murderer," I called out angrily.

Brian gave me and Gianna a death stare, and too late I remembered that we were supposed to have stayed back on the porch. "I'll thank you all to disperse and leave this woman in peace," he said.

"But she's a killer!" A man with a black Adidas beanie and bushy white eyebrows yelled and raised his hands over his head. "She should be stoned!"

"This isn't the Dark Ages," Brian retorted.

"She should burn in hell," a familiar voice grunted from behind the car. A tall woman stepped aside, and Gianna and I gasped as Mrs. Gavelli came into plain view. She was dressed in black, except for a delicate, white knit cap that covered her short hair. It had started to grow back nicely since the chemotherapy. She shook her fist at us in a menacing way.

"What are you doing here?" Gianna shrieked and went over to Nicoletta, placing a hand on her arm. "Johnny said you were playing Bingo today."

She grunted and jerked her arm away from my sister. "No Bingo. That for old people. I see about wake on TV. I knew Rosa not take me, so I ask my friend Mona to do it." She nodded at the woman with the bright red lipstick.

This was unreal. "Mrs. G, I'm surprised at you. You know that Josie's not a murderer," I said.

"Johnny's going to be very unhappy when I tell him about this," Gianna said reproachfully.

Mrs. Gavelli waved a wrinkled hand dismissively. "Ah, screw him. He no fun since he get mixed up with you. And if you marry, you best not wear white." She tapped a finger against the side of her white knit cap and gave Gianna a shrewd look. "I know things, missy."

Gianna's face turned crimson, and she stared down at the ground.

I went over to the side of the car to help Josie out. Her face was white and drawn, but she seemed unharmed. "Are you okay?"

She bobbed her head up and down slowly. "Shocked is more like it. I stepped out of the car for a minute to get some air, and suddenly they were everywhere. It felt like I'd been trapped in that old movie *The Birds*. Who the hell gets assaulted by a gang of old codgers like that? It's downright embarrassing."

Brian cleared his throat, or it may have been an attempt to cover up a laugh. "Okay, the fun's over, people. Please move away, and leave this woman alone."

"Who the hell are you, sonny?" A bald, thin man with white hair growing out of his ears snapped at him.

Brian calmly produced his badge, and a murmur of approval rose from the crowd. "*I'm* the *law*. And unless you all want to be arrested for harassment, you will leave this second."

"Bah," Mrs. Gavelli grunted as she strode off in the direction of the funeral home. "He cute but no fun either."

"Wait up, Nicoletta!" Gianna shouted and ran after her. "I want to talk to you!"

Mona walked over to Brian and wiggled her hips in a suggestive manner. "My word. You're a cop? I've always had a thing for men in uniform. Want to come over to my house for some hot chocolate, sexy?"

Brian bit into his lower lip to keep from laughing. "Ma'am, please do as I say."

"Stop trying to pick up the young-uns." The old man with the hair in his ears grabbed Mona's arm and steered her away.

"Pooh," Mona grunted at him. "I need some excitement

in my life. You stopped being hot thirty years ago."

They walked back into the funeral home, and their friends followed. Gianna was talking earnestly to Mrs. Gavelli on the porch. Josie exhaled a long breath and then looked from me to Brian with suspicion. "If either of you tells anyone about this, I'll track you down and hurt you."

Brian rocked back on his heels and grinned. "Just when I thought I'd seen everything."

"They scared the hell out of me," Josie admitted. "Do they lift weights three times a day? Drink protein shakes and Red Bull?"

Donna glanced around uneasily. I'd forgotten that she was there. "I'm glad you're okay, Josie. I should go inside and pay my respects now."

"Thanks for letting us know what was going on," I said.

She looked like she'd rather be someplace else. "I hate to tell you girls this, but it will save me a phone call later. Sally, I've decided to cut your show from the schedule. There have been so many protests about it online that I have no choice. People are very angry about what happened to Kelly. I've even received some obscene phone calls and death threats myself."

Although I was disappointed, it didn't come as a surprise. After the food fight had gone viral, I wondered if Donna might put us on the chopping block. "I understand."

"Did you report the threats?" Brian asked.

Donna nodded. "I'm sorry, Sally, but I must consider the reputation of my show first."

Josie's lower lip trembled. "It's all my fault. Sal doesn't deserve this to happen to her. It would have been such great exposure for the bakery."

"That's all right." I put an arm around her slim shoulders. "Your welfare is more important to me."

Brian observed Donna closely. "Wouldn't something like that draw more ratings for your show?"

Donna gave him a disbelieving look. "I suppose it's possible, but I'm not willing to take a chance that my show will be permanently damaged. If someone else comes forward and confesses to the murder, I'll reconsider."

"Have you found a replacement for Kelly? Or will you

hold off on hiring someone for a while?" I asked.

She frowned. "Yes, the show must go on. Kelly's replacement is named Anita Scranton."

My stomach muscles constricted. "Anita was there the day we were taping."

Donna studied me carefully. "That's right. She lives outside of Buffalo and also graduated from CIB. With the new position she'll be relocating to New York City permanently. She's got fabulous skills and the drive needed to succeed at this job. If Kelly's résumé hadn't been so impressive, I would have hired her."

Interesting. With Kelly gone, Anita was getting the job she'd been denied and most likely wanted in a bad way. "What does Anita do now?"

"She's the bakery manager for Groceries Galore in Colgate," Donna replied. "It's only about ten minutes from here. Of course it's not the most prestigious job, but that doesn't matter. I have to admit she had more culinary skills than Kelly did."

Josie snorted. "My eleven-year-old has more culinary skills than Kelly."

Donna ignored the comment. "Kelly ran her own bakery, which happens to be one of the most popular in Western New York. That would impress anyone. It made more sense for me to hire her." She fidgeted with the straps of her Prada bag. "I'm so glad that the tapings for Cookie Crusades' winners are almost finished. I've never cared for this section of New York."

Her remark stung like a wasp, and I had to count to ten before I spoke for fear of saying something rude. Josie opened her mouth, but I shot her a warning look. "Your work here is done?"

"Almost. I'm taping a couple of shows tomorrow and Tuesday. On Wednesday I'm accepting an award at the Culinary Institute and giving a speech." She wrinkled her delicate nose. "After that I can bid this section of New York adieu."

"Some of us happen to like this section of New York," Josie muttered.

Donna's eyes grew wide. "Sorry. I didn't mean to insult your hometown, but I'm more of a big city girl. The Big Apple suits me. I love my high-rise apartment and the fact that something is always going on there, any time of day or night."

"Let's get back to Anita," I said. "How upset was she when you told her at the last minute that she wasn't getting the job?"

She shot me a quizzical look. "How'd you know about that?"

I decided not to reveal my source. "Oh, we hear things."

"I see." Donna's nostrils flared. "Don't go there, Sally. I refuse to believe that Anita had anything to do with Kelly's death."

"I wasn't suggesting that," I lied.

Brian cleared his throat. "Ladies, it's freezing out here. Maybe you'd care to continue this conversation inside?"

Donna hesitated. "I do need to get in there. I'm late for a dinner meeting with my agent."

"All you care about is that stupid show." The color rose in Josie's cheeks, and it was as if new life had been breathed back into her. "Come on, Donna. Get off your high horse. I bet you have an idea who killed Kelly. Could anyone get backstage? Who would have had access to her insulin?"

Donna's jaw tightened. "There is a break room where we can store food and drink during the taping. Kelly always brought a smaller cooler along for her insulin and sometimes kept it in the fridge. Now if you're done interrogating and insulting me, I must go."

"Witch," Josie muttered as Donna walked away. "All she's interested in is her freaking show and its reputation. She should be careful about hiring Anita. If she's the one who killed Kelly, maybe Donna's next. What if it's her way of climbing the ladder of success, so to speak?"

The sky had already started to grow dark. I wanted to get home to Mike, but since we were in the area, I hated to waste an opportunity for some more snooping. "Hmm. I'm kind of hungry. Want to stop over at Groceries Galore for something sweet?"

A wide grin flickered across Josie's face. "Now that you mentioned it, I could use a doughnut."

Brian did not look amused. "You two had better not be planning to go question Anita."

"Of course not. I want something sugary and fattening."

He raised his eyebrows at me in disbelief. "You *own* a bakery."

"Well, there are times you want to sample someone else's goodies besides your own," I explained.

"Sally." Brian wagged a finger in my face. "How many times have I told you to stay out of this? The only reason I'm even investigating this murder is because you asked for my help. I thought that meant you'd steer clear of trouble if I did so."

Yeah, well, you thought wrong. "Brian, it's a Sunday night. Chances are she isn't even working. She's probably quit the job already."

Brian's phone beeped. He read the message and then reattached it to his belt. "I have to go. Don't get into any scrapes tonight because I won't be around to get you out of them." He gave me a long hard look. "I mean it, Sally."

Yes, Dad. "Okay, I promise."

Brian got into his squad car, and we started toward the porch where Mrs. Gavelli and Gianna were still deep in conversation. My grandmother's car drove into the lot.

"What's she doing here?" Josie asked.

I gestured at Mrs. Gavelli with a smile. "My guess is babysitting."

We walked over to Grandma Rosa's Buick Regal. I bussed her cheek as she got out of the vehicle. "Why did you come all the way out here? It's already dark, and the doctor said you shouldn't be driving at night."

"Bah," she scowled. "How does he know what I can see? He does not have my eyes. I am here to get my *pazza* friend."

"Crazy doesn't come close, Rosa," Josie remarked. "Nicoletta is a total whack job. She and her friends tried to assault me."

Grandma Rosa shook her head in disbelief. "Yes, I was afraid of that. Johnny called to tell me she was gone, and I thought she might come here. I managed to reach Mona, and she told me that Nicoletta was with her, but she did not tell me *where* they were. So I put one and one together."

"No, Rosa, it's two and—" Josie began.

My grandmother grunted at her. "Talk about people who

should not be driving. Nicoletta cannot back out of her driveway without hitting the recycling bin every morning. She almost ran Mr. Feathers over last month when he filled her gas tank."

Yikes. And Nicoletta liked Mr. Feathers.

"We need to get going," Josie said. "Sal and I have a quick stop to make, and she's in a hurry to get home to hubby."

"I know this." Grandma Rosa looked at Josie. "Would you let me talk to my granddaughter alone for a minute?"

"Of course," Josie said. "I'll go over and help Gianna before Nicoletta gives her a karate chop to the neck."

Grandma Rosa got back in her car and patted the passenger seat. "Get inside. It is cold."

I hurried around to the other side of the car and pulled the door shut after me. "What's up?"

She stared at me thoughtfully. "I wanted to make sure that everything was okay with you and your husband."

"It is. He came home about midnight and apologized to me this morning."

She nodded in approval. "It must have been some apology. You are blushing, *cara mia.*"

"Oh, Grandma." I laughed, in spite of myself. "Thank you for listening last night."

She patted my hand. "I am always here when you need me. Do not forget that. You must have patience with him, my dear. Mike must be very confused and does not know what to do."

"I wish that he would talk to me about it. I am his wife, after all."

"When we hurt, we do not want the ones we love to hurt too," Grandma Rosa said. "He is very protective of you. You are fortunate, *cara mia.*"

"I know." I was lucky—to have him and my wonderful grandmother, who in some ways was my other true love. She always knew exactly what to say to make me feel better. "But every time he hurts, I hurt too. I think that's the way marriage is supposed to be."

She smiled. "You are finally learning, my dear. Remember that love and trust can conquer any hurricane, though."

"Storm, Grandma," I gently corrected her.
She nodded. "I like that too."

CHAPTER THIRTEEN

———

After we had seen Grandma Rosa and Mrs. Gavelli off safely, Josie, Gianna, and I headed for Groceries Galore. I'd texted Mike to let him know I was running late, and he'd asked me to be careful not to let Gianna drive the car off any cliffs. Hilarious. The question remained, who was Thelma to my Louise—Gianna or Josie? It was too difficult to choose.

Gianna pulled the car to a stop in the parking lot of the grocery store, located on one end of the mini mall. The place looked deserted, with only a handful of cars nearby. Most people tended to do their shopping on Saturday or early Sunday mornings. Sunday evenings were a time to unwind for the upcoming workweek. At least that's how Mike and I felt since it was our only day off. We avoided grocery shopping whenever possible, picking up a couple of items here and there as needed. When we had children it would be different, though. My yearning gnawed away at me as I pictured myself pushing a baby in a grocery cart and then forced the vision away. *It will happen. Stop worrying.*

Josie broke into my thoughts. "I do need to get bread for the kids' lunches. I'd hate to think what Rob might fix if I left the job up to him." Her smile faded, and then she sucked in her cheeks at the mention of his name.

"Why don't I give Rob a call tomorrow?" I suggested. "Maybe I could ask how the kids are doing and—" I stopped when Josie's face hardened like stone. *Nice move, Sal.*

"I won't have it," she snapped. "This is my problem, Sal. I know you mean well, but there are some things that a husband and wife have to work out for themselves."

"Told you so," Gianna muttered.

Defeated, I blew out a sigh. "Okay, point well taken."

Large raised signs with black lettering were suspended from the ceiling and directed us to the bakery located at the rear of the produce aisle. We stood in front of the glass case as Josie peered in at the selection of sugar and chocolate chip cookies on display. She snickered. "Ours are so much better looking."

A woman was on the phone and glanced up at us while she finished writing something down on a piece of paper. She said good-bye to the person on the other end and walked over. Her gray hair was pulled back in a sloppy ponytail, and the white smock she wore was wrinkled and smeared with what I hoped was chocolate. She wore a white baseball cap with the letters *GG* on it.

"Help you?" she asked briskly.

Something assured me that this could not be Anita. She didn't seem stylish enough for designer-brand Donna's taste. "I—er—we were wondering if Anita Scranton was here."

"She's in the freezer doing inventory. Hey, Anita!" the woman yelled. "Someone's here to see you."

"Really, Jane. It's rude to scream in front of customers," a smooth voice reproached, and seconds later, a slim, petite woman appeared. She was attractive with light brown hair streaked with blonde highlights, an upturned nose, and tiny mouth. She smiled pleasantly at us. "Hi, ladies. Is this about an order?"

I hadn't expected to find her, and the ruse I'd planned at the last minute, pretending to be a local television reporter congratulating her on the job, didn't seem like such a good idea anymore. Might as well come clean. "We were wondering if we could talk to you for a minute. About your new job, that is."

Her intelligent, amber-colored eyes rested on my face for a minute then she turned around to address Jane who was watching the scene with intense curiosity. "You can go take your break. I'll cover."

"I'm good, thanks," Jane grinned.

Anita narrowed her eyes. "I said *go*."

Jane mumbled something under her breath but did as she was told. She brushed past us with a murmured "Sorry" and disappeared through a set of swinging doors at the end of the aisle.

Anita stuck her hands inside the pockets of her spotless white smock. Her eyes darted from me to Josie to Gianna and then back to me. "I know who you are. You appeared on Donna's show the day her assistant died."

Duh. Why had I not thought she wouldn't recognize us? We'd become marked women because of that stupid YouTube video. Maybe Mike was right. We were Thelma and Louise's twins, and everyone was looking for us. "That's right."

She looked Josie up and down. "And you're the one who was arrested for Kelly's murder."

Josie bit her lower lip. "Hell, I can't go anywhere without being recognized. It's like the reverse status of being a celebrity."

I gestured at Gianna. "This is my sister, Gianna Muccio. She's an attorney." Then I wondered why I had said that. Did I think Anita would divulge more information just because Gianna had a law degree?

Anita folded her arms over her chest. "I also know *why* you're here. You heard that I'm Kelly's replacement, and you're trying to pin her death on me. Well, save yourself the trouble and go home."

"It isn't like that at all," I insisted. "We heard that you went backstage to talk to Donna the day of the taping and wondered if you might have seen anything fishy going on. I want to prove that Josie was not involved." It was a partial lie, but she didn't need to know that.

She stared at me surprised. "How did you know I was there? Do the police know too?"

Not yet, but they will soon. "We were with Donna when one of her assistants said that you wanted to see her."

"Of all the worst days for me to go," Anita said bitterly. "I came to ask Donna if she'd put in a good word for me. I was applying for a position at a rival TV station. She told me it was no problem. Then out of the blue, she called two days ago and asked if I was still interested in the position as her assistant."

"And you couldn't wait to accept," Gianna said in an accusatory tone.

Anita glared at her. "Of course I accepted. I'm sorry

Kelly's dead, but that job pays three times what I make here. I'd have to be a moron not to take it. Plus it's always been my dream to work in television."

But how far would she go to make her dream a reality?

Anita seemed to guess my thoughts. "I'm not a murderer. Shoot, I've never committed one single crime in my entire life. I've worked hard for everything I've got and even had a full-time job back in high school. My father ran out on my mother and me. She died just before I started culinary school, and then I was on my own. While in school I held a full-time job so that I could pay my rent. For an entire year I barely slept, but it was worth it. When you want something bad enough, you'll make whatever sacrifices are necessary for it to happen."

Her words rang true as my thoughts turned to children once again. There wasn't much I wouldn't do to have a child of my own, with the exception of stealing one. I struggled to focus on the problem at hand. "When did Donna first offer you the job?"

Anita paused to think. "I interviewed with her in October. She called me the following week to tell me I had the position. When I said that I'd have to give two weeks' notice, she was fine about it. A couple of days later, she called me back and said she'd decided to hire someone else. To be honest, I was devastated. Fortunately, Groceries Galore was willing to let me stay on, but I'd already bragged to so many people about the new job that it was quite a humiliating experience."

Josie wrinkled her nose. "Did Donna give you any reason why she decided to hire Kelly instead of you?"

She shook her head. "Not really. She said someone with more experience had surfaced at the last minute. But I'm not a fool. Kelly had a popular bakery that won Cookie Crusades. She fit the profile much better than I did. From what I've heard that woman couldn't even make a decent cookie. She had her staff do it all."

"Sickening, isn't it?" Josie stared into the display case again.

"Oh, right," Anita smirked. "I read the story on Facebook about how she sabotaged your dessert in culinary school, and of course I saw the video. Have you viewed the comments people are leaving about you? They said you wanted to twist the knife in her back, so to speak. You know, even the score with her after all these years."

The color rose in Josie's face, and she sucked in some air. I put my arm around her shoulders in an attempt to steady her. "Breathe," I ordered.

"The kids are definitely going to hear about this at school," she wailed. "Maybe I shouldn't even send them tomorrow."

Anita glanced from me to Josie. "Look. I'm sorry for your trouble, but this doesn't concern me. Try to look at it from my perspective. I never met Kelly, so how would I have even known she was a diabetic or where she kept insulin so that I could tamper with it?"

Cripes. Was there *anyone* who didn't know how Kelly had died? So much for Brian wanting to keep the information a secret.

Anita raised her chin in defiance. "If you're so determined to find the killer, perhaps you should look elsewhere. What about Donna? What about the cameraman or Kelly's two-timing husband? I heard that Kelly was sleeping with one of the crew members. Have you talked to him or the other assistants who were lower than her on the totem pole? Maybe Kelly had a disgruntled employee at her bakery. Have you talked to any of them yet?"

Dang, she was good. Maybe Anita should partner up with us.

Josie scowled. "Doesn't it bother you to play second fiddle to Kelly?"

She shrugged. "I can't let it upset me. There's tuition bills that I still need to pay off. Maybe Donna's all about her show, but I'm all about the money. Do you really think I make much working here?"

"You must have had other offers when you finished culinary school," I put in.

"Not as many as you think. The market for pastry chefs isn't exactly booming right now." She stared down at the clipboard in her hands. "If you'll excuse me, I have to get back to work. It's my last night here, and I want to leave everything in order."

"Nice meeting you," Gianna said.

"Good luck with the new job," I added.

She gave me a sharp look and then disappeared into the direction of the freezer.

"What do you think?" Josie asked as we walked toward the exit.

"I don't know. Anita confessed she's all about the money, and I think that's the kind of person we're looking for." It seemed like an important piece of the puzzle was still missing. Somewhere along the way I must have overlooked something and wished fervently I knew what it was.

We dropped Josie off first then Gianna and I were silent on the short ride to my house. She finally spoke. "I'm sure you're anxious to get home to Mike after everything that happened last night. Sorry this took longer than we planned."

"No worries. I texted him already. He said he has dinner waiting for me." It was such a relief to know we were okay. Mike and I never really fought. The last argument I remembered us having was about the bail money a year ago. Sure, we'd had little squabbles like other married couples if he'd forgotten to bring home bread or milk, but this had been different. It had been painful and hit close to home. Life was too short to spend arguing with someone that you loved.

Gianna pulled into my driveway. Lights glowed from the front window and warmed my heart in the process. I leaned over to give my sister a hug. "Thanks for the ride. Are you going out with Johnny?"

"No. I need a break." She hesitated. "We're meeting someone for drinks tomorrow night, and he said he has something important to ask me. It's all a big surprise."

"Yes, I know." *Oops.* Me and my big mouth.

She stared at me sharply. "What do you know?"

I wanted to smack myself in the head. "He told Mike that he had something important to ask you but wouldn't say what it was."

Gianna closed her eyes and sighed. "If he proposes, I have no idea what I'll say."

This wasn't encouraging. "Do you love him?"

She nodded. "Yes, but I've barely gotten started with my career. I'm not ready to settle down yet, and if I tell him that, I don't know what Johnny will do. You know those Italian tempers."

I rolled my eyes. "Only too well. And his grandmother is the worst offender."

"The thought of having Nicoletta as a relative is an intimidating one," Gianna admitted. "Scary too. She loves Johnny more than anything, and I'll never measure up in her eyes."

"It could be worse," I said teasingly. "What if Johnny had wanted to marry me?"

"That," Gianna said, "would have given the woman a stroke."

We laughed as I got out of the vehicle. When she drove away, I hurried up the steps as Spike barked a welcome from inside. After I hung my coat by the front door, I reached down to pet him.

Mike came out of the kitchen dressed in a plaid shirt and jeans, freshly shaven and smelling of spicy aftershave. He drew me toward him and pressed his lips against mine. "I missed you, baby. Did everything go okay?"

I stroked his smooth cheek. "Well, we didn't drive off any cliffs."

"Always a good thing." He led me toward the table. "Come on. Let's eat. I picked up a pizza—your favorite kind. Hope that's okay."

"Anything sounds good right about now—I'm starving." I sat down next to him and immediately reached for a slice with white sauce and broccoli. It melted in my mouth. "Delicious."

Mike grabbed a chicken wing out of a box. "I've been thinking about some things while you were gone." He blew out a breath. "Maybe I should let my father say his piece and then be done with it."

I put the pizza down and reached for his hand. "What about *your* piece? I wish you'd talk to me about everything that happened back then."

He wiped his mouth with a napkin and gazed into my eyes with a sad smile. "I don't want to remember, Sal. That was a very lonely period in my life, and I'm done looking back at the past." He brought my hand to his lips and then reached out to pull me onto his lap. "Everything I need is right here. My present and my future."

My eyes started to water as I placed my arms around his neck. "Me too. But I'm your wife and want to help you get through this."

Grave emotion showed on Mike's finely featured face. "You do help. As long as I have you, it will be fine. I'll talk to my father, and then hopefully that will be the end." He reached up a hand to stroke my hair. "I've never been very religious but feel like God sent you to me at a time when I desperately needed you. You give my life meaning, Sal. Don't ever forget that."

A tear rolled down my cheek, and Mike brushed it away with his fingertips. He brought his mouth down hard on mine, kissing me passionately until desire had invaded every part of my body. I gripped his hair tightly and ran my fingers through its silky texture, not wanting him to ever stop—not being able to get enough of him.

When we finally broke apart, Mike flashed that sexy, teasing grin at me and gestured at my plate. "I thought you were starving?"

"To heck with the pizza. We can eat anytime."

CHAPTER FOURTEEN

———

Monday morning dawned bleak and gray, accompanied by a sleet-filled mixture that proved to be more treacherous than the fluffy white stuff. I hated this time of year. The holidays were long gone, and I was literally counting the days until spring.

The weather along with Josie's uncertain plight had started to affect us both and I hated to see my friend hurting. To make matters worse, it was as if the bakery didn't exist to the public anymore. We'd only had a handful of customers this morning. The newspaper continued to run articles about Kelly's death, and the last time I'd looked, the YouTube video had more than two million views. I would not allow myself to read the comments.

"This is all my fault," Josie sighed as she made up a batch of lemon crisps. They were a new recipe she had invented over the holidays that had become very popular with our customers. Well, back when we had customers, that is.

"Things will get better." I hummed a little tune low in my throat as I washed the mixing bowls.

From the corner of my eye, I caught Josie staring at me. "What?"

She gave me that sly grin of hers that I'd been missing lately. "By the look on your face and that carefree attitude, there must have been a great makeup session in the Donovan household last night."

"Oh, cut it out," I laughed, grateful that Mike had finally started to open up to me.

"I'm so glad things are okay between you guys," Josie said.

"What about you?" I asked.

"What about me?" she echoed. "Rob stayed at his mother's last night. He arrived at the house about ten minutes before I left for work this morning to take care of the kids. We didn't say one word to each other."

I shook my head in disbelief. "You guys need to talk this out."

She tossed her head defiantly. "There's nothing to say, except that he owes me an apology. Never mind about him anyway. What time is it?"

Resigned, I glanced at my watch. "Eleven thirty." The day stretched out in front of us, long and senseless like my father's blog.

"Hmm." Josie observed me closely. "Isn't Kelly's funeral this morning?"

"Yes. I think it was scheduled for eleven."

"I wonder if her bakery will be closed today."

A light switch flicked on in my brain, and I reached into my jeans pocket for my phone. "Let's find out."

On the second ring a pleasant woman's voice answered. "Naturally Delish. How can I help you?"

"Hi, I was wondering what time you close tonight."

"We're open until six o'clock, ma'am."

I mumbled a thank you and disconnected. Hey, why not. My bakery was deserted, so it was a great time to go over to Kelly's shop and do a little snooping. "With Barry, Shelly, and Kelly's friend Olivia at the funeral, we'll be able to check the place out, and no one will be the wiser."

Josie's eyes gleamed with that familiar look of excitement, which had disappeared the last few days. She ran to place the *Closed* sign on the front door. "Let's do it."

Uneasiness settled over me as I glanced at my friend. "Maybe you should wait in the car."

She shook her head vehemently. "No way. I want to see this place and what all the fuss is about."

"Someone could recognize you and start trouble. Say, maybe a bunch of lively eighty-year-olds trying to kick your butt. Then what would you do?"

Josie's mouth twisted into a pout. "Very funny. Been

there, done that. Does Gianna still have those wigs from the time the hairdresser mixed the wrong colors for her highlights?"

Gianna lived in the apartment over my bakery. She was at work now, but I had a key to her place, and we always shared everything, as some sisters do, so I knew she wouldn't mind if I rummaged about her things. "There's a good chance. She never throws anything away. I'll look in her bedroom while you finish closing up down here."

I ran upstairs and hunted around in Gianna's closet. I found a hatbox in the back that produced two wigs and hurried downstairs with them. I showed the hairpieces to Josie. There was a short, black pageboy style and a curly, shoulder-length redheaded wig.

Josie made a face as she handed the curly red-haired wig to me. "Figures they have to be the colors of our own hair. I guess we'll have to play switcheroo."

I narrowed my eyes. "*I'm* not wearing one."

"What if they recognize you too?" Josie asked. "I'm sure everyone at Kelly's shop has seen the video. You and all that curly black hair don't exactly fade into the background, girlfriend."

She had a point. I grumbled for a second then grabbed some hairpins from inside the box. I quickly pinned up my almost shoulder-length hair, grateful that the wig was longer in length than my own. Gingerly, I arranged the piece on my head. Josie held up her compact mirror while I pushed in the stray, dark strands that stuck out underneath the curly red mass. Although my complexion was olive, the wig was dark enough with its red shade so that it didn't look completely ridiculous.

"It makes you look feisty." Josie grinned as she fussed with the black wig and attempted to cram her red locks underneath it. She had a more difficult time as her hair was longer than mine. I'd always admired Josie's auburn color that was striking against her alabaster skin. "Why would your sister get a short style?" she groused. "This is a pain in the butt to fix."

I held the mirror for Josie and handed her some more pins. "It's better than nothing." After she was satisfied with the do, we locked the back door and got into my car. "Gianna was desperate for anything that day, and the store only had one wig with long hair." She'd been relieved to cover up the green color with anything until her regular hairdresser could fix the mess a few days later.

Josie studied her reflection in the overhead mirror. "If that sleaze Barry really had a life insurance policy on Kelly, he's my number one suspect. Who else do you think could have done it?"

"This is only a hunch," I said, "but I'd like to check out that assisted living home, Mount Eden, where Kelly worked right after she finished culinary school."

"Do you want to go tonight after we close up?" Josie asked.

I shook my head. "We're having dinner at my parents."

She snorted back a laugh. "Well, nothing compares to that, for sure. So what's Pops up to these days?"

"Dad filmed a commercial for a funeral home today. He called us at two o'clock in the morning and wanted to know if I had any fortune cookies handy. Guess he was a bit nervous." And he'd managed to make me jittery as well. Anytime the phone rang in the middle of the night, I was positive that someone had died, and frankly, I'd had enough deaths in my life recently.

Josie rolled her eyes. "I love your father, but some days he's a serious whack job."

"Yeah, well, Mike had another name for him when he woke him out of a deep sleep," I quipped. "I'll go to Mount Eden tomorrow. It seems that Kelly's best friend Olivia worked there as well." "The one you said was having an affair with Kelly's husband?" Josie asked.

I nodded. "Maybe we can find an employee who remembers either one of them."

Josie gave her wig a final fluff and settled back in her seat. "Do you think it's worth the trouble to go out there?"

"As my grandmother would say, I hate to leave any rocks unturned."

Josie barked out a laugh, and then we both fell silent until I had stopped the car in front of Naturally Delish. The bakery was situated in between a bookstore and a sandwich shop on one of the busiest streets in Colgate. It was a location I would kill for—well, almost.

Since a funeral was being held for the owner today, I'd expected to find the place deserted, but there were actually several customers waiting in line. A young woman in a spotless frilly, pink bib apron waited on them. I could see another woman in the back room decorating a cake, and an elderly woman was cashing people out.

The main storefront was double the size of mine. Teakwood walls gleamed with various awards and framed photos of Kelly everywhere. The Pergo floor underneath our feet was spotless and shone in the sunlight. There were two separate display cases—one for cookies and assorted pastries while the other held cakes and pies. There was even a limited sandwich and soup menu. Several square oak tables lined the front of the room for patrons to enjoy their food, and there was even a flat-screen television mounted to the wall.

How I longed to have a lunch menu and more room like Kelly's. Mike had promised to expand the main room for me at some point, but right now his paying customers had to come first.

An 11x14-sized photograph of Kelly adorned the wall above the coffee station. Underneath it someone had framed a message in black letters. *Our beautiful owner. May she rest in peace and always enjoy sweet things.*

Although I was certain the message had been well intended, it made me curious why they had used the term *sweet*. Everyone here obviously knew that Kelly was a diabetic, and she had been very offended by the fortune cookie saying she'd received in my shop. Anita's words from last night played back in my head. Who else didn't like Kelly besides Josie? Could one of her employees have hated her enough to kill her?

"What the heck are we going to say?" Josie whispered as we got in line behind two teenage girls who couldn't decide between sticky buns and vegan chocolate chip cookies. After a brief debate, the cookies won out.

"As it should be," Josie murmured.

When it was our turn, the young blonde behind the counter smiled at us. "Hi, ladies. What will it be?"

"Who's in charge today during Shelly's absence?" I

asked.

The girl's grin faded. "That would be Amy. She's in the back icing a cake. Would you care to speak to her?"

"Yes, please," I said, still not sure what the heck we were going to say to the woman.

A woman of about forty emerged from a side entrance. She had short, black hair in a blunt cut underneath a white *Naturally Delish* visor and an infectious smile that lit up her entire face.

"Hi, girls," she said briskly. "I'm Amy. What can I do for you?"

I cleared my throat. "We're, uh, from Donna's show. We need to know what to do about Kelly's personal effects that she left behind on the set."

"I see." Amy wrinkled her brow. "Why doesn't Donna call Shelly herself? Isn't she at the funeral today?"

Josie shrugged. "We don't know Donna's schedule."

"Didn't you say that you worked for her?"

Uh-oh. Please don't blow this, Josie. "Is there any chance we could talk in a more private area?" I asked. "Do you have an office or something?"

Amy looked at her watch. "There's a birthday cake I need to finish decorating, and the customer will be here within the hour. But I guess I have a couple of minutes to spare. Let me check the oven first."

She disappeared into the back prep room area, and Josie nosily peered in behind her retreating figure. There was a small thud, and I heard Amy curse. Josie moved out of the doorway and nudged me in the side. "What?"

"Tell you later," she mumbled before Amy joined us.

"We'll go back to Kelly, er—Shelly's office and chat." Amy led the way down a narrow hallway. There was a set of bathrooms on one side and a door marked *Private* on the left. She opened the door, and we followed her inside. The office was large and sunny, with windows plentiful. A treadmill and small fridge occupied one side, while an enormous mahogany desk and a five-shelf, matching bookcase ruled the other. A large display of cookbooks and recipe files dominated the shelves.

Amy nodded toward two comfortable-looking easy

chairs in front of the desk. "I'd offer you a seat, but I'm on a tight schedule. Okay, so you wanted to know what to do with Kelly's stuff? I can't answer that. You need to talk to Shelly."

"Is she the new owner?" I asked.

Amy pressed her lips together. "Looks that way. Were you two friendly with Kelly? Do you know Shelly as well?"

"We weren't exactly best buddies," Josie said dryly. "I have to confess that Kelly didn't strike me as having a lot of knowledge about running a bakery."

I shot Josie a warning look. We didn't know this woman well enough to be sharing confidences with her. Actually, I'd hoped for the other way around.

Amy glanced nervously from Josie to me. "You didn't like Kelly?"

Josie spoke up again before I could say anything. "Nope. Sorry to speak ill of the dead, but I didn't like Kelly and don't care for Shelly, either."

Ouch. I waited for Amy to order us out of the office in a rage, but instead she seemed relieved, almost as if she'd been hoping we'd say those exact words. She lowered her voice and leaned toward me. "Look. Between you two and me, no one here cares for either sister. Kelly thought she was better than everyone, and Shelly basically lived off her sister's business. I'm the only one who's had the guts to stand up to them—not that it's ever done me any good. At least Kelly knew something about the baking process, although she never did much of it herself. I never went to culinary school, but my grandfather owned a bakery years ago, and I helped out every day after school, until the place went bankrupt. I've also been baking in the kitchen with my mother since I was three years old."

A slow smile spread across Josie's face. "Sounds like me, except I'd bake with my grandmother or with Sal's—*ouch!*"

She gave a small yelp as I stepped on her foot, and immediately realized her mistake. "I meant to say, it *shall* always be one of my favorite memories."

Good grief. She'd almost blown our cover. "How do you like working for Shelly?"

Amy sniffed. "Well, it's better than working for that loser Kelly called a husband. I'm sure he'll be around though.

Barry always came in with his hand out. He's even emptied the register then gone on his merry way. It drives Shelly nuts, but what can she do? As soon as I find another job, I'm out of here. Too much drama for my taste."

"Could Barry wind up with the bakery instead of Shelly?" I asked.

Amy's face flushed crimson. "I can't believe that Kelly would be so stupid as to leave it to him. Then again, she was stupid enough to marry him, so who knows? The will hasn't been read yet. The only way Kelly was even able to buy the place was because of her mother. She died around the same time that Kelly finished culinary school. The woman was a state employee who just keeled right over at her desk one day. Kelly said it was a massive heart attack. Her mom received more money because she died on the job, and Kelly was sole beneficiary."

"That must have gone over well with Shelly," Josie remarked.

Amy's mouth twitched into a grin. "Oh, yeah. Kelly thinks her mother meant to change the will but never got around to it before her death. Apparently Shelly and her mom had a huge blowout a few years before which left Shelly out in the cold. Kelly laughed about it when she told me. Can you believe it?"

"Yes, I can," Josie said soberly.

I couldn't imagine doing something so hurtful to Gianna. "So Kelly got all the money while Shelly got nothing?"

"Pretty much." Amy folded her arms across her chest. "But just so you don't think that Kelly was a selfish bitch, she did offer Shelly a permanent job at the bakery. Thoughtful, huh?"

Josie shook her head in apparent disbelief. "Wow. Who needs enemies when you have a sister like that?"

"Exactly. And I'll tell you something else. I've been working here since Kelly opened the doors about eight years ago. Those two may have been twins, but there was no love lost between them. I've heard them arguing about money, customers, men—"

A chill ran down my spine. The thought that Shelly could have killed her own sister made me physically ill. I couldn't comprehend how anyone might hate their own flesh and blood enough to kill them. But I'd encountered a similar scenario before when Colin had been murdered.

"Was there any chance that Shelly was involved with Barry?" Josie asked.

Amy did a palms-up. "I suppose she could have been, but Shelly always acted like she hated him. Half the time I never knew what was real and what was fake with the twins. They were so plastic."

"That's obvious," Josie snorted.

"Barry had women on the side," Amy continued. "Kelly knew about them, and she had her own lovers too. She was crazy about Barry at first, but lately she seemed indifferent to him." She lowered her voice. "They had a total open marriage. Sick, huh?"

My skin crawled at the comment. Why would two people stay in a loveless marriage like that? There was only one reason I could think of—money.

Amy tossed her head angrily. "This may sound a bit pompous, but if it wasn't for me, there would be no bakery. I'm the only one who does anything around here. Kelly practically begged me to come and work for her after I put on a baking demonstration to apply for the job. I showcased several of my sugar free recipes and she fell in love with them. I always wanted to open my own place but never had the capital. Four years ago I finally had enough money and threatened to quit. Then Kelly promised to make me a partner in a couple of years."

"It never happened?" I asked.

Her face turned crimson. "Nope. Like a fool, I continued to stay here though, and kept waiting. Then when Kelly got that job with your boss and made Shelly manager, it was the last straw for me. By the way, Shelly is useless. She sits in the office during the day and counts the profits. I'm so done with this place."

As we listened to her tirade, it became apparent to me that there was yet another person with reason enough to kill Kelly. As if the list wasn't long enough already.

Why, if I had the money that they did—" A gleam came into Amy's eyes. She blinked rapidly, and then it disappeared. "Some of us in this life have to work for everything we've got.

I've never had anything handed to me like those two pompous bitches."

Josie and I exchanged glances. Okay, I hadn't expected to find Kelly's employees sobbing over her death, but a little remorse might have been nice. As I tried to figure out how to phrase my next question, Josie saved me the trouble. "Do you think Shelly could have had something to do with her sister's murder?"

Amy looked startled and glanced down at her watch again. "Uh, I hate to do this, but I need to get back to my cake. I'll let Shelly know you were here. She'll probably stop in later. What'd you say your names were again?"

"Thelma and Lou—" *Oh my God.* Thanks to Mike, I couldn't get those names out of my head. I cleared my throat. "Thelma and Lou Ann. But that's not necessary. We'll stop by to see her tomorrow. You don't even have to mention our visit."

Once we were inside the vehicle, Josie turned to stare at me. "Really? Thelma and Lou Ann? Where the hell did you get that combo from?"

I scowled and started the engine. "Never mind. It's pretty obvious that lots of people disliked Kelly and her sister. Barry's still at the top of my list, but we need to take a good hard look at Shelly too."

Josie placed her seat belt around her. "I wouldn't rule little Miss Baker out either."

"Amy? Because Kelly lied about making her a partner?"

"Exactly. Or maybe she was stealing from them. Didn't you notice those huge diamond earrings she wore? They had to cost a small fortune."

"They might have been a gift."

Josie pressed her lips together. "Wait, there's more. I was going to tell you inside but not with Amy so close by."

"Oh, yeah." I left the car idling in drive. "Why did you nudge me?"

Josie stole a glance back in the direction of the bakery. "That thud you heard? Her purse fell off the counter, and everything fell out. And guess what I saw? A backstage pass like the ones we had for Donna's show."

I shrugged. "She could have gone to a taping at some

point. Maybe Kelly handed them out to her staff. It doesn't mean she was there the day of the actual murder."

"Why are you defending her?" Josie cried. "I don't want to go to trial for this, Sal. I have to think of my kids. This would ruin their lives."

"Okay, okay." I tried to shush her before she became hysterical. "We won't let that happen. I'm trying to keep an open mind here. There are a lot of people who had a motive to get rid of Kelly."

My phone buzzed, and I glanced down at the screen. My parents' number popped up. "Hello?"

"*Cara mia*," Grandma Rosa said. "Mr. Donovan was just here."

Confused, I wrinkled my nose at the news. "Mike's dad? But how did he—what was he doing there?"

"I believe that he saw the sign on the lawn for the open house and all the cars. At first he thought that your parents were selling their house, until your papa told him it was an opportunity for people to look at the new casket he'd bought." She clucked her tongue in disapproval. "Your papa bought a second one. It is upstairs in your old bedroom."

My childhood home was becoming an undertaker's fantasy. I winced and shut my eyes. "Ugh. Sam must have been so impressed to meet Mom and Dad."

"I wanted to warn you," my grandmother cautioned. "After he talked to your mama and papa, they invited him to join us for dinner tonight."

"Oh, no!" Grandma Rosa was making Mike's favorite soup, pasta e fagioli. He had told me earlier how much he was looking forward to it. Yes, we had talked about him giving his father a chance, but as far as I knew, he hadn't reached a decision yet. Forcing my husband into a dinner he wasn't ready for—especially with *my* family—was definitely not the way to go. "Does Dad have no memory at all? Why didn't he check with us first? Couldn't you have stopped him?"

My grandmother snorted into the phone. "First of all, your papa is a *pazza* old fool. All he thinks about is that ridiculous blog of his. And coffins. This morning he had to go tape his commercial, and then this afternoon he talked about coffins while I handed out coffee and cake. His dream job, he called it. Do these people have nothing better to do? A few even asked for his autograph."

My father, the local celebrity of death. It was too much to comprehend.

"They made your mama an extra in the commercial too. She has been prancing around all day talking about it. This is a nutsy cookie house that we live in, *cara mia*."

"You mean world, not house."

"I know what I mean," my grandmother grunted.

"Aargh." I was tempted to pound my head against the steering wheel.

"Maybe the dinner will not be so bad," Grandma said hopefully, a note of optimism in her voice.

"Oh, right," I scoffed. "Dad will be his usual blunt self and ask Sam him why he ran out on Mike. Then he'll ask him to pass the eggplant Parmesan."

"What I meant," Grandma Rosa said, "is that it may help break the ice between Mike and his father. There will be other people around, so perhaps your husband will not feel so uncomfortable. I will do everything in my power to make it a nice evening."

Why did I have to have the only set of parents in the universe that refused to grow up? "There's too much going on in my life right now. Between Mike's Dad, Kelly's murder, and no business at the shop, I'm having a serious dessert attack. Please tell me you're making cheesecake tonight."

"For you, yes, I will do this. But cheesecake will not solve your problems, *cara mia*," Grandma warned. "Do not let it make you a hot mass."

I blinked at the phone. "I hope you mean mess."

"That is good too."

CHAPTER FIFTEEN

"What's going on?" Josie wanted to know.

I pushed the button for my husband's number. "My father invited Mike's dad over for dinner tonight. The you-know-what is officially about to hit the fan."

"Holy cow." Josie's eyes grew wide with alarm. "Yeah, that definitely won't go over well with hubby."

Thankfully, Mike answered on the third ring. "Hi, princess. What's up?"

"Your dad was at my parents' house today. You know that open house my father was doing?" *A casket tour. For God's sake, who does that?* "They got to talking, and he ended up inviting your dad over for dinner tonight. I'm sorry. I don't know what the heck he was thinking."

A deafening silence met my ears. Panicked, I started to babble. "We don't have to go, sweetheart. My grandmother called me and—"

"Whoa. Slow down," Mike said quietly. "So you're telling me that we're having a big dinner tonight to welcome my father into the folds of the Muccio family?"

Ugh. It was bad enough that Mike had to share the table with his father, but now we also had to worry about what might fall out of my father's mouth during the meal, besides food. One never knew quite what to expect when dining with Maria and Domenic Muccio. "My father means well. He probably thought he was helping the situation. But don't worry. I'll call Grandma and cancel."

"It's all right, Sal." He sounded weary and somewhat defeated. "Let's just get it over with."

"Are you sure?" I hated that he had to go through this.

Sure, I loved my father, but as Grandma Rosa often said, some days he needed a swift kick to the seat of his pants.

"Yeah. Look, I'm going to be working past six at this job, so I'll meet you there. Tell your grandmother I'm sorry we won't be staying long. I'd rather be alone with my beautiful wife tonight, but since she went to all that trouble for me, I'm not about to disappoint her."

My heart melted and ached for him at the same time. "Love you," I said softly into the phone.

"Love you too, princess." He disconnected.

"That could have been much worse," Josie remarked. "I didn't even hear any screaming."

I checked the mirror and drove away from the curb. "He isn't sure he wants anything to do with Sam, and I understand that. I can't imagine what it's like to go through your entire life knowing that your parents never wanted you."

Josie stared out the window. "Yeah, I know something about that too, remember."

"Of course you do." Josie had seven brothers and sisters and always seemed to be the forgotten child. Growing up, she'd spent more time at my house than her own.

She was silent for a moment before continuing. "When I was about nine or ten, I came downstairs late one night for a drink of water and heard my parents talking. They'd decided to send a couple of us away to live with relatives because they couldn't afford to feed us all. As it turned out, my grandmother ended up coming to live with us shortly afterward and helped them out financially."

"I remember your grandmother. I always liked her." More so than Josie's parents, but I would never have said that.

Josie bit into her lower lip. "Guess whose name was the first one mentioned that night?"

"Why didn't you ever tell me about this before?"

She shrugged. "I didn't want you to feel sorry for me."

I reached over to squeeze her hand. "Jos, that's awful. I don't know what to say."

Josie forced a smile to her lips. "If I'd gone away, we might not have stayed in touch. And we probably never would have run a bakery together."

"You're wrong. Our paths would have crossed again. It was written in the stars—er, I mean, the fortune cookies," I teased.

* * *

"So," my father said as he refilled his wineglass, "what do you do for a living, Sam?"

Sam stopped eating and wiped his mouth with his napkin. "This is delicious, by the way." He nodded to my grandmother who sat at the end of the table, hands folded primly on the handmade tablecloth. "You're quite a cook, Rosa. My wife could barely boil water. Isn't that right, Mike?"

You could have heard a napkin rustle to the floor. Mike reached over his still full plate to polish off his second beer in less than ten minutes. "Yep. Her specialties were Budweiser, Michelob, and Coors."

Ouch. Oh yeah, this is going well.

My father was seated at the head of the cherrywood dining table, with my mother to his left and me on the right. Mike was on my other side and Sam across from him, next to my mother. Grandma Rosa sat alone at the foot of the table.

My mother reached over to pat Sam on the hand and giggled low in her throat. "I can't get over the family resemblance. Sweetheart," she nodded at me. "If you want to know what your husband will look like in 25 years, here you go."

I shot her a murderous glance. Dear, sweet Mom who always thought she was helping.

"Unless he has a facelift like some people," Grandma Rosa muttered, making a veiled reference to my mother's cosmetic surgery a few years ago.

My mother ignored her. "It's too bad you couldn't meet our other daughter tonight. Gianna's a lawyer," she added proudly.

"Really?" Sam mused. "Sounds like you have two very successful children."

"Oh, I do. They take after their mother," she bragged. "In fact, *I* was in a commercial today."

Here it comes. I glanced worriedly at Mike who seemed

distracted as he stirred his soup with his spoon. He'd barely touched it or the eggplant parmesan. Grandma Rosa had also made homemade Italian bread that was still warm from the oven. I spread butter on a second piece and took a bite. It melted in my mouth.

Mike dropped the spoon and reached for a glass of wine. It looked like I'd be the one driving us both home tonight. I whispered in his ear. "Are you okay?"

He squeezed my hand but said nothing. I glanced down at my watch. How much more did he have to endure before we could make an excuse to leave?

"A commercial, huh?" Sam smiled at my mother. It was impossible not to be bowled over by her beauty and sunny disposition. She always looked at life through rose-colored glasses, although I'd recently learned this was also her mechanism for dealing with tragic events in her life. "What kind of commercial?" he asked.

My father broke in, his mouth full of eggplant parmesan. "That's right. We didn't have a chance to tell you about it earlier. I did a commercial for a funeral home this morning and talked them into giving Maria a part as an extra."

Mom stared at him in surprise. "What are you talking about, Domenic? They were practically begging me to be in it as soon as I walked through the door."

"Of course, baby." My father drained his glass and reached for the wine bottle.

I winced inwardly, but to Sam's credit, he smiled politely at my mother. "I can see why they'd want you. You must have wowed them with your looks."

Ew. I thought I'd noticed Sam checking out her legs earlier when she walked into the kitchen.

My father puffed out his chest. "She wows everyone. Best looking girl in the room. No offense, Sal."

Jeez Louise. I rolled my eyes. "None taken, Dad."

My father untucked his napkin from his shirt. "So, who wants to see what I got for part of my payment?"

"I'd love to." Sam's gaze drifted from my mother to my father with obvious interest. He might as well have been talking to deaf ears because my father had already left the room, whistling what sounded like "Don't Fear the Reaper."

"I can't wait to see this," I told Mike.

He put an arm around my shoulders but said nothing. I saw his gaze shift to his father, who was busy making polite conversation with my mother. Grandma Rosa remained sitting in place, a rarity for her since she was never idle. Her large brown eyes roamed the room, and I knew that sharp brain of hers was busy taking inventory.

My father returned to the dining room with a brass urn tucked under his arm. It was a foot high and had a gold ring design set within a black background. He placed it on the dining room table and spread his arms open wide. "They're even going to throw one in for your mother."

My mother made a face. "I'm happy for you darling, but really, I don't want one."

"No, but you will *need* one someday," he assured her. "We have to face the facts of life here."

Sam laughed out loud. "Well, I've never seen anything like this. Did they give you a family burial plot too?"

My father grunted. "No need. When I go, one of my kids will keep the urn on their fireplace."

"Um, yeah, that's so not happening," I whispered. It was a good thing Gianna wasn't here. She had no patience for my father's antics and would have blown a gasket by now.

"That's not all." My father rubbed his hands together in delight. "We have more news. I've decided to write a book."

For the first time all night, a smile formed at the corners of Mike's mouth. He stood, shook his head, and pushed his seat back. "Well, I think this calls for another beer."

Grandma Rosa rose from her seat. "Let me get it for you."

Mike put up a hand up to stop her. "No thanks, Rosa. You've done more than enough already. Please don't bother." He headed toward the kitchen.

"That's right." My father turned to my grandmother. "Instead, you can pass down the Frangelico chocolate pie and cheesecake, Mother dear."

Grandma Rosa gave him a death stare. "You can save your silly sentiments for that *pazza* blog of yours."

"Jeez," my father muttered. "Everyone has an attitude these days."

"Excuse me." Sam rose from his chair and followed Mike into the kitchen. He shut the door behind him while we all watched, openmouthed. I glanced at my grandmother nervously, and she reached over to pat my hand.

"Let it go, my love. They need to talk alone."

She was right, of course. In a little while, this would all be over, and if Mike didn't want to see him again, that was his decision. It was better for me to stay out of it, unless Mike asked for my help.

"The poor man," my mother said piteously as she studied her reflection in a handheld compact. "He told us earlier that he had just come from Colwestern Hospital."

My grandmother placed a piece of cheesecake in front of me, and I wasted no time digging in. "Did he say why?"

My mother leaned forward across the table and spoke in a low tone. "No, but I think it must be serious."

Grandma Rosa gave a loud harrumph. "I am not so sure."

"What do you mean?" I asked.

My grandmother stirred the coffee in her demitasse cup. "*Cara mia*, I do not want to ruin this chance for Mike to get to know his father. But I am—what do you say—worn of the man."

I had to think about this for a minute. "Do you mean wary, Grandma?"

She shrugged. "I like that too."

"Oh, pooh." My mother's lips twisted into a pout. "Ma, you're suspicious of everyone."

My father was tracing the pattern on the outside of the urn with his fingers. "True. She didn't like me when we were dating."

"I still do not," Grandma Rosa declared.

My mind was busy concocting a plan as I listened to their banter. Brian's girlfriend, Ally Tetrault, was a nurse at Colwestern Hospital. Ally and I had gone to high school together. We weren't exactly chummy, especially since she knew that Brian had been interested in me at one point, but we'd seen each other in passing a few times this winter and always exchanged pleasantries. Would Ally tell me anything? There were laws that protected patient information, so I guessed probably not. Still, it might be worth a try.

Mike came back in from the kitchen alone. His handsome face looked tired. A hard day's work, the stress with his dad, and the beer had all probably come into play. "Are you almost ready to go, princess?"

"Sure." I wiped my mouth with my napkin and then glanced at the kitchen door. "We'll come by and get the truck in the morning. Where's your dad?"

"He left." Mike looked over at my grandmother. "He said to thank you for the wonderful meal and that he enjoyed getting to know everyone."

Grandma Rosa started to clear the dishes from the table, and Mike and I went to help her. "How did you leave things?" I asked.

Mike raised his eyebrows and then stared over at my parents, who both had an ear tuned in to our conversation. "We'll talk about it when we get home." He gave my grandmother a kiss. "Thank you for dinner, Rosa. It was amazing as always."

She patted his cheek. "Anytime, my dear boy."

"Uh-oh," my father said suddenly.

We all turned around. My father had removed the lid from the urn and was staring inside. "I think I'd better call the funeral home in the morning."

My mother looked up from the nail she was filing with an emery board. "What's wrong, honey? Did they give you a broken one?"

My father shook his head, and a slow grin spread across his face. "Nope. They gave me a *used* one."

CHAPTER SIXTEEN

———

Mike leaned back in the seat and chuckled. "I'll say one thing for your parents. There's never a dull moment in their house."

That was the understatement of the year. Although the whole incident had been disgusting, at least it had managed to put Mike in a better mood. "Can you believe he's going to blog about it tomorrow?"

He closed his eyes. "And he'll probably get ten thousand hits."

"Did your father tell you about his visit to the hospital today?" So much for my trying to stay off the subject of dear old Dad.

Mike opened one eye and looked at me. "No. He simply said that he was proud of me and that you were adorable. He said I'd done well for myself."

"I do love a good compliment," I teased.

The grin faded from his face. "Dear old dad asked if we could spend some time alone together tomorrow."

"What did you tell him?" I slowed to let another car in front of me.

"I'm laying carpet in an empty builder over on Howard Street with a couple of guys I've hired for some upcoming jobs," Mike said. "He told me he'd come by around noon and bring lunch. What could I say? I'm tired of fighting it, Sal."

"Did he—was—" I paused and tried to find a subtle way to ask. "Was Sam like Ray?"

"No." Mike's voice sounded as if it was coming from inside a bubble, faint and far away. "I don't remember him ever hitting me. I was only five when he split, but all he and Mom ever did was fight. He gave family life a shot, and it failed. There are some people in this world who just aren't meant to be parents, Sal."

I said nothing. Personally, I couldn't imagine someone not wanting children in their lives but knew not everyone shared my view. Heck, even my own sister was on the fence about having kids. Mike's father has risen slightly higher in my opinion now that I knew he wasn't a child abuser. Still, he'd had a responsibility to his son and failed miserably. If he had stuck around, Mike might not have been subjected to the abuse he went through with Ray.

We stopped for a red light, and out of the corner of my eye, I saw him watching me. The vivid blue of his eyes shone from the reflection of the nearby street lamp. It had started to flurry out, and there wasn't a soul or another car in sight. The overall effect of the empty street resembled a Christmas picture postcard, covered in fine snow that sparkled on the ground like diamonds. It was difficult not to get emotional when I stared at this man who was not only part of my life but my soul as well. He was hurting, but I couldn't do anything about it.

Mike must have guessed my thoughts. "It's all right, baby. Here's my take on the situation. I've done plenty of dirty jobs during my lifetime—pumped septic tanks, fixed toilets, dug out basements. As far as I'm concerned, this is just another dirty job for me to finish."

I understood his philosophy, but comparing Sam to a leaky toilet didn't exactly fill me with optimism. Maybe something positive would come out of tomorrow's meeting. At least he was willing to talk to his father. That was something, right? "I hate seeing you go through this."

His voice grew soft. "You worry too much. That's the problem. You worry about everyone but yourself. I'll be fine. And Josie will too. We both have you, so what else do we need?"

Hot tears spilled down my cheeks, and I brushed them away with my hand. "If you keep this up, it will take us forever to get home."

"Why?" Mike asked, puzzled.

"Because I won't be able to see where I'm going."

He laughed. "Okay, princess. You win."

I drew a deep breath. "Rob and Josie are having a rough time. I don't know if you've spoken to him lately, but maybe you could say something?"

Rob and Mike were good friends, although they didn't see each other very often. Most of the time it was when the four of us went out together, and that was rare as of late. Rob had also been best man at our wedding.

Mike hesitated for a second. "I'd rather not interfere, Sal. Give them some time. I'm sure he's just concerned about the kids."

"He should be concerned about his wife too." My tone sounded a bit defensive. "And she's worried about the kids as well."

"They'll work it out. Kids always have to come first. We'll find that out before long."

"I hope so." Why did life have to be so tumultuous all the time? Mike and Josie were both going through family issues, Gianna was having relationship problems, and my parents were…well, they were my parents. Nothing was ever *normal* in their world. The irony of the situation was not lost on me. For once, I may not have been directly affected by the turmoil, but all my loved ones were. The worst part was that I couldn't do anything to help them.

Or could I?

* * *

Business at the bakery continued to be nonexistent the next day. I didn't say anything to Josie but had started to worry about sales—or lack thereof. Josie spent most of the day making cookies for an upcoming bridal shower. At least we still had a couple of orders trickling in. She tried to stay out of sight if anyone came in so as to avoid their natural curiosity. I hoped that the visit to Mount Eden Assisted Living tonight might reveal something that would benefit her. She was running out of time until the grand jury was scheduled to meet.

I spent most of the afternoon giving the bakery a good cleaning, which consisted of washing windows, mopping the floor, and cleaning both the espresso and Keurig machines. My cell phone buzzed as I finished. My husband. "Hi, sweetheart."

His tone was low and sexy. "Hi, princess. I'm running behind on this carpeting job, and one of the guys helping me went home sick. I think I'll be pretty late tonight."

"That's okay. I may be late too."

"Oh?" I caught a note of curiosity in his tone. "Something up at the bakery? Does the local school need 10,000 chocolate chips for tomorrow?"

"Ha-ha. I wish." He was not going to like this. "I'm going to an assisted living home in Datson."

"Jeez, I thought we had a few years before we needed to start making those kinds of decisions," Mike teased.

"You're a regular comedian today. Kelly Thompson used to work there, and I want to check out a few things."

A deafening silence met my ears. "Check out means to snoop for you. I thought we discussed this. You're not taking Josie along, are you? What if she beats up one of the residents?"

"Will you stop? Gianna's going with me. I'm not going to sit by and watch my best friend go to prison for something she didn't do."

Mike sighed. "All right. Promise me you'll be careful."

"I will." Since he wasn't volunteering any information, my inquisitive nature kicked into gear. "Did your father show up today?"

"He was here," Mike said quietly.

From his tone it was difficult to tell if things had gone well or not. "What happened? Did you get a chance to talk?"

He sighed. "We talked. He was here for about an hour. Another reason I'm running behind today. But I aired some of my feelings, and he told me a few things as well. I was going to talk to you about it later, but God knows what time I'll be home. I promised I'd have this job finished today."

"Did your father tell you why he left?"

"I've always known why he left," Mike said. "He and my mother didn't love each other anymore. I'm not certain that they ever did. Dad said he worried about uprooting me from the only life I'd ever known and thought it was better for me to stay with Mom."

I refrained from comment, but it sounded like a crock of

bull to me. Mike was only five years old at the time. He would have adjusted well anywhere at such a young age. How could Sam possibly think that leaving him behind with a mother who was drunk half the time was better for his son?

As usual, he was attuned to my thoughts. "Yeah, I know it sounds like a load of crap, but it's his story, and he's sticking to it. Maybe I should thank him."

"Thank him for what?" I asked in disbelief.

His voice softened. "If I'd gone with him, I might never have met you."

This man always knew how to turn my heart into a pile of mush. "We would have met somehow. We were meant to be together."

"I know." Mike was quiet for a second. "Sam—er, Dad, hasn't worked for a while and as we thought has some health problems."

Fear settled in the bottom of my stomach. "Did he say what was wrong with him?"

"Not exactly, but he did mention that he wished he'd never started smoking. It makes me think that he might have lung cancer."

I closed my eyes. After 25 years Mike had finally found his father and started to make peace with him. Now he might be taken away again but by a different type of force. Life could be so cruel at times. "I'm sorry, baby."

"Sal." Raw emotion filled his voice. "He asked if he could come and stay with us for a couple of weeks, until he gets some financial things straightened out on his end."

The request shocked me, although I probably should have seen it coming. In truth, I hated the thought of Mike and me giving up our privacy, even if it was for a limited amount of time. We had just gotten married, were in love, and trying to have a baby. "What did you tell him?"

"I said I had to talk to you first. This is a lot for me to digest," he said honestly, "and I really don't know what to do. What do you think I should tell him?"

"I want whatever will make you happy." Deep down, I figured Mike would end up saying yes to his father. My husband had a large heart, and even though Sam had run off on him, he was still all the family he had, except for my own. "Why don't you think on it for a couple of days?"

He blew out a long breath. "I really don't know how I got lucky enough to find you."

"That's funny. I was thinking the same thing."

"I have to run, princess." His tone was lighter now, perhaps due to the fact that he'd gotten this boulder off his chest. "Maybe I'll wake you up when I get home, and we can spend some quality time together that doesn't involve *any* talking."

I suppressed a giggle. "Sounds great to me. Love you."

"Love you too. Be careful tonight. And Sal?"

"Yes?"

"Thank you." There was a brief pause before the line went dead.

Josie was standing in the doorway of the back room with a piping bag in hand, watching me. "Someone looks pretty serious. Want to talk about it?"

"Mike's father asked if he can move in with us for a while." I bit into my lower lip. "He's not well and isn't working, so it's kind of a desperate situation."

She grimaced. "Wow. I love Rob's parents, but I'd never want either one of them living with me. I don't think we could coexist under one roof. I give you a lot of credit for considering it, Sal."

I followed her into the back room. "What else could I do? There's no way I'd ever tell Mike no. I guess the honeymoon's over if Sam moves in."

Josie's eyes twinkled with mirth. "Nah. You guys will think of something. Maybe you can go off in Mike's truck and find a secluded spot in the woods."

"Good God. What, are we back in high school again?" I was grateful that she seemed more like her old self now. "How's everything at home?"

Josie squeezed frosting out of the bag onto a batch of strawberry cookies. "Not great. A couple of kids confronted Danny at school yesterday. They asked him what it was like to have a mother who murdered people in cold blood."

My breath caught in my throat. "I don't know how kids can be so cruel. What did you do?"

She cocked her head to one side. "Rob and I are going to homeschool him for now. It hasn't touched the other kids yet, but if it does, you can bet your butt they'll be out of there too."

"What did the school say?"

Josie sniffed. "The principal said they hadn't actually attacked him, so there was nothing that could be done. Can you believe that crap? It's like the other kids have more rights than mine. Once this blows over, we may decide to send him elsewhere." She bit into her lower lip. "*If* it blows over."

I winced. "It will. How did Rob take it?"

"Not well." Her blue eyes, full of pain, met mine. "The kids come first. Sal, I may need to take a few days off. Danny's real upset about this, and I'd like to spend some time with him."

Why did this have to happen to Josie? Hadn't she been through enough in her life already? I was careful to guard my expression because she didn't want my pity. "Of course. Whatever you need."

She watched me thoughtfully. "Are you still planning to go to Mount Eden tonight?"

"Yes. Gianna's going with me. She'll be here in an hour."

Josie frowned. "It may not do any good, but I appreciate your trying. I wish I could go, but I want to get home to Danny as soon as possible."

"You can take off whenever you like. It's dead in here anyway."

Her lower lip trembled. "I'm sorry, Sal. This is my fault that you don't have any business."

"Stop it." My voice shook with anger, and Josie's eyes widened in response. "This is *not* your fault. Someone is setting you up. And for the record, I wouldn't even have a business if it wasn't for you. We're going to find out who's responsible for Kelly's death."

Her mouth turned upwards at the corners. "Damn, girl. I'm so proud of you. I used to hate it when you'd let people walk all over you, like skanky Amanda back in high school. But you've really come into your own. I mean, telling *me* off? Not many people can get away with doing that."

My phone buzzed from my pocket. "Well, you'd better get used to it, girlfriend. We don't take anyone's bull around here."

She howled with laughter as I glanced down at the screen. My parents' landline. Ugh. What now? Was my father teaching a class in embalming and wanted fortune cookies for his students? "Hello?"

"Hi, baby girl." My father's voice resonated through the line. He hardly ever called, so my alarm antenna went up immediately.

"Hey, Dad, is everything okay?"

He cleared his throat. "I went to the funeral home this morning to return the urn. They were able to match that baby up with its true owner."

Gross. "Well, I'm glad it all worked out. Especially for his family."

"Her family," my father corrected. "By the way, the owner thinks that the commercial is going to be a huge success, so they've decided to have an urn custom made for me. My initials or full name in raised gold letters with any kind of design I want."

Some people longed for swimming pools, hot racing cars, or a mansion. Then there was my father, who wanted his own personalized urn. "That's great, Dad. Well, I've got to run. Talk to you later."

"Wait, Sal," he interrupted. "Did I tell you at dinner last night that it's the same funeral home where your TV friend was being laid out?"

He had my full attention now. "No, you didn't. You went to Gavin Funeral Home?" Come to think of it, I vaguely remembered him telling me the other day that the parlor was located in Colgate, but I'd dismissed it from my mind. "Did you happen to see who was at the funeral?"

"No. The commercial was filmed at a different location. Like I said, I was over there this morning. While I was talking to the owner, his receptionist came in. She was all upset and said that the deceased's husband had already been complaining about the bill. He claimed they overcharged him and refused to pay."

"Are you sure about this?" I asked.

"Yep. What a lousy thing to do, huh? I mean, your life partner gets killed, and all you care about is how much their casket costs? That could make a great slogan, though. 'You can't put a price on a casket.' Hey, I think I'll blog about that."

"Whatever works, Dad."

He chuckled. "More like, whatever fills your urn. Man, I'm full of them today."

Ew. "Dad, I think people might get offended if you say that."

"Nah. Your old man is a big success, baby girl. Wait until the book comes out."

Good grief. If a publisher ever bought that monstrosity, Gianna might pull her own *Thelma and Louise* and drive off the nearest bridge.

"But in all seriousness," Dad continued. "Your wife is dead, and all you care about is the bill? What kind of a man stoops that low?"

I said nothing, but the words rang out loud and clear in my head, similar to a chorus of church bells.

A man who killed her, that's who.

CHAPTER SEVENTEEN

———

It was about six thirty when Gianna and I arrived at Mount Eden Assisted Living. The sky was pitch black, and the temperature hovered around zero degrees as we hurried toward the handicap accessible entrance. Lampposts on both sides of the paved walkway shone in welcome while lights blazed from the interior of the one-story, brown, brick veneer building.

We stepped through the automatic doors and spotted a middle-aged woman seated at the receptionist counter. A giant corkboard occupied the wall space behind her with various flyers and posters announcing bake sales, movie outings, and several other activities.

The woman's name tag identified her as Laura. Her friendly brown eyes crinkled at the corners as she smiled at us. "Can I help you, ladies?"

"Hi, we're looking for some information," I began.

She immediately handed me a pamphlet with pictures of white-haired women and men laughing while they played shuffleboard, enjoyed meals in the dining room, and snoozed peacefully in king-size beds. "Is this for your parents or grandparents?"

"Grandmother," Gianna said quickly.

I winced. We'd discussed our plan of action on the drive over, but the thought of Grandma Rosa in an assisted living facility was almost comical. The woman was more self-sufficient than I was most days.

She smiled in understanding and picked up the phone beside her. "Of course. I'll get Phoebe to give you a quick tour. She doesn't leave until eight."

While we waited for Phoebe, Gianna and I turned our

attention toward a large room adjacent to the receptionist area where several seniors were seated in armchairs before a large flat-screen television. Familiar music met my ears, and I guessed that they were watching *Seinfeld*.

"Hi, girls," a squeaky, female voice greeted us from behind. Phoebe was tinier than me at about five feet tall, with long, dishwater-colored hair and oval gray eyes. She wore a blue blazer paired with jeans and looked like she belonged in high school. "Would you like a tour? Did you bring your grandmother with you?"

"No," I said quickly. "She's not very receptive to the idea." Boy, was that putting it mildly.

Phoebe nodded sympathetically. "Of course. We see that a lot." She gestured at the room where the seniors were watching television. "This is our entertainment room. There are also two loaded bookcases, a pool table, and shuffleboard. We offer bowling outings on Saturday nights and shopping trips three days a week. We even go to the theater. There's a trip scheduled for New York City next month to go see *The Lion King*. Our motto is that a busy resident is also a happy resident. I'm sure this will be the perfect place for your grandmother."

Gianna rolled her eyes, and I pretended not to notice. Phoebe showed us the dining room, which held between 15 and 20 tables with seating for six people at each one. A female employee was vacuuming the rug while another busied herself removing dirty tablecloths from what appeared to have been tonight's dinner.

"We offer three different choices of entrees for dinner," Phoebe said proudly. "What type of cooking does your grandmother prefer?"

Her own. "Ah, she favors pasta and braciole."

Phoebe wrinkled her nose. "I've never heard of braciole, but we can ask in the kitchen, if you like. Let me show you the living quarters. Every resident has a private room with an adjoining bathroom."

We walked down a wide hallway with doors on both sides, some with names on them while others sported decorations that looked as if they'd been made by a child. Phoebe stopped in front of Room 16 and opened it, allowing us to enter first. "This one was recently vacated—unexpectedly."

"Oh, I'm so sorry," I murmured.

Gianna shivered and drew back from the door.

Phoebe laughed. "It's not what you think. Mrs. Ellington didn't pass on. Her son moved into a larger house, and she went to live with him and his family. Such a lovely lady. Do you think this room might suit your grandmother?"

I glanced inside. There was a double bed, an oak dresser and desk, and a small flat screen television on the wall. I could see another door that must have led to the bathroom. The comforter was a beige floral design, with overhead lighting that was dim, casting the room in shadows. Sure, this would suit Grandma Rosa. If she liked claustrophobic spaces, that is.

Gianna glided her boot back and forth over the dark, brown carpeting. "The flooring is very thin."

"Commercial-grade carpeting," I explained. "It's safer and durable for people who aren't very mobile." Mike had discussed this in detail with me when I'd accompanied him to Home Depot once to purchase some for a job he'd been working on.

Gianna glanced at me, impressed. "Wow. You never fail to amaze me with your knowledge, sis."

"Is your grandmother mobile?" Phoebe asked.

"Yes, she gets around quite nicely," Gianna admitted.

Phoebe beamed. "Fabulous. Come on. I'll show you the kitchen."

There was an older woman in a white smock wiping down the large, eight-burner gas stove. She looked up as we entered and attempted a smile. Two side-by-side refrigerators stood at each end of the beige Formica countertops, which ran around the room in an L-shape.

"Hi, Doris," Phoebe greeted the woman. "We're doing a tour. Hey, have you ever heard of braciole?"

Doris put down the bottle of cleaner and the roll of paper towels that she'd been using. "Sure. It's thin slices of beef you pan fry. Then you put cheese inside, roll the slices up, and dip them into sauce to serve with spaghetti."

"Interesting," Phoebe mused. "These ladies say it's their grandmother's favorite dish."

Doris's light brown eyes surveyed us with interest. She had short, curly, salt-and-pepper hair with deep-set crow's feet around her eyes. I judged her to be mid-fifties, but with the crow's feet she might have been older or slightly younger.

"How long have you worked here, Doris?" I asked.

Doris didn't seem to be much of a conversationalist and picked up the bottle of spray again. "About nine years."

My pulse quickened. Here was the contact I'd been hoping for. "Are you the chef?"

"Assistant chef," she replied. "I'll never get *that* job. Always a bridesmaid, never a bride."

The smile faded from Phoebe's face. "Well, we can see you're busy, Doris, so we'll let you—"

"My grandmother is interested in this place because her friend's niece used to work here," I lied. "I think she was an assistant chef."

Phoebe looked interested. "Really? What was her name?"

"Kelly Thompson." I noticed that Doris' pupils grew wide when I mentioned the name. She eyed Gianna and me suspiciously but said nothing.

"Huh. I don't know her," Phoebe said. "Then again, I've only been here about a year. When did she work here?"

"She started a few months before I did." Doris cut her eyes to Phoebe. "She's the one they found dead at the television studio the other day. Didn't you hear about it?"

Phoebe put a hand to her mouth. "Oh! I didn't realize. I heard a couple of other employees talking about the incident, but I never watch the news. It's too depressing."

My mother and Phoebe could have been kindred spirits. She hated the unpleasantness of real life too and preferred her own rose-colored world. *Hey, whatever works for you.*

Phoebe's phone buzzed, and she stared down at the screen. "Oh, shoot. I have to take this. Would you excuse me for a minute?" She didn't wait for our reply, and she hurried out the door.

Doris continued to watch me with accusing eyes. "I know who you are."

My mouth went dry. "I'm sorry?"

"The video." Doris's mouth turned up slightly at the corners. "It's your friend who's being accused of Kelly's death."

Damn. Why hadn't I thought to bring the hairpiece again? The jig was up, so I decided to level with the woman. "Look. My friend didn't do this. I'm only trying to help her. I thought there might be some clue in Kelly's past that would reveal why someone wanted her dead." This was beyond frustrating. "I'm sorry."

"Hang on," Doris said. "I admire you trying to help your friend. Want my opinion? I don't think she killed her. No one, except the head chef at the time, liked that little witch when she worked here. She was too uppity for my taste."

"How well did you know her?" Gianna asked.

"Kelly was assistant chef back then. And then there was me—a lowly kitchen helper who got to do dishes and mop the floor. Guess what. Since we've cut back on staffing, I still get to do those things." She gave a hollow laugh. "Kelly's death didn't exactly come as a surprise. She tried to pin a murder on me once, so you could say I wasn't exactly fond of the girl."

My blood ran cold. "Wait a second. You're telling me that someone was murdered—here? Inside the home?"

Doris glanced toward the double doors that led to the dining area. We could see Phoebe through the portholes, chatting away on her cell. "Since you don't really have a grandmother coming to live here, I'll fill you in. A woman by the name of Maude Norton was murdered about nine years ago. Stupid old fool." The bitterness in her voice was apparent. "She kept one of those small fireproof safes in her room and bragged about how much money she had inside it. Maude told me once it was about a hundred grand."

"With that sum I wonder why she didn't buy her own house," Gianna said.

"Who knows?" Doris shrugged. "I think she liked the interaction with other residents. Plus she was confined to a wheelchair and didn't have family, except for a granddaughter who had three small children and couldn't take her. At first, most of us didn't believe she had so much money, but she kept bragging about it—like she wanted attention. Maude didn't trust banks. There was this one time I went to her room to grab her tray because she didn't feel like coming down to the dining room. While I was there, Maude insisted on showing me the money, so she must have shown others too. It was stolen out of the safe the night she died."

"How did she die?" I asked.

Doris folded her arms across her chest. "You know those Russell Stover candy boxes? Someone had inserted rat poisoning into every single piece, and Maude polished off at least half the box. Someone came to check on her later that evening and found her lying on the floor unconscious. She was rushed to the hospital in an ambulance, but it was too late by then. The next morning, the police opened the safe and found it empty."

Gianna and I exchanged glances. "Was anyone arrested for the crime?" I asked.

"No. Let me tell you, I almost lost my job over that whole mess. Like a fool, I once mentioned to Kelly that I had seen Maude's money. Kelly wasn't working the day of the murder, but the cops questioned her as well. All the employees had to give a statement. Anyway, Kelly was only too happy to tell them that I had seen the cash on a previous occasion so of course, I got questioned again, and the police asked why I hadn't told them this." Doris's face colored. "I really believe Kelly was trying to pin the crime on me."

"Why would Kelly do that to you?" Gianna asked.

Doris's nostrils flared. "Maybe she's the one that did the deed. Besides, she never liked me. Kelly was always jealous of people who had more talent than her. What's even more interesting is that another worker swore they saw Kelly here that night. She had an alibi, though. She was with her boyfriend at a casino in Buffalo. She won over a grand, so they'd had to ID her."

A light bulb went on inside my brain. What if it had been Shelly and not Kelly who the worker had seen? Shelly had mentioned that they had often played switcheroo. "Does that person—who saw Kelly—do they still work here?"

"No." Doris bit into her lower lip. "Roger was killed in a car accident about five years ago."

I took a step closer to the woman, who watched me like a cat watches a mouse before they pounce. "Level with me. Who do you think was responsible?"

She looked amused. "I can't say for sure but will tell you this. I talked to Maude's granddaughter a couple of days after her death. She said that the police let her see pictures of the chocolates when she asked about them. What she couldn't understand was how they looked so perfect."

Perplexed, I stared at her. "I don't understand."

"What I mean," Doris said, "is that they didn't look like they'd been tampered with. The police didn't seem too interested when the granddaughter mentioned this, but I thought the whole scenario was kind of odd. Someone with cooking skills may have done it. It certainly would have required the person to have a great deal of patience because you wouldn't want any of the pieces to look like they'd been tampered with. Hey, it's only my opinion, but I'm sticking to it."

This all struck me as a weird coincidence. Both Kelly and Maude had died from lethal substances. One had injected herself with the source while the other had ingested it. What if Kelly had killed Maude, someone knew and had blackmailed her with the knowledge? Then perhaps this person decided to kill Kelly in a similar manner. Or could the same person have committed both crimes?

"I'm sorry she's dead." Doris's voice was flat and sounded anything but sorry. "Still, what goes around comes around, and in my opinion that witch got what was coming to her. Kelly used to walk all over people when she worked here."

If anything, I had to admire the woman for her honesty. "Did Maude have any visitors the night she died?"

Doris shook her head. "That's the first thing the cops looked at. No one signed in, but that doesn't mean they couldn't have snuck in. There's a back entrance for employees only. They wouldn't have been caught on the video camera either."

"Who else worked in the kitchen back then besides you and Kelly?" Gianna wanted to know.

The woman stared at the stucco ceiling above her and frowned. "Our chef was named Grace Patterson. She left here about five years ago when she had a baby. There was a food buyer too, but she wasn't around that day."

"Do you know where I could find Grace or the food

buyer?" I asked.

"Grace moved away after she had the baby. Last I heard, she owns a restaurant in Virginia." Doris's expression soured. "Man, I never liked that woman. She ran the kitchen like a drill sergeant. I never actually met the food buyer. I had just started working here, and she only came in a couple of times a week."

"What did Grace look like?"

"Blonde." Doris flung the used paper towels into the trash can. "Grace was very pretty—and very mouthy. She was about Kelly's age and had also graduated from a culinary school somewhere down south. They got along for the most part, which is surprising. Cut from the same cloth, if you ask me. They were both more than happy to step on anyone who got in their way. Maybe Kelly figured that she'd learn from Grace. Even though she graduated from culinary school, she never impressed me with the fact that she was a great cook. Average at best."

"What about Olivia Nigel, Kelly's best friend?" I blurted out. "She worked here at the same time as Kelly. She could have had access, right?"

"Yes," Doris admitted, "but she wasn't working that night either. As far as I know, the case was never closed. The police were looking at one of the other residents as a top suspect, but then she dropped dead shortly after Maude did. Natural causes."

Phoebe pushed open the swinging doors. "Sorry about that, ladies. Now where were we?" She cut her eyes from us to Doris and hesitated. "Why does everyone look so serious? I hope that Doris hasn't been telling stories again." She gave a halfhearted laugh, but I caught the warning look that she cast at the older woman.

Doris pointed at herself and grinned. "Who, me? Of course not. I was telling these ladies that their grandmother is in good hands. Life's pretty sweet around here."

Phoebe stuck her nose out proudly in the air. "It sure is."

"Yep." Doris gave me a sly wink. "Sweeter than candy."

CHAPTER EIGHTEEN

———

On the way back home, Gianna's phone buzzed. She answered and then mouthed "client" to me, so I stayed quiet. Lost in my own thoughts, I concentrated on the road. Colwestern Hospital came into view on the right, and on impulse, I veered into their parking lot.

Gianna covered the phone with her hand. "What are you doing?"

"I want to talk to Ally Tetrault for a minute if she's here. Do you mind?"

She waved me off dismissively, and I left the car running for her. The air was bitterly cold as I hurried toward the lower level entrance. I cursed myself for forgetting my gloves in the car. Once inside, I passed the cafeteria and decided to forego the elevator, running up the stairs to the main floor where the emergency room was located. Last I knew, Ally had worked there. I asked the woman at the receptionist desk in the waiting room if she was here.

"Let me see if she's with a patient." The woman disappeared through a door, which led to the small curtained-off treatment areas I'd become very familiar with in the past couple of years. After a minute the woman returned with Ally behind her.

Ally Tetrault and Brian had started dating shortly before my wedding last summer. Dressed in pink scrubs and black Crocs, she was tall and slim with short red hair the same shade as Josie's. She seemed a bit surprised to see me but gave me a warm smile. "Hi, Sal. What's up?"

"Sorry to bother you," I said, "but I need to ask you a quick question."

"Sure." Her gray eyes appraised me with caution. "Is this about Brian?"

Cripes. Not again. I was afraid she'd think this had something to do with him. Ally had been worried last summer that Brian might still have been carrying a torch for me. I hoped we were past all that now and was quick to reassure her. "No, it's not. I need some information. Mike's father was in here for a physical recently."

"Oh?" She raised her eyebrows slightly. "What's his name?"

I blew out a breath. "Sam Donovan. I was wondering if—well, he told us that he's very sick but wouldn't say what's wrong. Mike and I are concerned and hoped that you—"

"Might fill in the blanks?" Ally interrupted.

I nodded. "Something like that."

She frowned. "I'm sorry, Sal, but I can't help you. We're bound by HIPAA, and I can't give out personal information like that."

I bit into my lower lip. "Right. I only hoped that if he was sick, you could tell me what was wrong. We're worried that it's cancer."

Ally stuffed her hands into her pockets and leaned back against the wall. "He may have a reason for not wanting to tell you. I know he's family, but that doesn't matter. You don't have any rights to the information unless Mike's father wants you to have it."

Dejected, I hung my head. "Sorry. I didn't mean to put you on the spot."

She laughed. "No worries. For the record, I did see Mr. Donovan when he was in and wondered if he might be related, but of course I couldn't ask." Her voice softened. "I hope it works out for you. Are he and Mike close?"

I shook my head. "Sam took off when Mike was five. The first time I saw him was when he showed up at my bakery the other day. We're pretty sure his illness is what caused him to seek Mike out—before things get worse."

For some reason, Ally's eyes turned wary, but her voice was still smooth as silk. "Oh, wow, that stinks. I'm sorry for you guys."

A blonde nurse also in pink scrubs approached Ally, a purse slung over her shoulder. "Sorry, I don't mean to interrupt. Al, if you're busy, I can bring you back a coffee."

Ally glanced at me and hesitated.

"It's fine," I assured her. "I think we're done anyway."

Ally flashed me a sympathetic smile. "Good luck with everything." She turned to the other nurse. "Let's go, Judy." On their way out of the waiting room, they held the door open for me, and I followed at a respectable distance. As I waited for the elevator, they proceeded down the stairs to the cafeteria together, laughing and talking.

When the elevator finally arrived, I noticed that a button had popped off my coat. I must have snagged it on something. "Shoot!" I went back into the emergency room and scanned the floor but didn't see it there. Then I went back out and checked the hallway again. Nothing. The button was nowhere to be found. Mike had given me this coat for Christmas. It was a black Michael Kors with a down-like material that came to my knees and a big furry hood that kept me cozy in the freezing Northeastern temperatures. My grandmother might have a matching button in her sewing kit, but maybe not. Resigned, I decided to check on the ground floor where I had entered the building and headed in the same direction as Ally and Judy. I had just reached the stairway when I heard voices coming from below and recognized Ally's immediately.

"His name is Sam Donovan. Sounds like he's running some type of scam."

My pulse quickened at her words. I hoped she'd continue but didn't want to take a chance that they'd see me. As their voices grew louder, I glanced around in panic for a place to hide. Nothing. I quickly climbed the stairs to the next level and prayed they wouldn't look up and see me. What kind of a lame excuse could I give if they spotted me—*Oops, I forgot my way out?*

"That really bites," Judy said. "So you think he's trying to swindle money out of them by pretending to be sick?"

"Sounds like it." Both women came into view and started down the hallway toward the emergency room, coffee cups in hand. "I wish there was some way to tell her that the guy's in perfect health," Ally continued. "Hopefully things will work out for them."

My blood ran cold as they disappeared out of my line of vision. *What the heck was going on?* Sam wanted us to believe that he was sick, but in truth he was fine. Anger bubbled dangerously close to the surface for me. What kind of a father would do such a horrible thing to his son?

My phone buzzed with a text from Gianna. *Are you coming back out today?*

The sarcasm in her message was evident. I hurried down the stairwell then out the doors by the cafeteria, the button all but forgotten. I had more important matters to deal with now.

Gianna watched me closely as I got into my car. "How'd you make out?"

Frustrated, I shook my head. "We'll talk about it later." I was so angry with Sam that I could barely see straight. How could I confront him with the news? Worse yet, how would I tell Mike the news?

"Sal." Gianna gently touched my arm. "What's wrong?"

"Nothing," I lied. "Want to go for a drink?"

She laughed. "You don't drink. But I do have some anisette up in my apartment. It would go great with some of Josie's black and white cookies."

"Sounds like a plan." Within ten minutes we were settled at one of the little tables in my bakery. Spread out in front of us was a bottle of anisette, shot glasses, and a plate of cookies that included many of our specialties—jelly, fudgy delights, lemon crisps, chocolate chip, and genettis.

"Yum." Gianna reached for a black and white cookie. "These will hit the spot. I think I'm premenstrual. Or it's Nicoletta getting under my skin. Whatever the case, I need chocolate really bad."

"Coffee? Or would you rather have espresso?" I stood before my Keurig and waved a paper cup in my hand.

Gianna finished chewing before she spoke. "Decaf, or I won't be able to sleep tonight."

After I finished brewing Gianna's coffee, I handed her the cup and then sat down across from her. "Aren't you in a hurry to get home to Mike?" she asked.

"He's working late. I'll probably end up beating him

there." I hadn't thought to do anything for dinner. We had some leftover lasagna in the freezer from Grandma Rosa, so Mike could have that if he was hungry. My appetite had pretty much disintegrated after learning the news about Sam, but I reached for a jelly cookie anyway.

Gianna finished her cookie and grabbed a genetti. "I had no lunch today and am so hungry I could eat two trays of cookies. I know I'll regret this later, but right now I don't care. What's your theory about that old lady Maude's death?"

"I'm not sure what to think," I confessed. "For some strange reason I feel that her death and Kelly's connect. Maybe Kelly killed Maude, and then someone found out and killed Kelly. When I get some free time, I'm going to read through the articles on Google about Maude's death and see if they can provide any clues. I should tell Brian about my findings too."

Gianna stretched her long legs out over the seat between us. She was still in her gray business suit from work that she had paired with black, knee-high leather boots. "My feet are killing me. I'm going straight to bed after I finish one more cookie."

I laughed. "Not even a phone call for Johnny?"

She bit into a fudgy delight and uttered a low moan in her throat. "You and Josie can bake for me anytime. Johnny's with Nicoletta tonight. She's nursing some very hurt feelings as of late."

"I'll bet."

Gianna finished the cookie and grabbed another. "Johnny and I had a talk last night. He—uh, asked me a question."

"Oh my God." Without thinking, my eyes stared down at her left hand. It was bare. "Where's the ring? Did you refuse him?"

Gianna gave me an arrogant smile. "It wasn't *that* question."

"Oh." I tried to gauge her reaction, but unlike me, she'd always had a good poker face. "How does that make you feel?"

"Relieved," she admitted. "Don't get me wrong. I love Johnny, and yes, I've known him my entire life, but hey, what's the rush? We've only been dating six months. There's plenty of time for marriage—and other things. Plus I don't even know if I want kids."

"Did you mention any of this to Mom?" The woman was dying for a grandchild, and so far, I hadn't been able to produce one. *Stop it, Sal. It's only been six months*. Like Gianna said, there was plenty of time.

She narrowed her eyes. "Do I look like a fool? She would have freaked out and called the Colwestern Country Club right away to book the date."

True enough. "So what did Johnny ask you then?"

Gianna nibbled at the chocolate frosting on top of the cookie. "Now that Nicoletta's cancer is in remission, Johnny wants to buy a house and get out on his own again. He doesn't want to be too far away from his grandmother though. Nicoletta blames me and says I'm taking him away from her. She's always checking up on him, and God forbid if she finds him here with me late one night. That's why she's been so snarky to me."

"She's snarky all the time," I protested.

Gianna flashed me a superior grin. "To you, maybe. Most of the time, she's okay with me. Johnny found a house that he really wants, and it's in his price range. He brought me with him to the showing, and I liked it too. The bad news? It's only two streets away from Mom, Dad, and Nicoletta. Over on Johnson Road."

"You're kidding."

My sister rolled her eyes. "Don't I wish. Oh, and Johnny asked me to move in with him. *That* was the question he wanted to ask me."

Although this didn't come as a surprise, the hopeless romantic in me had been wishing for a different question that involved a diamond. "Wow. That's a pretty big step. Of course it might be the death of Mrs. G. What will she do without him?"

Gianna picked up a genetti and gnawed at some of the nonpareils. "A friend of Nicoletta's is moving here from Italy. Her husband passed away a few months ago, all of their kids are here in the States, and I guess she's lonely. Allegra is planning to move in with Nicoletta for a while. They were very close when Nicoletta and her family lived in Italy, and they've remained friends all these years."

"It's weird to think of Mrs. Gavelli as having friends," I

remarked.

"I know!" Gianna's brown eyes grew wide. "They even Skype weekly."

"Mrs. G Skypes?" Somehow I couldn't take it in.

Gianna extended her hands, palms up. "Go figure. Apparently Allegra wants to open a store when she gets here. I guess she's quite the cook, so it will probably be something related. Whatever it is, you can bet that Nicoletta will be involved too."

"This has to be a huge relief for you. I always figured that when Johnny flew the coop, he'd have to bring his grandmother along." Although I couldn't imagine Nicoletta leaving her house.

Gianna sucked in some air. "I would *never* live with that woman. I can tolerate her most days but wouldn't want to start my life off with Johnny that way. He'll be enough for me to get used to."

I raised my coffee cup in salute. "Congratulations."

Her face creased into a smile then disappeared. "That's not actually what I wanted to talk to you about though. Do you remember Jackie Freemont?"

My eyebrows shot up. "Of course. We worked together at Sunny's for a while."

Sunny's had been a local ice cream parlor that was now out of business. They had employed me during my brief stint at the local community college, and I'd managed to quit both within a year. Resigned to being in the food industry, I had gone on to Starbucks and as a result had several years as a barista under my belt. To this day I still couldn't look at a mocha Frappuccino without cringing.

My sister drained her coffee cup. "Jackie's a real estate attorney now."

"Good for her. She always was a brain. How'd you meet up with her?"

Gianna leaned her elbows on the table. "Johnny needed an attorney for the house and asked if I knew anyone. He thinks that just because I'm a lawyer, I know everyone else in the business. A co-worker gave me a couple of names to choose from, and when I saw hers, Johnny and I arranged to meet her for drinks last night."

I wasn't sure where she was going with this. "How is she?"

"Great." Gianna looked at me nervously. "She asked about you, of course. I told her about the bakery, that you'd gotten married again, and she asked me what your new name was now. Blah, blah. All small talk."

I laughed. "Okay, what is it you're not telling me? Did she date Mike once upon a time?" I'd been down this road before and wasn't concerned. We were past all that petty high school stuff now.

"No." The color had disappeared from her cheeks, and my stomach twisted into a giant pretzel as I waited for her to continue. "But she knows Mike's father. It seems that he was in her office a few days ago. When I gave her your married name, it clicked, and she asked if you guys were related."

I thought about Ally again and the conversation I'd overheard. "Is she allowed to reveal details about her clients?"

"He's not her client," Gianna said. "Sam was only looking for some free information."

"Oh?" This was interesting. "Does he have plans to get a house soon?" Sam mentioned that he hadn't worked in a while, so I wondered how he would scrape together funds for the deposit.

Gianna squared her shoulders, and her eyes bore straight into mine. "Yes. He wanted to know if he still had any rights to yours."

CHAPTER NINETEEN

———

For a moment I thought someone must have punched me in the stomach. Gianna's statement had managed to knock the wind right out of me.

She placed a hand on my arm. "Are you okay?"

"I can't believe it," I gasped. The man had totally blindsided us.

Her expression was grim. "I'm so sorry. I figured I'd wait until after our trip tonight to tell you. I can imagine how upsetting this is to hear and can't even begin to think of what it's going to do to Mike. His dad sounds like a real piece of work."

"They had lunch today. He asked Mike if he—" I couldn't take it all in and was afraid that I might cry. "It all makes perfect sense now."

Gianna leaned forward across the table. "What makes sense?"

I told Gianna what I'd overheard in the stairwell at the hospital. "Sam asked if he could move in with us for a while."

Her round, brown eyes were soft with pity. "Oh, Sal. He must have figured that if he could get you to feel sorry for him, you'd let him move in, and then maybe he'd find a way to take the house away. Maybe Sam and his shady mind thought he'd have more rights if he was already living in your house."

"Does he have any rights?" I asked nervously.

"I don't know much about real estate law," Gianna confessed, "but Jackie didn't seem to think so. She referred him to an estate attorney. I got the impression that Jackie thought he was a real jerk for doing this, but being professional, she didn't comment."

I massaged my fingers against my temples then took a

long swig of anisette. "I don't want to tell Mike, Gi. He's been hurt enough already."

She nodded. "I know, but you can't put it off. You have to tell him before he gives his father an answer. Can you imagine that guy living with you? He sounds like the type who'd sell your silverware to make a few bucks."

I winced at the statement. "I wanted to see this work out so badly for Mike's sake. The only family he has is ours."

Gianna grinned. "Yeah, and they're more than enough for anyone." Her expression sobered. "For the record, I do complain about Mom and Dad a lot. I mean—yeah, they're nuts, but at least they love us. They're—oh, what's the word I'm looking for?"

"Nutsy cookies, as Grandma would say? Free spirits or full of surprises? Take your pick," I laughed.

"Those all work."

I reached for a chocolate chip. "That reminds me. You haven't heard the latest."

Gianna cocked an eyebrow. "Do I want to?"

Someone tapped loudly on the front door, and we both jumped. I rose from my seat and walked over, carefully lifted the blind then stared out. A policeman looked back in at me. At least it was a familiar one. "It's Brian," I said to my sister and unlocked the door.

"Oh my." Gianna rose to get another cup of coffee. "Sounds like Ally couldn't wait to rat you out."

I wasn't sure how much more I could deal with today. My head was still spinning with the news about Mike's dad and what Gianna had told me, plus the details of Maude's murder that convinced me it connected to Kelly's death somehow.

"What are you doing here?" I asked, convinced that I didn't want to know the answer.

"Well, you sure do get around fast, Mrs. Donovan." His tone wasn't especially friendly, and my suspicion was confirmed. "I was on my way home and spotted your lights on, so I decided to stop and make sure everything was okay."

"Sit down and take a load off, Brian." Gianna stirred some sweetener into her cup. "Would you like some coffee?"

"No thanks." He sat in the seat that Gianna had vacated

and stared down at the half-eaten plate of cookies with a grin before grabbing the lone chocolate chip. "My one weakness." He took a bite and watched me. "I heard you were pumping my girlfriend for information tonight. If she'd told you anything, she could have lost her job, you know."

Here it comes. Bring on the lecture. "Mike's father was over at the hospital, and I wanted to know what was wrong with him. He just suddenly reappeared in Mike's life, so it seemed a bit suspicious. Turns out that I was right."

He wrinkled his brow. "What do you mean?"

I left out the part about the stairwell conversation in the hospital but told him the information that Gianna had just relayed to me.

Brian's jaw dropped. "Wow. I'm sorry to hear that, Sally."

"Let's not talk about it anymore," I sighed. "Please tell Ally I'm sorry. I didn't realize she'd be so upset that she'd call you." *And right away too.*

"She didn't," Brian said. "I happened to call her shortly after you'd left the hospital. For the record she wouldn't tell me anything about Mike's dad either. And I'm a cop for crying out loud."

Gianna and I both laughed. "Well, I'm glad she's not sore at me."

Brian finished the cookie and then flicked a couple of crumbs off the dark blue uniform jacket he wore. His green eyes sparkled. "That Josie does make a mean cookie. Her sarcasm and witty spirit shines through them."

"Stop that. By the way, *I* happened to make those chocolate chips."

He looked around the shop. "How's business been since Josie's arrest?"

I leaned back in my chair and tried not to sound bitter. "There hasn't been any. Listen. I found out something interesting tonight and would love to run it by you."

Brian folded his arms across his chest. "Shoot."

"Gianna and I drove out to Mount Eden Assisted Living in Datson. Kelly Thompson used to work there."

He raised an eyebrow. "How'd you find this out?"

"Her twin sister told me."

"Good sleuthing skills." Brian sounded impressed. "What did you learn?"

"Did you know that a resident died at the home? It was while Kelly was employed there, about nine years ago. The woman ate half a box of chocolates with rat poison in them."

He cocked his head sideways at me. "I can certainly check it out. Was anyone ever arrested for the crime?"

"No, and as far as I know, the case was never closed. The main person of interest died of natural causes a week after the death. I'm almost positive it links to Kelly's murder somehow. Maybe Kelly killed Maude—the elderly woman—and someone who worked at the assisted living home knew and decided to get even with Kelly by killing her in a similar manner. The interesting part is that someone stuffed the chocolates with poison in such a precise way that I wonder if they may have had some type of culinary skills."

Brian grabbed a small notepad out of his lapel pocket. "I'll see if I can find the officer who investigated that night. Nine years is a long time, and they may have even retired by now. But there has to be a list of employees and residents on file somewhere who were interviewed at the time."

"That would be a big help. Thank you," I said gratefully.

He eyed me sharply. "Since you're sharing information with me, I'll share some news with you as well."

My stomach clenched. "About Kelly's murder?"

He shot me a warning look. "This is strictly on the QT. You are not to reveal what I'm about to say to anyone. Understand?" Brian cut his eyes to Gianna, who was still standing by the Keurig machine.

Gianna raised her right hand as if she was on the witness stand of the courtroom. "Hey, I'm a lawyer. You can trust me."

Brian snorted back a laugh. "Right. We're very close to making an arrest in the case, and it happens to be Kelly's own cheating husband."

I sucked in some air. "Was it because of the life insurance policy?"

"That does come into play," he admitted. "There's also the fact that Kelly filed for divorce last week. He may have wanted to strike while the iron was hot—before she had a chance to change her will. Barry does have a prior record, you know."

Gianna placed her hands on her hips. "No, we didn't know. What was the charge?"

"Apparently he was involved in a barroom brawl when he was underage," Brian said. "He got into a fight with another guy, supposedly over a woman. Barry hit the guy over the head with a chair, and the blow paralyzed him permanently. Barry got off on probation."

"He never served any time?" Gianna asked in disbelief.

Brian shook his head. "Barry's uncle is a former state senator."

"Oh, well, that explains it," she said dryly. "Unbelievable."

"The life insurance policy was taken out a month before Kelly died," Brian explained. "When their home was searched, a letter was found among Barry's things from an apparent lover. The person wrote, 'As soon as she's gone, we can get married.'"

"But that could have been referring to the divorce," Gianna pointed out.

I snapped my fingers. "It must have been from Olivia Nigel, Kelly's best friend. Where is she now?"

He shrugged. "From what I've heard, no one knows where she is. Maybe she skipped town. She was at the wake but not the funeral. Barry might have been planning to leave and meet her somewhere, but that's not going to happen now. We're watching him around the clock." Brian studied my expression. "What are you thinking, Sally?"

"Barry definitely had a motive. Perhaps the biggest of anyone," I said. "But this seems more like a crime that would have been committed by a woman."

Brian leaned forward across the table with interest. "How so?"

I drained my coffee cup. "The sugar that was dumped on Kelly's head. We already figured out that the killer probably did that to frame Josie after the food fight. And it feels more like something a woman would have done rather than a man. Think about it. From what I've learned, Kelly was conceited and very shallow. It's almost like someone wanted her to be found dead in such an embarrassing position. Since they used sugar, it may have been someone who had connections to Kelly's baking world too. Lots of possibilities."

Brian made another note on his pad. "Good observations. Anything else?"

"Has Olivia been questioned?" I asked.

"Well, I had planned to question her at the wake, but she left before I got a chance." He raised an eyebrow at me. "If you'll recall, I had another pressing situation to deal with."

Whoops.

"Hey, that wasn't Sal's fault," Gianna protested. "Mrs. Gavelli and her gang started it."

Brian rolled his eyes at her. "Whatever."

"Did I mention that Olivia and Kelly worked at Mount Eden together?" I asked. "That's how they met. Maybe they were in on it together to kill Maude."

Brian rubbed his eyes wearily. "Even though the murders are somewhat similar in nature, there's no proof to tie them together."

Frustrated, I bit into my lower lip. "I know this. But it *feels* like they are."

He put his pad away. "We can't arrest people based on feelings, Sally. While I agree that Barry not committing the murder makes some sense, please remember this is not my case. The Buffalo force is being gracious enough to let me do some investigating because of my father's connections. It might be best if they go ahead and arrest Barry anyway."

Perplexed, I stared at him. "I don't understand."

"To put the real killer off guard," he explained. "Josie's already under suspicion, but if a second person comes into play, all the better for the real killer. They're bound to think they're safe in that type of scenario and therefore no one's looking at them. That's when killers might slip up and unintentionally end up giving themselves away. You know, say something stupid to the wrong person. I've seen it happen before."

"I'll keep that in mind." My brain was already so overloaded with details that making a list might help. It would not do to forget any clues at this stage of the investigation.

Brian and I walked toward the front door together. "By

the way, I ran into your mother at the drugstore this morning."
He grinned. "So the Muccios are celebrities now, huh? A
commercial—that's pretty impressive."

Gianna shut her eyes in dramatic fashion. "Can we
please not talk about that fiasco?"

"That reminds me," I addressed my sister. "There wasn't
time to tell you earlier, but Dad's planning to write a book."

Brian roared with laughter. "About what? Supernatural
experiences of the dead?"

"It's going to be blog related. My guess is somewhat
real-life experiences." *How embarrassing.* I could only pray that
he wouldn't mention me or the bakery.

Gianna shuddered. "Okay, that's it. If he makes the New
York Times list, I may have to drive off a cliff."

CHAPTER TWENTY

———

Determined to stay awake until Mike got home, I settled myself in bed with a cup of hot chocolate in one hand and Spike nestled against the other. After flicking through television stations for about five minutes, I found the classic movie *Fried Green Tomatoes* and snuggled down under the covers in an attempt to escape reality for a while. My eyelids started to droop, and the last thing I remembered was Kathy Bates yelling something about being older and having more insurance.

When I opened my eyes, the house was quiet and the room dark, with the exception of the full moon illuminating it through the half-opened window blinds. I glanced at the red digits of the clock on the nightstand. Three fifteen in the morning. Mike was beside me, his bare chest pressed against my back, one arm protectively thrown over my shoulder. He smelled of the spicy aftershave I adored and must have taken a shower when he arrived home. I turned my body slowly to study his face while he slept. The movement had no effect on him, and Mike continued to snore softly, his handsome face peaceful with no visible signs of distress. It broke my heart in two to think of what I had to tell him.

I thrashed around in bed for about another hour or so, part of me hoping that he would wake from the disturbance, while the other half prayed he'd stay asleep. Mike never stirred, and the unreasonable side of my brain was almost annoyed by that fact. My thoughts were loud enough to keep sleep at bay for a long while. I watched the digits change on the clock for what seemed like an eternity before sleep beckoned again.

Too soon, Mike woke me with a light kiss on the forehead. I opened my eyes groggily to see him sitting on the edge of the bed with a steaming cup of coffee in his hand. "Six thirty, princess. Time to rise and shine."

It was still dark outside, which only added to my bleariness. "Ugh." I took a long swallow from the cup while he grinned down at me. "When did you get in last night?"

"About midnight."

I paused for another sip. "Why didn't you wake me?"

He tucked a loose curl behind my ear. "I wanted to, but you looked so pretty and peaceful. Without a care in the world."

Yeah, right. If he only knew.

Mike gave me a soft kiss on the lips. "I have to get going. We're putting a bathroom in on Tyler Street today. I'll probably be pretty late again, ten o'clock or so."

My fingers curled into the front of his T-shirt, not willing to let go of him yet not wanting to relay my news either. "We need to talk."

"What's wrong?"

I swallowed hard. "Are you going to see your father today?"

Mike shook his head. "I told him I'd call him tomorrow and give him an answer." He studied my face, which was probably its usual road map of distress. "Something's bothering you."

"No," I lied. "Everything's fine."

"Sal." Mike's voice was gentle. "If you're not all right with this, I understand. Hell, I don't even know if *I'm* okay with it."

This might be the most difficult thing I'd ever had to say to him, and I struggled to control my emotions. "Your father—"

Mike's phone beeped. He reached down a hand to remove it from his pocket then stared at the screen and frowned.

"What's wrong?"

He cursed under his breath. "Jim and Pete are already at the house. I need to get moving."

I clung to his arm. "What's the rush? Would they mind waiting in the truck for a little while?"

Mike gave me a wry grin. "I'm sure they wouldn't mind. But *I* mind since I'm the one paying them." He watched me thoughtfully. "Are you sure you're okay?"

"Yes. See you tonight."

I stood at the window and waved as he zoomed down the road in his truck. Once he was gone, I pressed my forehead against the cold pane in resignation. Since he wasn't going to talk to his father today, I didn't see the harm in waiting until tonight to tell him what had transpired. If I'd relayed the news now, he would have been upset all day. *What does it matter?* Mike was going to take it hard whenever he found out, but at least if it were tonight we'd be together afterwards.

I showered, dressed, gave Spike fresh water and food, and took off for the bakery. The sun shone brightly in a royal blue sky with no signs of snow—a miracle in itself for the middle of January. Since it was Josie's turn to open, I arrived at eight thirty. She was taking a tray of ginger cookies out of the oven when I walked in the back door.

"Looks like another long day ahead of us," she announced.

Sadly, she was not wrong. We only had a handful of customers throughout the day, and I was starting to panic. Business needed to pick up and soon. I texted Brian to ask if Barry had been arrested yet, but he shot back a reply of no. Perhaps once word got out about Barry, the bakery would start making sales again, or so I hoped.

The sun started to sink into the clouds around four thirty. I sighed and added some more fortune cookies to the container in the back room. Josie was scrubbing the cabinets for lack of something better to do. "How's Danny doing?"

"He's great. Let me show you something." Josie reached for her purse on a shelf by the sink. She handed me a small white box. "He made this in art class a couple of weeks ago. It's for my birthday tomorrow."

Head smack. With everything else going on, I'd almost forgotten about Josie's birthday. I opened the box and stared down at a bracelet strung on taut string with pink and white colored beads. There were *Happy Birthday* and *My Mom is #1* plastic charms hanging from it.

The sweet but simple gift moved me. "Oh, that's so beautiful." I placed the bracelet back in the box and left it on the block table. I couldn't wait for the day my children would do the same for me.

Josie's mouth twitched into a grin as she turned back to the cabinets. "That kid of mine is tough."

"He takes after his mother." I leaned against the block table and wished I could tell her what Brian had relayed last night. "Something tells me that they'll make an arrest soon, and then this nightmare will be over for you."

Josie glanced up at me sharply. "What do you know, Sal?"

"Nothing for certain," I admitted. "So far, there's only some rumors flying around, but I promised not to reveal them until it's a sure thing."

She observed me closely. "That means Brian's been feeding you information."

I ignored her comment. "By the way, I tried to call you last night after Gianna and I got back from Mount Eden, but your mailbox was full."

"Oh. I always forget to empty that thing. We turned in early anyway." Josie blushed as she said the words.

"*We?*" I asked coyly. "So things are okay between you and Rob now?"

She nodded, the pink color rising in her cheeks. "Rob apologized last night. He knows he didn't handle the situation very well. We had a long talk, and then we made up in private after the kids went to bed."

I rolled my eyes. "Okay, way too much information, but I'm so happy for you guys."

Josie started to wash the cookie trays in the sink. "You and me both. For the record, my money is on Barry. He's the one who killed Kelly."

"Hmm." I rolled one of the fortune cookies between my forefinger and thumb. My mind was a thousand miles away.

"Sal?"

Startled, I glanced over to see Josie watching me with a puzzled expression. "Come on. Spill it. Something else is going on."

"I don't know. For some reason I'm not convinced it's Barry." I proceeded to tell her about the visit to Mount Eden last night but didn't mention Mike's situation. That was my own problem to deal with later. "I can't help thinking that the situation with Maude and the candy relates to Kelly's death somehow."

Josie dried the cookie trays with a dish towel. "You might be grasping at straws. Your mind is way too suspicious these days."

"Maybe." The cookie cracked apart in my hands, and I stared down at my dreaded message of doom.

The answer is obvious.

What answer? As far as I was concerned, nothing was obvious to me.

Josie glanced at her watch "Do you mind if I take off soon? I told Rob and the kids I'd make a special dinner tonight."

It wasn't even five thirty, but the sky was already pitch-black outside. Snow had begun to fall, and we were supposed to get a few more inches tonight. I sighed. The never-ending darkness at this time of the year had started to wear on me. "You can leave now if you like. I'll finish up."

"Are you sure?"

"Yeah. Enjoy yourself. Why don't you go ahead and take tomorrow off for your birthday—with pay, of course. It'll be my gift to you."

Josie's mouth opened wide in amazement. "Oh, Sal, I can't let you do that. I know how bad sales have been lately."

"I insist." What difference did it make at this point? She deserved the day, and I doubted it would be that busy anyway.

She smiled. "Well, Rob did mention something about us spending the day together and then taking the kids out for dinner, but I didn't want to ask for the day off. I told him we'd make plans for Sunday."

I put an arm around her shoulders. "You've been through a lot this past week. It's the least I can do. Have fun, and I'll see you on Friday."

Josie hugged me, the emotion heavy in her voice. "Thanks, Sal. You're such a good friend. I don't know what I'd do without you."

I started to choke up as well. "The feeling's mutual."

After she'd left I swept the floor and washed the outside of the display case with glass cleaner. It was a few minutes before six, and I had just placed the *Closed* sign on the door when my phone buzzed. My parents' landline.

"*Cara mia*, would you and Mike like to come for dinner tonight? I have stuffed peppers in the freezer."

"No thanks, Grandma. Mike's working late, and I'd rather go home, take a hot bath, and think about some things."

"You are worried about Mike's father."

How did she always know? "Grandma, he's been lying to us. The only reason he came back is for our house. He doesn't care about Mike." It pained me to say the words out loud.

She clucked her tongue against the roof of her mouth. "I was afraid of that. I am so sorry, my dear. Something about that man smelled rotten from the beginning. You know the saying."

"Something's rotten in the state of Denmark?" I asked.

My grandmother snorted. "Bah. Not that. Something is rotten in Emilia-Romagna."

I stared at the phone in confusion. "Who's that?"

Grandma Rosa laughed. "Not a 'who.' It is a region in northern Italy and the birthplace of Parmigiano-Reggiano that is, what you say, the king of all cheeses. Someday I will take you there. Now what have you found out about that woman Kelly and her killer?"

"Brian said they're close to making an arrest, but I can't say who it is."

"You do not have to. It is the husband," she replied simply.

She'd done it again. "Well, maybe. But something tells me it's *not* him. This feels more like a woman committed the crime."

"Yes, because of the sugar on her face. Kelly also had some sugar, no?"

"She was a diabetic, if that's what you mean. Someone put antifreeze in her insulin vial. That's how she died."

Grandma Rosa snorted into the phone. "I already know this, dear girl. It has been all over the television. This is, what do you say, a double tender."

She was really confusing me. Usually I could figure out her mixed-up cliché sayings, but not this time. "As in chicken tenders?"

Grandma laughed. "No, silly Sally. When the words

have more than one meaning."

"Oh! You mean a double entendre."

"That is what I said." My grandmother paused. "Someone may have put the sugar on Kelly because Josie used it during their fight. This person must have seen them fighting and wanted Josie to be blamed. The entertainment people on the television yesterday said that Kelly was getting some sugar on the side, and everyone laughed." She made a *tsk-tsk* sound. "That is not a very nice thing to say."

"I see what you're getting at now," I said. "Yes, Kelly was having an affair, and so was her husband."

"Or perhaps this was another way for the killer to make fun of Kelly, since her bakery does not serve anything with sugar," Grandma commented.

Her last comment struck a chord with me and made me certain that there was something I had failed to put together. My head ached with lack of sleep from the night before. "Grandma, what you're saying makes sense. I'm just too tired to figure it all out right now."

"Go home, and get some rest. When Mike comes home, talk to him about his father. It will hurt him yes, but he is a tough man. You will both be fine."

"Marriage can't be a bed of noses all the time, right?" I teased.

My grandmother was silent on the other end. "I do not get it. Ciao, bella." She disconnected.

I went into the back room to grab my coat. When I reached into my pocket for my keys, I drew out the brochure from Mount Eden and thought briefly of my grandmother living there. *Yeah, right. Never in a million years.*

At that moment the bells jingled over the front door. Yes, I needed business, but why did it always have to be at the very last minute? Too bad I hadn't remembered to lock the door. Resigned, I placed my phone and coat down on the table and went out into the storefront.

The streetlights outside shone on a black BMW parked at the curb. Donna was standing in front of my display case in her full-length Burberry coat, complete with black stockings and heels. She was about the last person I had expected to see right now. "Hi, Donna."

She gave me a genuine, warm smile. "Sally, I'm on my way to the airport and wanted to talk to you for a minute."

I noticed the black, sequined dress underneath her unbuttoned coat and remembered about the award. "Weren't you at the Culinary Institute today?"

She flushed with pride. "That's right. I just came from the ceremony and told the driver I'd drop the car at the airport myself. He moves too slowly for my taste in the snow. Anyway, I signed autographs for almost an hour. Such a fabulous time— you should have come." She glanced around the shop. "How's business?"

She might as well know the truth. "Not very good."

Her face was sympathetic. "Well, I'll bet that it improves soon. Did you hear about Barry Thompson?"

I wasn't about to share Brian's information with her and kept my expression guarded. "What about him?"

"Shelly came to see me yesterday. She thinks that they're close to arresting him. It looks like his skanky girlfriend, Olivia, skipped town, and I guess Shelly's been giving the police various bits of information about him. Hopefully Josie will be off the hook soon."

"It would be wonderful if that happened," I breathed.

Donna hesitated. "There's something else I have to tell you. You're probably going to take it as a lecture, and maybe it is, but I was very upset to learn of your dishonesty."

Surprised, I blinked at her. "What are you talking about?"

Donna gave me a sharp look of disapproval. "The head baker at Kelly's—or shall I say Shelly's now—told her that two women were in Naturally Delish the same day as the funeral. They claimed that they worked for me. Shelly studied the footage from the video camera later that day, and guess what. She recognized you and Josie, even with your lame wigs on."

Damn cameras. I hadn't thought about that. Still, I made no excuse for our actions. "We did what we had to."

"Look," Donna said. "I appreciate you wanting to help your friend, but don't drag my employees into this. No disrespect to Kelly, but I'm glad this nightmare is over. It has hurt ratings on my show severely. I also wanted to tell you that once Barry is arrested, I'll go ahead and air your episode."

"Thank you. That means a lot, but to be honest my main concern is for my friend right now. I'm glad the nightmare is over for *Josie*. Or will be soon." I really didn't care about Donna's show or how it had been affected. When Barry was arrested, Josie's life should get back to normal and hopefully our bakery would too.

Donna eyed me suspiciously. "I know what you're thinking. Who cares about my show? I'm just some spoiled celebrity who leads a pampered life. Your friend had to leave culinary school when she was pregnant. Very sad. That never happened to me, but believe me, I've had my rotten shakes too."

Was Donna trying to throw herself a pity party now? "I'm sure you have."

She stared into the display case. "I'd love some of your fortune cookies to take with me, but it looks like you don't have any more."

"Oh, sure we do. They're in the kitchen area. I'll get you some out of the container."

Donna followed me into the back room. "Like I said, I worked my way up from the very bottom. My parents both died when I was a teenager. I put myself through culinary school and worked a variety of dead-end jobs to help pay for it but still had to take out student loans. Cashier, short-order cook, food buyer, bakery counter helper. You name it, I did it."

I placed a dozen of the cookies into one of my little pink boxes as my mind reverted back to the day that Donna had shown up in her chauffeur-driven limousine. Donna had come a long way from her food buyer days. A chill ran down my spine, and I sucked in some air.

Oh, Sal. How could you have not known?

All of a sudden, everything fit. Again, I thought about the chocolates that had killed Maude. As I suspected, someone with culinary skills had filled them. Kelly, Anita, and even Amy could be considered, though I didn't know what Anita or Amy's motives would be for killing Maude. Olivia had worked at the home but not in the kitchen. Even though Donna was a previous food buyer, that didn't necessarily mean she had worked at

Mount Eden. Then I recalled the day we'd first met Donna and
Josie's words—words I had long forgotten.

She only hires people with the most experience.

Kelly, with her popular and successful bakery, was
indeed a fraud, and surely Donna had seen through her façade.
Amy had developed several of the winning recipes while Kelly,
in return, had promised to make her a partner but failed to come
through. Amy did the grunt work in the bakery, while Kelly took
all the credit. And why would Donna hire someone like Kelly
when Anita had more experience and persona? If given the
choice, I would always hire someone who was more
knowledgeable—a person who worked hard, enjoyed their craft,
and had earned their degree at culinary school without sleeping
with the instructor.

"Sally, is something wrong?"

Her words made the hair on the back of my neck rise. I
swallowed hard. "Oh, no. A couple of these cookies have cracks
in them, and I was trying to figure out how that happened." I
took a few seconds to pull myself together before I turned
around. *Please don't fail me now, face.* I felt in my jeans pocket
for my phone. Not there. Oh, right. It was on the block table less
than six feet away, but next to where Donna stood.

Donna waved something in her hand at me. It was the
pamphlet from Mount Eden. When our eyes met, I saw the
monster in hers begin to emerge—the creature she had managed
to keep hidden up until now. Icicles chilled my blood. "Aren't
you a little young to be thinking about assisted living?"

Think fast. Think fast. "Oh, that's for my grandmother."
My heart thumped loudly against the wall of my chest. Why
hadn't I figured it out before? Donna had killed the old woman
and Kelly. I didn't know what her motive was yet but suspected
it was money related. Kelly must have known about Maude's
murder and somehow used it to blackmail Donna into giving her
the job. This was why she had hired Kelly at the last minute and
not Anita.

"Well, I guess I'd better be going. Take care of yourself."
Donna gave me a brittle smile and turned her body toward the
storefront. As soon as her back was to me, I reached for my
phone on the table and looked up to see Donna rushing toward

me with my rolling pin in her hand. I attempted to duck but wasn't fast enough and the wooden handle came crashing down hard on my forehead. My legs gave out from underneath me, and I staggered to the floor, my mind reeling with thoughts of double entendre and the music from *Someone's in the Kitchen with Donna* rolling around in my head.

CHAPTER TWENTY-ONE

With all my strength I fought against the impending darkness as I lay there on the floor, dazed from the blow. Gingerly, I reached a hand up to my forehead and felt something warm and sticky. Blood. My head thundered with severe pain as I tried to open my eyes.

Heavy breathing circulated in the air above me as someone grabbed hold of my legs. My eyelids finally fluttered open as Donna began dragging me across the floor. Panic kicked in as I noticed we were headed for the walk-in freezer. Any lingering feelings of pain subsided as I realized that this crazy woman intended to lock me inside.

Desperate, I glanced around wildly, looking for something to grab hold of. My life hung in the balance, and I needed to work fast. As we approached the doorway of the freezer, I reached out my hand and grabbed the leg of the small silver rolling cart sitting nearby. The doorway was wide enough for both the cart and my body, and I dragged it inside with me. Donna shouted something in anger at me that my fogged-up brain couldn't decipher. I pushed the tray forward with all my strength and was rewarded with an, "Ow!"

Slowly I rose to my feet. My stomach did somersaults, and bile rose in the back of my throat. The room needed to stop spinning because I had to get out of there. Like a drunk, I stumbled toward the freezer door, which had already closed. As I reached for the push bar, Donna grabbed me by the hair and pulled me back with a vengeance. I let out a low moan as my head connected with the gray, resin-coated floor.

"Sorry, Sally," she said with a victorious smile that looked anything but apologetic as she pushed the handle to open the door. It didn't budge.

Annoyance and then terror quickly crept over her face. "What the—" She pushed the bar again, over and over, but the door did not release. It was just desserts for the woman, so to speak, except for one thing. I was stuck in here with her.

"The handle's been sticking." My voice was feeble, and I lay my head back down on the cold surface for relief.

Donna started to scream at the top of her lungs until I thought my head was going to explode. "Help me! Someone! Please!"

"No one's going to hear you." Sick, cold fear settled in the bottom of my stomach. We were doomed. I was going to freeze to death—and with a killer nonetheless. "Do you have your cell?"

She whimpered and pounded on the door with both hands. "I left it in the car. Oh my God. I can't stand being in here. I'm claustrophobic!"

I glanced around the inside of the freezer. It was small, only six by eight feet, with metal racks of shelving that we used to store the frozen dough on. The racks lined both sides of the walls, and I searched for a potential weapon or even a piece of cloth that might keep me warm, but there was nothing, save the dough. Defeated, I raised myself into a sitting position. Dear God, I had been in some awful predicaments before, but this might be the worst one yet.

Donna leaned back against the door and started to weep. "No one's even going to be looking for me until tomorrow. My plane leaves in two hours. They'll never think to find me here." She looked over at me hopefully. "Did you put the *Closed* sign up?"

I blew out a long breath. "Yes, but I didn't lock the door." Who was I kidding? It was after six o'clock, and the snow was probably coming down at a heavier pace. The only way anyone would get in was if they tried the door, and with my luck it would be someone looking to rob the place. Still, money was the least of my worries now.

"Your husband." Optimism filled Donna's voice. "He'll be looking for you."

Mike wasn't due home until ten. I glanced at my watch.

That wasn't for another four hours. He might try to call or text me before then, but it was doubtful since he was trying to complete a bathroom installation by tonight. I'd already spoken to Grandma Rosa and told her I was going straight home. My parents were off to dinner with a casket maker. Gianna, my last hope, was working late and then going to dinner with Johnny afterward. My guess was that she wouldn't make it back here until about midnight. Too late for Donna and me.

"My husband will be home around ten, and when he sees I'm not there, he'll come looking for me."

Donna's eyes bulged out of her head. "That's four hours from now!"

How long could we survive in here? "The temperature is always set at zero degrees. We should be okay until then." Or so I hoped.

Donna blinked back tears. "No. I changed the control before I dragged you in. I brought it down to minus 15 degrees."

My gasp filled the small room. I didn't know much about logistics here but figured with the small space and less oxygen to share between two people, we might be gone within a couple of hours. No one would even hear us if they walked into the storefront. My only hope was that someone might spot my car in the back alley or Donna's BMW at the curb. Since no one was looking for us, the chances weren't very good though.

I wiped away a lone tear and began to walk in a circle, trying to think of ways to keep myself warm. Donna had her heavy coat on while I was wearing only a T-shirt and jeans. I didn't expect the woman to offer to share the coat and thought I might rather freeze to death than ask her.

She watched me suspiciously. "How did you figure out it was me?"

"I didn't figure it out until tonight, after you came in."

"You were at Mount Eden," she accused. "I told you I was a food buyer. That's how you knew, isn't it?"

I shrugged. "The clues were there, but I didn't put them together at first. I was unsure of your motive. Then I remembered something that Josie said the first day you came into the bakery. She mentioned that you were known for always hiring the most experienced people. It didn't register with me, until today, why you would have hired Kelly over Anita. But now I'm guessing that Kelly knew you had killed Maude."

Donna leaned against the wall, her arms wrapped around her middle. "And you would be correct."

"Kelly blackmailed you into giving her the job?"

She cast cold, angry eyes upon me. "I had no choice. Then I made up some lame excuse to Anita. I really wanted to hire her. She had real talent, unlike Kelly. Kelly's one of those people who's made her success at the expense of everyone else. I hate people like that."

You hypocrite. "So by killing Maude and stealing her money, *you* didn't make your own success."

Furious, Donna straightened up. "Look. I did what I had to do. She was old and had cancer. I was doing her a favor—that's all. Besides, the woman was so stupid. Who keeps one hundred grand in a safe in their room? She even opened it once to show me the money. It was almost like she was bragging about it. I managed to memorize the combination over her shoulder. She liked me, the dumb twit. If she saw me in the hallway, she'd always ask me to stop in and talk. 'Oh, Carol. Come in and sit for a spell. Tell me all about your day.'"

What a twisted psycho. "So you had a different name back then."

Donna stifled a laugh. "Yeah. You didn't actually think that Donna Dooley was my real name, did you? I figured it would go well with the whole 'in the kitchen with Dinah' theme song. Plus Dooley was my mother's maiden name. I had it legally changed later on. It seemed like a good idea anyway when I got the host position for *Delicious Dishes in Twenty Minutes*. I wasn't scheduled to stop by the home the day Maude died, and there were no video cameras by the employee entrance. Of course I was questioned by the police, but they didn't even look at me seriously. A resident across the hall from Maude didn't like her, and someone told me they were always getting into arguments. The best part? She dropped dead a week after Maude did, and from natural causes. The whole thing couldn't have worked out better if it had been planned."

"You're sick," I muttered under my breath. "Why kill Kelly now? Did she threaten to reveal what happened?"

Her nostrils flared. "Kelly threatened to tell the police that she saw me coming out of the room that night. I couldn't afford to take a chance and had no choice but to give her the job. That witch kept it a secret for nine years—nine years! She knew she'd have an opportunity to use it against me at some point. Even though I couldn't stand her, I have to admit she was smart. But I knew that there would be more trouble. *Bide your time, Donna. Just bide your time*, I told myself. The day she met you, she immediately started complaining about Josie and how she didn't want her on the show. Um, hello, *whose* show is it again? Then it dawned on me—kill Kelly, and let Josie take the rap. A sweet opportunity. Pardon the pun."

It was so cold that I was starting to lose the feeling in my legs. I desperately tried to pay attention to what she was saying, but it was becoming more difficult.

"The day of your taping, I asked Kelly to be at the studio extra early," Donna continued. "Then I sent her out on a bogus errand. She always gave herself a shot of insulin at the same time—around six o'clock every night. I figured we would have finished taping by then, so that worked out well. While she was out on the errand earlier, I took the vial to my dressing room, removed the insulin, and put antifreeze in that I had concealed in a water bottle inside my purse."

I put a hand to my mouth and yawned. This wouldn't do. I had to stay sharp and focused. The injury to my head probably wasn't helping. "Well played."

"Yeah." She smiled, but the color had drained from Donna's face, and her teeth started to chatter. "The icing on the cookie, if you will? That was when Kelly started the food fight with Josie. I knew that some idiot in the crowd would end up taping the whole thing. It all worked out perfectly." She scowled at me. "Until you had to stick your fat nose into the mess."

"There's no way I'd stand by and let my friend go to jail for a crime she didn't commit," I said. "At least she's off the hook now."

Donna's lower lip trembled. "Yeah, and I'm the one who's doomed. I'm so cold that I can't even feel my feet anymore." In a sudden frenzy she started to pound on the door again. "I don't want to die like this! Please help me!"

Her screams didn't bother me as much as they had before. I closed my eyes for a little while, then opened them with a start. I glanced at my watch. It looked like the time said seven o'clock, but I couldn't be sure. There was fog built up on the inside of the crystal of the watch face because of the severe cold. We weren't going to last much longer at this rate. I leaned my head against the wall and wrapped my arms around my knees, starting to rock back and forth. I thought of Mike and started to weep silently. *Why didn't I remember to have him check the door?* The health department had been in for their annual inspection of the bakery only two months ago, and it had worked fine then. "Now it breaks," I whispered.

Donna looked at me funny. "What did you say?"

I shrugged and didn't answer. I was unbearably cold and needed to sleep. With a sigh I closed my eyes and tried to remember what day it was. Monday? No, wait, it was Wednesday. Mike would find me eventually. It would have to be Mike because I'd given Josie the next day off. Why had I done that? Right, because it was Christmas. Or some other holiday. Fourth of July? My brain refused to let me focus. Nothing seemed to matter anymore.

A vision of Grandma Rosa popped into my head. "Why does trouble always follow you around, *cara mia*?" she asked. "You are such a good girl."

"Thanks, Grandma," I whispered. "I'm going to take a little nap, and then everything will be fine. Don't worry."

A loud noise punctured my dream. There was shouting and scuffling sounds, but I was too tired to open my eyes or even care. Someone half dragged, half carried me across the cold floor—Donna? This time I was too weak to do anything about it.

When I finally managed to lift my eyelids, I was lying on the blue and white checkered vinyl floor in the front room of my bakery. Josie was bending over me, her face white as powdered sugar.

"What's wrong?" I asked.

"Oh my God, Sal." Tears were in her eyes as she covered me with her coat. "Don't move, honey. You're going to be okay."

I tried to raise my arms but without much success. They were too heavy. Suddenly I remembered the freezer. "Donna—

she's the one. She killed Kelly."

Josie was on her cell phone, talking very fast. "Yes. We're at 13 Carson Way. Sally's Samples. Please hurry." She paused. "I don't know. At least an hour, maybe more. Please hurry." She disconnected. "Don't move, Sal. I'm running upstairs for blankets. I'll call Mike too."

"No." I started to lift my head off the ground, but it would not cooperate. "You have to go after her." Josie was already up the stairs and hadn't heard me. This wouldn't do. Someone had to catch that evil monster.

The sound of shoes clattered on the wooden stairs, and Josie was back, covering me with several blankets. "I just called Mike. He'll be here soon, honey. You're going to be okay."

My entire body started to tingle. "Where's Donna? You need to go after her."

She frowned. "I don't give a crap about Donna right now. All I care about is that you're alive. Thank God I came back for Danny's bracelet. He was so upset when he found out I'd left it here that after dinner I decided to run back and grab it."

"But where—" My brain was a mass of jumbled confusion and couldn't seem to comprehend anything.

"I saw your car and immediately knew something was wrong," Josie said. "Why would you be here so late, unless we had gotten a big order at the last minute? When I tried your cell and didn't get an answer, it scared me. So I called Brian and asked if he'd meet me here. He wanted me to wait for him before I went into the building, but I couldn't stand it anymore. Finding the front door unlocked was the worst—I know you'd never forget to do that! Then I came into the back room and saw the blood on the floor—" A sob rose in her throat.

"She hit me with a rolling pin." I reached a hand up to my forehead to show her.

Josie gently pulled my hand down and tucked it underneath the blankets. "I thought she'd killed you. When I opened the freezer door, Donna charged at me like a mad bull and knocked me right over. It was either follow her or stay with you. An easy choice."

"No," I said in desperation. "They need to find her."

She wiped at her eyes. "I'm so glad I didn't wait for

Brian. You might have been—" She didn't finish the sentence. "Oh God, Sal!"

"I'm all right, thanks to you." Yes, it sickened me that Donna had gotten away, but if I'd been in Josie's place, I would have done the same thing.

A siren sounded in the distance, and lights reflected off my front window. Car doors slammed, and within seconds Brian and his partner, Adam, were inside the shop. Brian knelt down next to me. "You okay?"

I nodded weakly. "Thanks to Josie."

He said nothing, but his face was etched with concern as our eyes met. Adam ran back to their cruiser and brought in another blanket as Brian gently touched my cheek with his fingertips for the briefest of seconds. He then rose to his feet and moved back as Adam covered me with the blanket.

"The ambulance should be here any second," Adam assured me.

It was becoming easier to talk now. "I figured out it was Donna Dooley but not soon enough. She saw the Mount Eden pamphlet and figured I knew. She used to work there as a food buyer. Then she tried to drag me into the freezer, but we ended up getting locked in there together."

"Stop talking," Josie ordered. "Save your strength."

Brian stooped down again to examine my forehead. "That's a nasty gash. You might need stitches."

Josie pressed her lips together tightly in anger. "That cooking monster hit her with a rolling pin. Wait until I get my hands on that freak."

"I don't want to go to the hospital." My voice sounded like a whiny five-year-old's.

Brian's voice was soft and reassuring. "It's necessary, Sally. You probably have hypothermia."

"You need to put out an APB for Donna," I said. "She's the one who killed Kelly Thompson. She also killed Maude Norton nine years ago at Mount Eden."

Brian and Adam exchanged a glance. "That won't be necessary." Adam grinned.

Josie glanced sharply at him. "What's going on that you're not telling us?"

"I answered a call when I went back for the blanket," Adam said. "Apparently Miss Dooley wasn't in much better shape than Sally. How she even managed to pull her car away from the curb is the real mystery, but rest assured, she didn't get far. We ran the plate Josie gave us earlier and found out it was a rental charged to her."

"And?" I asked.

Adam's mouth twitched at the corners in a slight smile. "Donna didn't even make it down the street before she crashed into Mrs. Gavelli's car. It seems the woman was on her way here to look for her grandson."

"I hope she's okay." The elderly lady was a proverbial thorn in my side, but despite everything, I still cared about her.

"She's fine," Adam said." "Not a scratch on her."

Josie grunted. "I could have told you that. The woman is indestructible."

We all laughed at that one.

CHAPTER TWENTY-TWO

———

Despite my protests, the doctor who attended to me at Colwestern Hospital insisted that I remain overnight. I'd needed five stitches in my forehead and was told that I had also suffered from a mild case of hypothermia. We discovered that Donna was in the same hospital, but Brian had assured me that a policeman would be posted outside her room all night. Tomorrow she would be on her way to the nearest jail cell.

Before Josie left, she'd checked all the social media outlets, and apparently Donna was the top story of the day. People had already started to rename her show with such catchy titles as *Poisoned Candy Crusades* and *Someone's in the Kitchen with a Killer.*

Mike had met us at the bakery as the ambulance pulled in. He'd ridden to the hospital inside it with me. They'd offered to move a cot into the room for him, but he'd assured the nurse that it wasn't necessary.

"I won't be able to sleep." His voice quivered slightly as he wrapped his strong hands around one of mine and held it against his chest. "I can't believe I almost lost you like that, Sal."

I smiled up at him from the hospital bed. "Thank God for Josie." She'd promised to stop and see me in the morning before she went to the bakery. She had checked our voicemail messages while at the hospital and told me that we had three new cookie orders for the weekend. It looked like business might start picking up again. The doctor didn't want me to go back to work for a few days, so Grandma Rosa had offered to help Josie at the bakery if necessary. I felt bad about messing up her birthday plans, but Josie assured me it was fine.

"I already have my birthday present," she'd told me in a

choked-up voice. "You're okay, and I'm not going to prison. What else do I need?"

"It was wrong of me to ask you to stay out of things and not get involved with her mess," Mike said. "She saved your life."

I placed a finger on his lips. "It's all right."

He handed me a paper cup that held hot tea. "Have some more, princess."

I took another sip, grateful to be warm, with my husband, and above all, alive. "I really didn't think we'd make it out of there."

"This is all my fault." Mike ran a hand through his hair in visible distress. "If I'd fixed that damn door, this never would have happened."

I stared at him in shock. "You didn't even know. I forgot to tell you about it."

He gazed down at me soberly. "I'm betting that the lock mechanism on the handle was out of adjustment and caused some type of damage. I'll look at it tomorrow." His midnight blue eyes were dark with concern. "As soon as you're back home with me, safe and sound."

There was a knock on the door, and Grandma Rosa came in. She gave me a light kiss on the forehead. "Gianna is waiting for me downstairs. Johnny has already taken his grandmother home."

"How is she?" I asked.

Grandma Rosa snorted. "Nothing will ever kill that woman. She is too mean to die. Wait until you meet her friend, Allegra, who is coming here to live with her. She makes Nicoletta look like a Girl Scout."

Mike and I both chuckled at this. "She should get a reward for what she did tonight," I said. "I'll have to make up a special batch of fortune cookies for her—all with good messages inside."

My grandmother waved a hand dismissively. "Bah. If there were only good messages, she would complain about that too. It is part of the fun for her, not knowing what to expect." She looked from me to Mike. "Those cookies are a little bit like life sometimes. You never know what is waiting for you next."

"Well, that's true enough," Mike admitted.

Grandma Rosa observed my face closely. "Would you like me to stay for a while? I could get a taxi to take me home later."

I knew what she meant. My grandmother was aware that I hadn't told Mike about his father yet, and this was her subtle way of offering to help relay the news. But I couldn't keep running to my grandmother every time I had a problem. I was a big girl now—a married woman, in fact, and this was the first real problem we had encountered during our life together. I had learned many times before that there were ugly truths in life and no possible way to stay away from all of them.

"No thank you, Grandma." I glanced at my husband. "We'll be fine."

She nodded in approval. "I know that you will."

Mike gave her a kiss on the cheek. "Thanks for coming, Rosa."

"I have been thinking," Grandma Rosa said, "that I need a vacation. I am not sure that I have ever had one before."

"Not even a honeymoon?" I asked.

She shook her head. "There was no money for one when your grandfather and I got married. He was too cheap anyway."

Mike and I laughed at this.

There was a faraway look in my grandmother's eyes. "I was wondering if you both would like to come with me."

I turned to Mike, and he nodded approval. "Of course," I said.

Grandma Rosa wagged a finger at us. "Not a word of this to your parents. Gianna and Johnny may come too if they wish. But your parents, God love them, are part of the reason I need a vacation."

I tried to hide my smile. "I think we understand."

"No argument there," Mike muttered. "Where would you like to go, Rosa?"

She looked at him thoughtfully. "I am not sure. It would be nice to go back to Italy one last time before I die. But then again, I would also like to go to Las Vegas and see what all the fuss is about."

"I've never been there." I handed Mike the cup of tea.

"But I honestly can't picture you sitting on a stool for hours on end, pulling the lever on a slot machine."

Grandma Rosa waved her hand dismissively. "Sometimes in this *pazza* world we live in, it is good to not be practical. For once, I would like to waste a few hours on a mindless task." Her eyes widened with pleasure, and I pictured her as a young girl—wild, passionate, beautiful, and carefree. As much as I loved her now, I wished I'd known her back then. Grandma had once told me that she had done things she was not proud of. She had told lies to her parents to be with an older man they didn't approve of before she'd met and married my grandfather. Although not ashamed of the relationship, she regretted the hurt it caused her family. I suspected that there were many other stories of tragedy, heartbreak, and happiness my grandmother had not shared as well. Hopefully someday she would.

"You'd be a real rebel in Vegas, Grandma," I teased.

She smiled. "A rebel without a pause."

Mike managed to hide his smile. "I think you mean cause, Rosa."

"That is good too." She blew us both a kiss and closed the door quietly behind her.

Mike heaved a long sigh and sat down on the side of my bed then gathered me into his arms. "Your grandmother is right, you know."

"Meaning?"

He smoothed the hair back from my face. "About not always being so practical. You and I work hard at our jobs, but we need to take more time to enjoy ourselves. Someday soon we'll have kids, and like Rob and Josie, we'll have to make sacrifices for them."

"Those are sacrifices that I won't mind making." The longing for a child had started to develop into an enormous ache in my chest. "I just want it so badly."

"It will happen, Sal," he promised. "I feel it in my bones. I can even visualize what our children will look like in my head—just like my princess."

"They have to have your eyes." The time had come, and there was no putting it off any longer. "I need to tell you something."

His eyes shone with such vivid blue rays of happiness that I immediately regretted my choice of words. "Not *that*. It's about your father."

The expression on his face turned serious. "What's wrong, baby?"

There was no easy way to say this. "Gianna met a woman that I used to work with years ago. She's a real estate attorney now. Your father came to see her for a free consultation. When Gianna told her my married name, she asked if we were related."

Mike drew his eyebrows together. "Go on."

"He asked questions about the house. He wanted to know if—" I stopped and bit into my lower lip when I saw the confused look in his eyes. No, it was pain—pain so transparent that it almost blinded me.

"I think I can wager a guess here," Mike said softly. "He wanted to know if he had any rights to our house. Is that it?"

My head bobbed up and down in misery. "How did you know?"

He wove his fingers through my hair. "Well, he kind of gave himself away at lunch the other day. At first, I thought I'd give him the benefit of the doubt. Dear old dad asked me a lot of questions about what I had done to the place. How old was the roof, did I replace the hot water heater, would I consider adding another bathroom, and so on. He almost sounded like a real estate agent himself."

My heart sank at his admission. "That isn't all. I discovered that he's not really sick either."

A muscle ticked in Mike's jaw. "I see. How did you find that out?"

"I asked Ally, Brian's girlfriend, the other night when she was on duty at the hospital." I couldn't stand the hurt look on his face. "She wouldn't tell me anything, but on my way out of the building, I overheard her talking about it with another nurse. It seems that he's in perfect health." A tear rolled down my cheek. "I'm so sorry, honey."

He didn't say anything for a moment then reached out and pulled me against his chest while I sobbed quietly, overwhelmed by all that had transpired in the last few days.

Mike kissed the top of my head. "It's all right, Sal. I had my suspicions too. I was angry when he first came back—very angry. Then I decided to take your grandmother's advice. Don't judge a book by its picture."

I hiccupped back a sob and turned it into a chuckle. "Did she really say that?"

"Yes. Before Josie called to tell me about you, my father phoned and wanted to know if I'd made a decision. Then I asked him point-blank why he was really here. After he insisted it was to get to know me, I decided to help him out. I told him that he had lost all claim to the house after my mother died. She left it to me in her will. He then quickly mumbled something about going out of town for a while and asked that I tell you good-bye. He said he'd call when he gets back."

Sure he would. I moved back against the pillows so that I could see his face. "I hate that you have to go through this."

He sighed. "I'm okay, Sal, really. I carried a lot of anger around inside of me for years. Most of it was directed against him. Maybe I felt that if he hadn't left, my life would have been better. But who really knows for sure? I felt sorry for myself for a long time. You remember how I was when we first dated in high school."

"Yes." He'd been so insecure and jealous back then, but I'd seen past his façade and knew there was a loving, passionate man underneath. In my innocent teenage brain, I thought I'd be able to fix everything when, in truth, he'd needed to figure things out for himself.

"I never understood why my father would ditch me like that. Topping it off was my mother divorcing him and marrying a guy who smacked me around. She was too drunk all the time to even do anything about it. So I blamed Sam for leaving me. I let it affect my life in so many ways. The worst part was letting you slip through my fingers. After that, I started to wake up—slowly, but I finally got there."

My voice grew shaky. "I wasn't perfect either, you know."

"It doesn't matter anymore," Mike said. "We have each other, and that's what's important. I won't lie and say it doesn't hurt that my own father never cared about me, but I won't let that define who I am. I love you, and someday we'll have children of our own to love. Let's not waste any more time worrying about what could have been. Life is too short."

"You're right." I snapped my fingers. "Hey, I think you've just given me a new slogan for the bakery."

"Oh yeah?" He looked amused. "And what would that be?"

I grinned, proud of my unusual wittiness. "Life's short— eat the cookie."

Mike smiled and gave me a light peck on the lips. "Sounds like great advice to me."

RECIPES

———

LEMON CRISP COOKIES

INGREDIENTS:

½ cup butter, room temperature
1 cup (7.1 ounces) granulated sugar
½ tsp. vanilla extract
½ to 1 tsp. lemon extract, depending on how lemony of a flavor
you want
1 egg, room temperature
1 tsp. lemon zest
1 tbsp. fresh lemon juice
1½ cups (7.5 ounces) all-purpose flour
½ tsp. salt
¼ tsp. baking powder
¼ tsp. baking soda

For rolling dough:
½ cup granulated sugar

Do not preheat the oven yet. The cookie dough will need to chill first. Line baking sheet with parchment paper. In a medium-size bowl, whisk together the flour, salt, baking powder, and baking soda. Set aside. In the bowl of a standing mixer, whip the butter and granulated sugar together until fluffy, about 2 minutes on medium speed. Add the egg and beat until fully incorporated. Mix in the vanilla, lemon extract, lemon zest, and lemon juice. With the mixer running on lowest speed, slowly add the flour mixture. Beat until it is just fully incorporated. Cover the cookie dough with plastic wrap, and allow to chill in the refrigerator for 1 hour or even overnight. Preheat oven to 350 degrees Fahrenheit. Place remaining ½ cup granulated sugar in a shallow bowl. Form cookie dough into small balls, about a heaping teaspoon. Roll the balls in the granulated sugar, and place on the parchment-lined baking sheet, at least 2 inches apart. Don't crowd the cookies, as they tend to spread. You should have 12 cookies per baking sheet.

Bake for 9 to 11 minutes. The edges should be turning light golden, and the tops should be crackled. Remove from the oven, and allow to cool on the baking sheet for 5 minutes before transferring to a wire cooling rack. Cool completely, and store leftovers in an airtight container at room temperature for up to 3 days. Makes 30 - 40 cookies, depending on size.

TIRAMISU

INGREDIENTS:

⅔ cup of coffee
⅓ cup plus ½ cup maple syrup
16 ladyfingers
3 ounces of mascarpone
½ cup nonfat sour cream
1½ cups of whipping cream
1 tbsp. unsweetened cocoa powder

Combine coffee and ⅓ cup maple syrup into a small bowl and mix well. Spoon the mixture over the ladyfingers. Coat an 8 x 8 dish or pan lightly with nonstick spray. Then line the bottom and sides with ladyfingers. Combine mascarpone, sour cream, and ½ cup of maple syrup in a bowl, and beat together until smooth. Fold in the whipped topping. Spoon mascarpone mixture over the ladyfingers, and then cover with plastic wrap. Refrigerate for about 15 minutes. Remove plastic from the dish, and sprinkle or sift cocoa over the top just before serving. Makes 6 servings.

FRANGELICO CHOCOLATE PIE

INGREDIENTS:

8 ounces instant chocolate pudding mix
½ cup Frangelico liquor
¼ cup dark Crème de Cacao
¼ cup chocolate syrup
2 cups heavy cream (plus additional cream to serve pie with)
19-inch graham cracker pie shell

Mix pudding, liquor, and syrup together until it forms a thick paste. Whip the heavy cream until stiff, and then fold the chocolate paste into the whipped cream. Spread mixture into the pie shell and freeze. Remove from the freezer about 30 minutes before you wish to serve it. Top with whipped cream. Make 6 to 8 servings.

Note: This pie can also be made with Scotch. Substitute the Frangelico with between ¼ and ½ cup of the whiskey, depending on how strong you like your dessert to taste.

DOUBLE CHOCOLATE CHIP COOKIES

INGREDIENTS:

⅔ cup shortening
1½ cup sugar
2 eggs
1 tsp. vanilla extract
2 cups all-purpose flour
½ cup unsweetened cocoa powder
½ tsp. baking soda
½ tsp. salt
2 cups miniature chocolate chips

Preheat oven to 375 degrees Fahrenheit. Line cookie sheets with parchment paper. Cream together shortening and sugar in a bowl for about three minutes or until light and fluffy. Mix in eggs, sour cream, and vanilla. Sift flour, cocoa, baking soda, and salt on waxed paper. Add to wet ingredients in the bowl, mixing well. Fold chocolate chips into bowl, careful not to over mix. Drop dough by teaspoonfuls onto the prepared baking sheets at two inches apart. Bake until cookies start to puff up, about ten minutes. Cool on wire racks. Makes about 72 cookies.

ABOUT THE AUTHOR

USA Today bestselling author Catherine Bruns lives in Upstate New York with a male dominated household that consists of her very patient husband, three sons, and assorted cats and dogs. She has wanted to be a writer since the age of eight when she wrote her own version of Cinderella (fortunately Disney never sued). Catherine holds a B.A. in English and is a member of Mystery Writers of America and Sisters in Crime.

To learn more about Catherine Bruns, visit her online at: www.catherinebruns.net

Enjoyed this book? Check out these other fun reads available in print now from Gemma Halliday Publishing:

www.GemmaHallidayPublishing.com

Made in United States
Troutdale, OR
01/11/2024

16898431R00130